KU-342-329

THE ICE LANDS

THE ICE LANDS

STEINAR BRAGI

Translated by Lorenza Garcia

MACMILLAN

First published 2016 by Macmillan
an imprint of Pan Macmillan
20 New Wharf Road, London N1 9RR
Associated companies throughout the world
www.panmacmillan.com

ISBN 978-1-4472-9881-6

Published by agreement with Salomonsson Agency.

1 3 5 7 9 8 6 4 2

A CIP catalogue record for this book is available from the British Library.

Typeset by Palimpsest Book Production Ltd, Falkirk, Stirlingshire
Printed and bound by CPI Group (UK) Ltd, Croydon, CR0 4YY

THE DESERT

1

ICELANDIC FLORA

Hrafn

Over the highlands all was still. The shadows on the horizon darkened, growing sharper against the sky, before dissolving into the night.

All four of them were silent. The only sound was a low murmur coming from the radio. On the back seat, Vigdís was reading a book, while Anna, awake after a brief nap, had just opened a beer. Between them lay Trigger, Anna's Icelandic sheepdog, which she had acquired a few months before.

'Let's play I Spy,' said Anna, breaking the silence. 'I think of a thing, inside or outside the jeep, on the road or the sands . . .'

'Yeah, I'd forgotten that one,' Egill broke in, his voice oozing a childlike eagerness after three beers and a dozen swigs from his hip flask.

'Interesting,' said Hrafn, ignoring Egill. He glanced at Anna in the rear-view mirror, her dark silhouette and the faint glimmer of her eyes. 'What do you mean by "thing"? Would it count if I thought of your boyfriend's integrity, or of blood?'

'Sicko,' replied Anna mockingly.

Egill gazed out of the passenger window, and it occurred to Hrafn that he might be looking in the wing mirror, at Vigdís, who was sitting behind him.

'No, blood doesn't count. Only things you can see around you are allowed.'

'What are you talking about?' asked Vigdís, closing the book she had been immersed in: *Icelandic Flora*. Anna explained the rules of the game to her and announced that she would start.

'Go for it!' said Egill, and the game commenced.

Hrafn kept his eyes on the road, which was becoming increasingly difficult to see as darkness set in. The summer evenings were no longer as light, and the sky grew dim for a few hours now at night. Winter was starting to impinge on his thoughts, rising like a huge wave on the horizon, fuelling the anxiety he had been experiencing in recent days. Since noon, he had felt an overwhelming urge to drive back to town as fast as he could.

'The driver's eyes?' asked Vigdís, as the jeep rolled between the marker posts that glowed in the dark.

Hrafn pressed the button to open his window, poked his head out and saw that the sky was filled with unusually low, thick clouds. But then they were in the *high*lands.

'Do you think you'll find the answer up in the clouds?' Anna's voice rang out behind him, laughing.

'You've got to help me here, guys,' said Vigdís. 'I've run out of ideas.'

'Marker posts,' Hrafn suggested, closing the window again. Anna said no. *Arctic winter*, he thought. Was that a thing? They could see signs of it all around them, at any rate. Rocks cleaved apart by ice, no greenery, no colours, no *flora*. Only sand and gravel in varying shades of black and grey.

Soon the clouds sank to the ground, and they drove straight into them. The jeep's headlights cut two cones in the fog, which turned white but remained dark grey to the sides across the black sands. Visibility was only ten or twenty metres, and Hrafn's eyes began to smart from staring into the fog. He wouldn't have minded a rest from driving, but Egill was too drunk to take the wheel, and as for the girls, he scarcely trusted them in town let alone out there on the sands.

He stopped to take a piss outside and wake himself up, and stared into the thickening fog as its cold moistness settled on his face. None of them had any experience of travelling in the mountains, or the remotest idea what to do if the jeep broke down. Vigdís had pointed that out when they were planning the trip, but he and Egill had reassured her with some nonsense they couldn't deliver on, and had installed a satnav, which went on the blink soon after they left Askja, although they couldn't be sure as none of them really knew how it worked.

Hrafn imagined how long a person might survive out there on the sands. A few days in summer, providing they had access to water and shelter from the wind, but in winter at most a few hours, or even minutes. The fear of being lost would increase blood flow to the skin, cooling the body; they would become disoriented, the tension would be too much for their system and they would basically die of fright.

He climbed back into the driver's seat and set off again. The marker posts shone blankly through the fog like deep-sea fish eyes. Out of the corner of his eye he saw Egill light a cigarette then thrust the hip flask into his face yet again, and heard him laugh. They were still absorbed in their game, and it struck him how absurd this was, the four of them gliding across the sands north of Vatnajökull, through darkness and fog, as if nothing were more natural; swigging Mexican beer, dressed in summer clothes in the heat they controlled by turning a knob on the dashboard, to the sound of music; borne along, motionless, across the landscape, oblivious to the crunch and rasp of tyres rolling over gravel, without a care. Not about the *trip* at any rate, but rather about something completely different: their relationships, what someone said or did to them once, yesterday or twenty years ago, or about their bank balance, as they watched the landscape go by outside . . .

Emerging from his reverie, Hrafn tried to focus on the road, but sensed instantly that something had changed. He drove on for a few minutes, steering in one direction then the other, before slowing down and finally coming to a halt.

'What's wrong?' asked Egill.

'Can you lot see any marker posts?'

Hrafn tried to remember when he last saw one, but

couldn't. For a while now, they had started to become more spaced out as the fog thickened.

'Fuck,' said Egill, sitting up in his seat and staring through the window. Anna appeared between the front seats and asked if they were lost.

'I wouldn't mind if we were,' she added. 'Lost in the fog, like in an adventure story.'

'How long is it since we saw a post?' Hrafn asked, looking at Vigdís in the rear-view mirror. She raised an eyebrow.

'No idea,' she said. 'I was busy playing the game.'

Hrafn gazed ahead into the lights at the pale wisps of fog, stepped on the accelerator and moved off again slowly.

'How did you manage to lose the road?' asked Egill.

'I'm sure we'll find it again,' said Anna, leaning through the seats.

The smell of alcohol on her breath was pungent, overpowering. They couldn't have left the road that long ago. Hrafn had the vague impression that he had turned a bit too far to the left, which meant the road had to be on their right.

He swung the wheel to the right and tried to hold his course. Vigdís asked what he was doing and he explained.

'Then we'll just have to hope the *road* doesn't also bend to the right,' she said, and Anna giggled.

Hrafn kept driving until he was sure he had gone too far for the road to be on their right. What's more, he had doubtless turned the wheel so sharply that they had gone round in a circle, albeit a smallish one – possibly several. The others were too drunk to notice, or they didn't care.

He stopped the car again, switching off the radio so that

he could concentrate better, and reached for the compass in the glove compartment.

'That's that, then,' drawled Egill. 'No mercy.'

Hrafn placed the compass in his lap and set off towards the east.

'Why are you doing that?' asked Anna.

'So that we don't drive round in circles,' he said, looking alternately at the compass and at the sands ahead of them.

'But are we driving in the right direction?' asked Vigdís.

'The road we were on was north–south,' he said. 'I know we didn't veer off to the east. That means we are to the west of the road, and we're heading east to find it again. Do you agree?'

Vigdís raised her eyebrows again, and Hrafn had the impression that she was irritated.

'It sounds logical,' she said. 'Unless of course we drive back across the road between two marker posts without realizing it . . .'

'Then we'd better keep our eyes peeled, hadn't we? You two look to the right and we'll look the other way.'

His old despair was starting to resurface, his claustrophobia. He wound his window down and saw the fog continuing to thicken, as the stench of alcohol congealed . . .

'How did you manage to lose the fucking road?'

Aware of Egill whingeing beside him, Hrafn decided he was fed up with ignoring him.

'Why did *you* lose it? Aren't you sitting next to me staring out of the same fucking window?'

'Yeah, but I'm not *driving*, am I?'

'Now, boys,' said Vigdís, touching Hrafn's shoulder, 'let's calm down, take a deep breath or something. It'll all work out, and sooner than we think.'

They fell silent. The dog was sitting up on its haunches, and occasionally gave a low whimper as the hiss of sand beneath the tyres reached them through the open window. Hrafn scanned the darkness on his side, but saw nothing. After driving east for ten minutes, he no longer knew what to do for the best. Remembering his first instinct, it occurred to him that he hadn't driven far enough west, and he glanced down at the compass to make sure they were heading in the right direction. Surely if they stayed on course they would end up finding the road again.

'Are there any ravines or crevasses around here?' said Anna. 'Shouldn't you put your seat belt on, Egill?

'Or quicksand,' said Vigdís.

'Ugh. You mean the ground might swallow us up?'

'Yes. They dug up some horses around here dating back to the Middle Ages, perfectly preserved. And men too.'

'A jeep would be a great haul. With four passengers, a dog, mobile phones, text messages and fillings. A specimen of twenty-first-century life preserved for later generations.' They laughed.

There was no sign of the marker posts or the road. Rather than turn round and risk being questioned about whether he was doing the right thing, Hrafn decided to keep going east; they should probably stop and wait for a couple of hours until it got light, or until the fog lifted. On the other hand, that would be incredibly stupid if the road was only a few metres away. He drove on. He didn't want to give up too soon, or perhaps he had he lost all sense of time, was caught up in his thoughts – either that or he didn't care. Perhaps none of them did, he reflected, as they stared silently into the fog, which was grey at the edges and illuminated in the centre, giving Hrafn the impression that he was driving through a shiny white opening, an ever-deepening tunnel.

At some point he glimpsed a faint, golden light through the fog. Almost instinctively, he turned towards it, gripping the wheel tightly. The darkness began to swirl about them, and he murmured to himself, squinting at the light, which disappeared suddenly as something came hurtling out of the fog and crashed into the jeep.

2

ON ALL FOURS

Hrafn

The windscreen shattered, cracks spreading across its surface, as a white bubble expanded over the world, swallowing up his head. Inside the bubble were luminous fish – whole banks of tiny fish with piercing red eyes fixed on him. Ejected from the bubble, Hrafn saw Egill hit the passenger window; a red trickle ran down his cheek as he flew out of his seat, a grin on his face.

Now there is blood, Hrafn thought as the car listed to one side, and he felt the shock absorbers judder before everything went quiet. He took a deep breath, blinked and was aware of a pain in his chest where the seat belt was cutting into him. The air bubble had vanished. The jeep was filled with a grey vapour that tasted of petrol, and white specks floated in the air. Raising his hands to his face, he felt for any shards of glass, and found none. Then he undid his seat belt and all at once found himself outside the car, the fresh air flowing into his lungs.

The first thing he did was reach into the back seat and help Vigdís out. She assured him she was all right. Anna was screaming out Egill's name as he lay, now slumped over the driver's seat. The window on his side was also broken.

Beyond the car, the darkness had congealed, like a great rock stretching up to the sky, looming over them, sinister and silent. Hrafn wondered when the sun would come up, whether it would manage to scale this black colossus, as he dragged Egill from the jeep and laid him out flat on the sand. The dog ran yelping in circles around them.

Vigdís knelt beside Egill and shouted at Hrafn to fetch the first-aid kit from the boot. A light went on in the upper part of the rock, one light then two.

'He's only been knocked out,' he heard Vigdís say as he passed her a bottle of surgical spirit. Anna cradled Egill's head while Vigdís wound a piece of gauze around it and staunched the blood.

The headlights were smashed and had gone out. The grey vapour inside the car had dissolved and was now pouring out from under the crumpled bonnet. Hrafn crouched down beside the front tyre that wasn't plunged into darkness, and heard a faint, steady hiss, as though an animal had crawled beneath the car to hide.

The fog in his head began to clear, and he glimpsed the outline of a house, a black house on the black sands, into which they had driven. He heard the sound of soft, unsteady footsteps and saw a beam of light dart across the sand. The dog barked. Someone appeared from behind the corner of the house and shone a torch at them.

'Who's there?' a woman's voice enquired out of the darkness.

Vigdís replied, saying they needed help. The beam alighted on Egill's bloody head, and then a second torch appeared out of the darkness. The woman's voice gave a groan, and Hrafn could make out her shape against the light – hunched back, wispy hair – and behind her a scrawny old man, smiling the way Egill had when he hit the window.

'Into the house,' a voice said.

'*Into the house*,' the crone repeated and told them to hurry, swinging her torch and scolding the old man. Anna was sobbing. Hrafn picked Egill up under the arms while Vigdís held his ankles. Between them they carried him round the corner, up a steep flight of stone steps and into the house.

The old woman beckoned them into the front room, where they laid Egill out on the floor. He started to come round, mumbling incoherently and smiling with his eyes closed. Anna called out his name.

Hrafn felt Vigdís loom close to his face, almost as if the world had become two-dimensional, and she asked him if he was all right.

'I think so, a bit dazed,' he said, and they clutched hold of one another. Over Vigdís's shoulder he could see the old woman tottering around what looked like a kitchen.

'How about you?'

Vigdís told him that she was fine as far as she knew, disentangled herself from his arms and said she was going out to the car to fetch the first-aid kit and the whisky to perk Egill up.

Soon afterwards, there was a commotion, and Hrafn

went through to the hallway where he found Vigdís arguing with the old woman, who was standing in front of the door, barring her way.

'I need to get some things from the car,' said Vigdís.

'Are you locking us in?' asked Hrafn. 'What do you think you're doing?'

The old woman didn't reply. She shook her head and gazed at them with wide-open, pleading eyes.

'Let's keep calm,' said Vigdís, clasping Hrafn's hand. 'I understand that you and your husband are upset. We drive into your house in the middle of the night, make an almighty din and scare you half to death . . .'

'Will you open this door!' said Hrafn, sounding to himself as if he were on the verge of laughter. A strange atmosphere of hostility hung in the house; where it came from, or why, he didn't know.

'We're all perfectly calm,' said Vigdís, and Hrafn was astonished to see that she was looking at *him* not at the old woman.

Then he found himself back in the front room. Anna was leaning over Egill, speaking to him in hushed tones and gazing down at him like a lovesick girl . . . *Sick, sick people,* thought Hrafn. Somewhere in the house he heard the sound of hammering.

Vigdís appeared in the front room, dragging the dog behind her; it clearly wanted to go back outside. She passed Anna a plastic bag containing a blanket and a bottle of whisky. Anna spread the blanket over Egill, who had opened his eyes, and poured some whisky into the lid, which she placed to his lips.

Hrafn felt the old craving wash over him, and heard Egill cry out, pointing a finger at him and yelling angrily:

'You did this on purpose! But you forgot the air balloon!'

He carried on babbling – drivel to which Hrafn turned a deaf ear. Anna leaned across Egill, preventing him and Hrafn from looking each other in the eye.

Appearing once more, Vigdís asked: 'Are you sure you're all right? You look rather pale.'

Hrafn nodded.

'I'm positive. It was an accident, an unfortunate accident.'

He lit a cigarette, inhaled deeply, and watched Anna tip more whisky into Egill's mouth, before lifting the lid to her own lips.

'But clearly it's crazy and *preposterous* that we should be in this house, in this room.'

He remembered his mobile phone, fished it out of his shirt pocket and checked the reception.

'Do you have a signal?' asked Vigdís.

He shook his head and something told him that the thing they called a signal no longer meant anything, not after this – that it belonged to his former life, concerns of a previous existence. He could make no sense of his thoughts, which seemed to fuse with the buzz from the nicotine, and he decided to sit down and rest. He slumped onto the sofa, and heard Trigger the dog whining somewhere in the house.

Vigdís brought him a glass of water, which he gulped down. His eyes followed her into the kitchen where she started to chat with the old woman. He glanced about the room, at the brown lino and the red blanket they had spread over Egill. There was a shelf lined with books, and a framed photograph hung on the wall. On a table next to the sofa was a vase of red, green and blue glass, with a pattern that seemed familiar.

They weren't guests there, he reflected as the ash from his cigarette dropped onto the blanket. Despite her insistence on locking them in, the old woman wanted to be rid of them as soon as possible. They weren't welcome.

He needed an ashtray, and, walking out of the room to find one, he noticed that the front door had been bolted.

'They've said we can stay,' said Vigdís when he came to a halt in the kitchen doorway. She and the old woman were sitting at a table. 'We'll spend the night here so that Egill can rest. And anyway, we can't see about the jeep until it gets light.'

'That's kind of you,' said Hrafn, beaming at the woman.

He introduced himself and she mumbled something in turn which sounded like Ása. When he asked her if that was an abbreviation of a longer name, she didn't reply. The old man seemed to have vanished.

'I assure you we won't hang around, Ása,' he said. 'I understand that we have to leave here as soon as possible.'

'Make yourselves at home,' said Ása. Her voice sounded elderly and shrill, and yet Hrafn had difficulty guessing her age. Her face was wrinkled and leathery, and her dark hair, which hung in a ponytail down her back, was streaked with grey. She could have been sixty, although her eyes possessed a sly watchfulness more appropriate to someone younger. 'You'll spend the night here,' she went on, nodding as if to convince herself. 'It's best for all. There's no other choice. I'll show you to your rooms, and in the morning all will be well and you can move on.'

'It must be awkward for you to have unexpected guests like this,' Vigdís said. 'You must have had a shock.'

'Possibly,' said Ása, rising from the table. 'That was an almighty bang.'

The old woman had what looked like eczema in the corners of her eyes, a raised patch of redness that ran down the sides of her nose to the corners of her mouth.

The rooms they were allotted were on the top floor, facing each other at the end of a long corridor. As instructed by Ása, Hrafn and Vigdís fetched a mattress from the cupboard, and put it in their room, which was empty apart from a small table and an oil lamp. Anna and Egill's room contained a chair, a table and a double bed for the patient to sleep in.

While the girls helped Egill upstairs, Hrafn waited in the kitchen. Finally, his dizziness was beginning to wear off. Ása told him that if their jeep wouldn't start the next day, there was one at the farm they could use to drive to the nearest village. Hrafn perked up even more when he heard this. Everything was going to be all right.

Ása provided them with blankets and pillows, lit the

lamp in Hrafn and Vigdís's room, and told Anna she could keep Trigger in the room overnight, adding that she would be down in the kitchen if they needed anything.

Hrafn lay on the mattress on the floor, lit a cigarette and stared up at the ceiling. The mattress had a musty smell, but the lamp cast a warm glow on the walls. Out in the corridor, Anna and Vigdís discussed how safe it was for Egill to sleep after being knocked out, and why the front door had so many locks and bolts.

'Four. As if she were expecting . . .' Anna started to say, then lowered her voice.

Hrafn closed his eyes and heard Vigdís enter the room. She walked across the creaky wooden floor and lay down beside him on the mattress, put her arms around him and nestled her head in the crook of his neck. He stubbed his cigarette out on a cork on the floor and turned towards her.

'I don't mind if you have a drink,' he said.

'I know, but I don't feel like it – I'm too sleepy,' she said, after a brief silence. 'Of course I know you don't mind. Do you want one?'

Hrafn shook his head. With hindsight, it seemed odd that the old woman hadn't asked them about events leading up to the accident, or offered them refreshments: coffee, biscuits, a sandwich, even. What had happened to the time-honoured hospitality of country folk? On the other hand she had agreed they could stay the night, and yet it was obvious she was up to something, he could see it in her eyes. The old woman was *hiding* something, obliged to shelter them against her will.

He opened his mouth to discuss it with Vigdís, but thought better of it. She undressed, spread the blanket over them and snuggled up to him. They started kissing; he told her he loved her, but she didn't reply. She gave a sigh, and before he knew it, he had unzipped his trousers and pressed himself into her. After a moment, she turned over onto her stomach, and he raised himself to his knees, holding onto the windowsill to steady himself.

Glancing out of the window, he noticed that the fog had lifted. Every now and then, the moon broke through the clouds, casting its pale light onto the sands. Towards the horizon, the glacier rose up from the plain, heavy, motionless and white, like an unexposed photograph.

Their bodies were moving faster, and somewhere far below him Vigdís let out a wail. As he came, Hrafn glimpsed someone streak across the sands outside: the misshapen, hunched figure of a man running from the house, stumbling and then disappearing into the night, on all fours.

Hrafn lay on his back on the mattress; the room was spinning before his eyes and his heart was pounding. *On all fours*, he thought, and soon afterwards he fell asleep.

3

THE CARCASS

Hrafn

When Hrafn woke up he was alone in the room. He lay still for a while, trying to order the previous night's events, which were jumbled in his head. It reminded him of the old days, back when he drank.

Down in the kitchen Vigdís sat poring over a map. On the table was some sliced meat, cheese and bread, along with three used plates. Vigdís told him that the others were up and had eaten breakfast.

'Egill and Anna went for a walk, to take a look around . . . The jeep's a write-off.'

'Says who? Egill?'

'See for yourself.'

Hrafn went outside, descended the steps, which were broader than he remembered, and rounded the corner of the house to where they had abandoned the jeep. The bonnet on the passenger side was buried in the wall, and both the front tyres had burst. They were probably lucky the wall hadn't collapsed on top of them. Hrafn reached inside the car and turned the key in the ignition to try to start the engine, but nothing happened. The windscreen had shattered, as had the window on the passenger side; a deflated airbag hung over the steering wheel and another over the glove compartment. On Egill's seat was a patch of congealed blood.

The engine was flooded with oil, as was the sand underneath the car. The sleeping bags, tents and fishing tackle on the roof rack were undisturbed.

Hrafn went back inside, sat down at the table and buttered a piece of bread which he ate with some cheese.

'Ása is going to lend us a jeep,' said Vigdís. 'There should be a road going north from here to Askja.'

'Do you know where we are?' He gestured with his head at the map, and she nodded.

'Sort of . . . The old couple were both here just now. I reckon he must have late-stage Alzheimer's. What do you suppose they do?'

'No idea. Farmers, I expect.'

For some reason he remembered the eczema on the old woman's face. Someone had told him that country folk age more quickly, their skin weathered by the sun, frost and rain.

'I didn't like to ask.' Vigdís frowned. 'But, farming out here on the sands doesn't seem plausible, does it?'

Hrafn poured himself some coffee from the pot on the table.

'Did we check to see if they have a telephone?'

'I did ask. She said the line was down.'

'Down!' He cursed. 'How close are we exactly to a proper road?'

'I've no idea . . . That depends how far we strayed yesterday. I can't work it out. We left Mývatn just after two. Drove for a couple of hours, stopped for two hours to buy provisions, then drove south for another three or four hours, I think.'

'More like four, I reckon,' said Hrafn. 'And we were driving round in circles for about an hour. We missed the shortcut east, which would have taken us to Askja. Wouldn't that put us about an hour or two south of there? In which case we should be able to see the glacier.'

'I showed Ása the map, and she seemed unsure of their or our location.' Vigdís grinned. 'Either that or she's never seen a map before – which is quite possible, judging by her expression.'

Hrafn pushed the plate away, took his coffee over to the window and lit a cigarette. The advantages of country life: people still smoked indoors – they didn't worry about the walls turning yellow after a couple of decades. He had started smoking again the day after they left town, and instantly regretted every single day he had given up.

The sky outside was blue. He felt the numbness flow out of the cigarette and down his body. The kitchen was on the same side of the house as the bedroom, and yet he saw no sign of the glacier anywhere.

Egill and Anna appeared in the yard, the dog sniffing at the ground around them. Hrafn went out onto the steps to greet them. They carried on laughing about something they had been discussing.

'What's so funny?' said Hrafn. 'Have I missed something?'

'They're waiting for us,' said Anna. 'In the barn.'

'The jeep is ready,' said Egill. 'Also a six-hundred-litre barrel of moonshine, which the old woman rations out to the old boy.'

Anna hurried into the house to use the toilet and pack her things, leaving the two men standing there. Egill's head was still bandaged.

'Are you OK?' Hrafn asked as he sat down on the steps and lit another cigarette.

'A slight headache . . . Forgive my behaviour yesterday. Anna told me I yelled at you. I don't know what came over me, maybe the blow to the head mixed with something else, the beer . . . I should have put my seat belt on, like Anna asked me to do. I know you're a good driver, it was the fog, of course, and the poor visibility . . .'

'It doesn't matter. Let's just forget it.'

They shook hands, in what should have been a playful gesture, Hrafn realized, but it felt clumsy, awkward and foolish.

They walked over to the jeep, and Hrafn packed his clothes and cigarettes in his rucksack. Then he knelt down beside the hole in the wall, but it was too dark for him to see inside the house. He climbed into the driver's seat, turned on the satnav and tried to make it work, but, as before, couldn't get anything but a map of downtown Reykjavík.

Egill gathered his stuff together from the back of the car, then appeared at the broken passenger window and leaned inside, holding a bottle of beer.

'What's up, man, what are you doing?'

'Checking out this crappy satnav. I've followed the instructions, done everything it tells me to do, but it keeps saying we're in Austurvöllur.'

'Exactly my sentiments,' said Egill, raising the beer bottle and gesturing towards the house. 'Outside Hotel Borg.'

'Already on the juice?'

Hrafn wanted to draw Egill's attention to his own blood on the seat and the dashboard – which he seemed not to have noticed, or was ignoring – but he resisted the temptation and climbed back out of the jeep.

'We all have to work together as a team now – we need to travel light,' said Egill, and grinned at him.

The girls were ready in the yard. They pulled on their rucksacks and set off towards an outhouse two hundred metres to their left – a peeling wooden structure with a battered corrugated-iron roof – and next to it another, taller building, probably the barn.

The weather was calm, the visibility couldn't be better, and Hrafn was amazed that they still couldn't see the glacier. Being two floors up could scarcely have made that much difference.

'Do you think they keep cows or sheep?' he asked no one in particular.

'I haven't seen a single animal here,' said Egill. 'But they must do something with the hay. They can hardly eat it themselves.'

'Aren't cattle sheds empty during the summer? Don't farmers put animals out to pasture to fatten them up?'

'Assuming there is any grass up here. If you ask me, there isn't a field within miles. But then, wouldn't they have to buy hay from other farmers?'

'You two don't really know much about anything, do you?' remarked Anna, showing that mischievous streak which, as the trip wore on, Hrafn had quickly realized could become increasingly unbearable or delightful. He had never understood what made Anna tick, or who she was, even. She seemed full of contradictions: when you first met her she gave the impression of being perfectly charming, almost childlike; someone who functioned on a purely emotional level. And yet when she felt that her light-heartedness was preventing her being taken seriously, or that she wasn't being shown the respect she was due, she was liable to turn prickly, aggressive and coldly analytical to the point where Hrafn scarcely recognized her as the same person.

'What's that?' said Vigdís, pointing in the distance. They veered off the path, and a few minutes later came to a streetlamp, which rose up out of the sand.

'A streetlamp! There's no working phone on this farm but plenty of streetlamps,' said Anna, chuckling.

The pole was somehow rooted in the sand, and stood straight up, before arching over the ground, with no apparent purpose. Gathering round the streetlamp, they gazed up at it. The light was switched off.

'Do you suppose it works?' asked Vigdís. 'Could this be the light we saw yesterday, before we drove into the house?'

'It's too far away,' said Hrafn. 'Besides, why would they keep it on in the middle of the night?'

'Perhaps it's here so that dogs have something to piss on,' said Anna, as Trigger trotted over, lifted his back leg and sprayed the lamppost with urine. They burst out laughing and the dog started to bark, looking about dumbly, until Egill scolded him.

'No, we could have strayed further from the path than we thought,' said Hrafn, after a brief silence. 'This reminds me of another streetlamp, in another faraway place – called *Narnia*. When they stepped out of the wardrobe, they gathered round a streetlamp in the snow . . .'

'There were four of them, too,' said Vigdís. 'Two girls and two boys.'

Anna had strolled on ahead and was calling to them to join her. She was standing over a dead animal on the sand; bloody shreds of flesh hung from the creature's thick, powerful bones. Bluish-green entrails spilled from its belly, and tufts of light-brown fur lay scattered about the carcass. From its head protruded a small pair of antlers.

'How disgusting,' said Anna, but remained rooted to the spot.

'A reindeer,' said Hrafn, and he had the impression that the carcass was relatively fresh, possibly from the night before. The animal's eyes were still intact, and it hadn't started to smell yet. Crouching over the carcass, he saw that there was plenty of meat left on it. Some of the bones bore traces of what looked like teeth marks. He touched the body, which was cold, then examined the chest and shoulders for any signs that the animal had been shot, but found none. When he was younger and lived in Suðurnes, he had shot hundreds of seagulls, a few geese and the odd swan. He had never come across a reindeer.

'It's been ripped to shreds,' said Vigdís. 'The animal must have died and foxes picked up the scent. Foxes didn't kill it, did they?'

'There's no evidence of it having been shot,' said Hrafn, rising to his feet and glancing about. 'Did you see anyone running away?' he asked Anna, who shook her head.

'"Anyone", you make it sound like a person . . .'

'I meant any*thing*.' He smiled. 'Perhaps we startled something in the middle of eating . . . Even so, it's strange that the deer would come this close to the farm to die, assuming it wasn't killed.'

They set off again.

4

THE BABY RAM

Vigdís

Through the open door of the barn they glimpsed bales of hay wrapped in green and white plastic. In the yard in front of the barn stood a sand-blown Willys jeep. The old woman was crouching beside one of the wheels in a pair of grubby overalls, poking a tool under the body of the vehicle. Clearly she was in charge of more than just the housework on the farm.

Clouds of blue smoke billowed from the exhaust pipe, and Vigdís had the impression the jeep was quaking under the strain of keeping its engine running. It had doubtless once been roadworthy, but was now covered in rust and even a few holes, moss grew on the rims of the windows, one of the headlights was smashed and the tyres were so worn that the cord showed through in places.

Next to the barn door stood a big, grey iron barrel that reeked of brennivín – the moonshine Anna and Egill had mentioned. A padlock had been fitted to the spigot.

The old woman stood up and Hrafn asked her whether she and her husband drove much on the sands.

'Less as the years go by,' she replied.

'By the way, thanks a lot for lending us the jeep,' Egill boomed. 'Of course, the distances here aren't exactly normal – it must take years to muster the energy to pop out . . .'

'Do you have sheep?' Anna broke in, gesturing discreetly to Egill to be quiet.

Ása nodded.

'Cows and sheep,' she said, gazing out across the sands. 'Sheep are unpleasant creatures, sluggish and dull-witted.'

'I once knew a man who grew up in the highlands,' said Anna. 'His father was a land surveyor, in charge of power cables and fencing – enclosures to stop the spread of scrapie. I guess there must be many different kinds of farmer. Have you lived here long?'

'Oh yes, a very long time,' said Ása, nodding without looking up.

'We saw the streetlamp. And we found a dead animal nearby. A reindeer – or that's what we thought it was anyway.'

Ása didn't answer. She walked round to the front of the jeep, opened the bonnet and leaned over the engine.

'Not in the least surprised,' Egill snorted. 'A dead reindeer near the farm!'

Anna hissed, and dragged him to the far side of the jeep where Vigdís could hear her pleading with him to stop drinking; she was scared, she said, and tired of seeing him drawling and bleary-eyed in the middle of the day. Soon afterwards, he sloped off to the barn. They would probably give each other the silent treatment for a while, which didn't mean much; they were quick to fall out, and even quicker to patch things up. Anna usually made the first move, acting like a lost little girl, which she wasn't, and asking Egill to help her with something stupid like opening a tin or a bottle, and before anyone knew it they were kissing.

In some ways Vigdís admired her ability to manipulate, and yet she felt like a sexless, prudish old woman when Anna turned on the charm, flirting with both men, making them so puffed-up they did whatever she wanted without realizing it. Sometimes it was just a matter of fluttering her eyelids a bit faster than usual and pouting imperceptibly. Doubtless it had become second nature to her, and Vigdís would do better to imitate rather than to criticize. And yet, Hrafn's willingness – ever since the trip started – to envelop Anna with his manliness, his warmth, his protectiveness, irritated her. She couldn't stand his cheerfulness when he was around Anna, the fact that he didn't even notice these changes in himself.

Trigger began to bark again. They saw something move on the horizon, two rust-coloured blobs, which drew closer, stopping near the barn.

'Foxes?' cried Vigdís, unable to conceal her astonishment. Anna grabbed hold of Trigger, pulled a leash out of her rucksack and fastened it to his collar. The foxes sat motionless, gazing at them, their fur glistening in the sun; they had long, bushy tails, and their ears were pricked. Every now and then, Vigdís thought she saw them bare their teeth slightly and snarl, but she wasn't sure.

'What's going on? Do they usually come this close?' Hrafn said to the old woman, who appeared unsurprised by the foxes. 'They feed on a dead animal a hundred metres from the farm, and then they come here? Have you seen them do this before? How did the reindeer die?'

'Do you feed the foxes?' asked Vigdís, but the old woman didn't reply.

They stared at the creatures in silence until Egill emerged whistling from the barn and opened another can of beer, which frothed over. The foxes took fright and vanished across the sands. Anna and Egill resumed their bickering and Vigdís decided to find somewhere secluded where she could have a pee before they set off. She slipped round the corner of the barn, where she discovered another, longer, lower building adjoining it: the cattle shed. Outside the shed stood a tractor and a trailer containing a pile of sand.

The central doors were open, and despite the stench, which in her mind Vigdís equated with the smell of the countryside, she ventured inside. As her eyes grew accustomed to the darkness, she made out row upon row of empty stalls. The floor was covered with muck – cow dung, she assumed – and she heard a mooing sound coming from somewhere further inside the shed. The dung was smooth and wet, not unlike a carpet, and she glimpsed wooden boards underneath.

Penetrating deeper into the shed, she was surprised to see a toilet in one of the stalls. The white bowl was pristine and the seat relatively clean. Vigdís peered inside and instead of water saw that it opened directly onto the dung-covered floor . . . *One more spurt won't make any difference*, she thought and felt a sudden thrill. She wouldn't take long, the toilet was hidden from view, and this was doubtless what country folk did when they were caught short.

She hurriedly pulled down her trousers and sat on the toilet. As she relieved herself with a soft tinkle onto the floor below, she glimpsed a figure close by her in the shadows. Stemming the flow, she sprang to her feet and fastened her trousers. Over by the wall, the old man was standing, smiling at her.

'Hello,' she said, as a door opened, seemingly from the adjoining barn. The old woman appeared in the doorway and asked her gruffly what she was doing there.

'I needed a pee,' said Vigdís, apologetically.

The old woman walked towards her and the old man fell in behind her. His features were delicate and he had a tremor; he smiled a lot but seemed unable to speak. The skin under his eyes sagged in startling folds, revealing the glistening flesh beneath his eyeballs, which threatened to pop out of their sockets if he leaned too far forward.

'Was he bothering you?' asked Ása. The old man drew nearer and gaped at Vigdís. 'He hasn't been well. He gets confused sometimes. I hope you won't take it to heart. We don't get many visitors here.'

'Of course not. I quite understand,' replied Vigdís, doing her best to ignore the old man without appearing rude. The old woman was relatively tall, but seemed to have a habitual stoop; her spine was crooked, and the vertebrae stood out, not unlike on a hunchback. 'Don't you get tourists passing through?'

Ása shook her head.

'Not so many. They deliver provisions, and hay for the animals in spring and autumn. And his medication,' she nodded towards the old man, 'they bring it by plane. But I wouldn't call people visitors when they don't stop.' She emitted a sound that reminded Vigdís of a rusty door opening slowly.

Vigdís became aware of something moving and looked down even as she felt the old man's palm pressing firmly against her belly, inches from her crotch. She gasped, recoiling, but the old woman leapt forward, seizing his hand, and addressed him in hushed tones.

She apologized to Vigdís:

'You needn't worry. It's just his way of saying hello.'

The old man extended his arm once more and Vigdís laughed uneasily before shaking his hand. His skin felt rough, his nails were dirty and his clasp unpleasantly tight. Vigdís introduced herself as the old man looked straight at her and tried with great difficulty, it seemed, to say something. His brow wrinkled with the effort, and his grip on her hand remained firm.

'What is he trying to say?'

'He wants to sing for you,' said Ása.

The old man straightened up, and his face relaxed as he sang in a bright, childlike voice:

Baby ram, my little lamb,
Fatten up as quick as you can.
For the lamb has no clue,
That it's bound for the stew.

He fell silent, and without taking his eyes off Vigdís, he smiled. His gaze was absent, but in a sly rather than a gentle way, unlike most old people she had known. She withdrew her hand, almost wrenching it from him, and at that moment the old man lost interest in her and walked away.

5

THE GARDEN

Vigdís

They drove slowly across the sands, on a road that was sometimes visible, sometimes not. Hrafn stared straight ahead in front of the jeep, occasionally glancing sideways through the open windows, and he stayed mostly in second gear, despite the engine's sputters and screeches. Trigger lay whining in Anna's arms, as if he didn't want to be in the jalopy.

'None of it makes any sense . . . And that house,' said Anna, 'how did it get there in the first place? Unless it's an old summer house. I once stayed in a stone house a bit like that one, on a hillock in the middle of a bog in Borgafjörður. The great-granddad of the guy I was seeing was a county magistrate, and had built it as a summer house. In those days summer houses were for rich people, not for the plebs.'

'At least it was a proper house. Made out of stone quarried from nearby cliffs,' said Hrafn, glancing at them in the rear-view mirror.

'Perhaps it was used for something else. Before it became a summer house,' said Anna.

'You mean a leper colony,' Egill said sarcastically from the front seat, but they ignored him.

'Like Möðrudalur,' Vigdís chimed in. 'Wasn't that a kind of crossroads?'

'Yes, but there's a farm at Möðrudalur,' said Hrafn. 'And the landscape is totally different. Moorland and fields, not like this desert.'

'*Desert*?' said Anna, assuming the expression of a frightened waif. 'Why do you call it a desert?'

'Because that's what it is. What else should I call it? The highlands are barren – or as good as – a windswept desert. No farm could thrive here, not without having to buy in fodder. Which means they have money.'

'Oh, so that's what they are, rich people in a summer house,' said Egill. 'Of course, it's all starting to make sense. The old couple came here on holiday and stayed on . . . for approximately fifty years.'

'I still think there must be a better word to describe it,' said Anna.

'*Wasteland*? Does that sound more picturesque?' asked Egill.

'A third of Iceland is defined as desert,' said Vigdís. 'The idea takes some getting used to, but there's no other way to describe it.'

'Why does this nation always think it's so special?' said Egill, getting irritated, perhaps because he didn't yet dare open one of the beers he had crammed into his rucksack. 'Everything has to be a little bit more unusual than in other places. Even the deserts.'

'That's not what I'm saying,' retorted Vigdís. 'Of course this is a desert. And yet, there *are* many reasons why the area is special. For example, most of the sand comes from *inside* the earth, from volcanic eruptions. Astronauts used to prepare for their trips to the moon out here. And studies of the sand have revealed that, aside from actual moon dust, no other soil on the planet is finer or more easily carried by the wind.'

'In other words, our deserts are made of dust,' said Egill. 'And the difference between them and foreign deserts is that ours are finer!'

'Who would want to have a summer house here, anyway?' asked Anna, throwing up her hands in despair.

'Did you notice how laid-back the old man was?' said Hrafn.

Except when they were parting – then he had clasped Hrafn's hand and mumbled something that seemed at once sincere and urgent, but came out as gibberish.

'Don't make fun of the old boy,' said Vigdís. 'He's sick.'

'If you ask me, they're both sick,' said Hrafn. 'Sick in the head. Take the foxes, for instance. What kind of farmer befriends foxes? And how that reindeer died is a mystery to me too.'

'They were beautiful,' said Anna. 'And I doubt there's much for them to eat around here. If they came scavenging round my farm in the middle of winter, half-starved and miserable-looking, I'd probably do the same.'

'They're too aggressive to be domestic animals, or some kind of cat-dog. That's their *nature*. No one befriends foxes!'

Hrafn scoffed. 'And what farmer would encourage them? Either you keep livestock *or* you run a fox farm, you can't do both.'

'You're right, it is odd . . . Perhaps they don't depend on farming. The more I think about them, the more intrigued I am,' Anna went on. 'You don't build all that without money, and if they have to buy in hay and fodder as well, they must have even more funds. I wonder what they did before they came here.'

'Astronauts, obviously,' said Egill.

He and Hrafn became absorbed in a discussion about foxes and fox farming, which Hrafn's father had invested in back in the nineties, and the girls fell silent. Vigdís felt a stinging sensation between her thighs from the urine that had dribbled onto her in the cattle shed. In fact, ever since she'd woken up that morning, her whole body had felt off-kilter; her heart was beating faster than usual and her breathing was shallow and rapid.

She wished she could chat with Anna. From the moment the trip started, all their attempts to talk had failed. They'd met for dinner a few times beforehand, and things had been less strained then because they both knew there was an end in sight. But right from the beginning of this trip, it was as if they'd realized everything had changed, and as a result they kept floundering: their exchanges were fraught with misunderstanding, affected politeness, silences that were too long or too short. Relations with Egill were easier, the demands less uncompromising, because naturally, as two women, she and Anna were expected to bond. They weren't expected to *bond* with each other's partners.

Perhaps because Anna was younger, Vigdís sensed a slight superciliousness in her; sometimes she suspected that Anna thought her too *conventional*, not impulsive enough, that she didn't express everything in evocative language. Doubtless she was imagining things. Trigger nudged against her, tongue lolling, eyes shining.

She decided to say the first thing that came into her head.

'I do like you,' she said, scratching the backs of Trigger's ears.

'What?' Anna leaned forward in her seat, smiling at Vigdís.

'You heard me!' Vigdís laughed. 'I said I like you. I just wanted you to know that.'

'Thanks, that's sweet of you. I was just this minute thinking about how everything is so . . . About how useless I am.'

'I often wish we could talk more, only I'm not always sure how. Sorry if I seem odd. I'm not drunk, perhaps it's all this fresh air . . .'

'You needn't apologize. I have a confession to make too, since we're on the subject: I feel awkward around you . . .'

'Awkward, why?'

'I don't know. Maybe because I started seeing a shrink a couple of months ago. I have the feeling that you can all see through me, that you think I'm hiding something.'

'I understand. And are you hiding something?'

Their eyes met, and Anna grinned.

'You're good at this! No, I guess it's just a general sense of shame, about nothing in particular. I don't know. When I leave the shrink I feel ashamed of myself, like a guy sneaking out of a brothel. I find handing over the money difficult too; I'm not sure you can ever pay enough for something like that. And money interferes with the illusion that I've been talking to someone who really cares about me. In other words, I want the whore to say I love you, or better still – I love you *truly*. It's pathetic . . . Am I comparing you to a whore?' Vigdís nodded and they both burst out laughing. 'I don't think I could do that kind of job, where you take your work home with you.'

'You can learn anything,' said Vigdís, 'for example, how to keep a professional distance. Although, coping with this line of work requires you to do many things: examine your own life, confront past problems, open up old wounds. Things I think that I've achieved.'

The moment she said this, Vigdís was aware that it was false, and she felt as if a crack were trying to open inside her head, which was filled with confusion and pain.

'And then of course you get used to it,' she added, gazing out of the window, at the sands passing her by. 'Isn't that the simplest explanation?'

Vigdís didn't remember where or in what context she had first heard the expression 'ordinary people', but she'd had the feeling ever since that it referred to her parents. Vigdís's mother was the daughter of a fisherman and a housewife.

She was brought up in Akureyri until the family moved to Hafnafjörður when she was a teenager. She met Vigdís's father, who was older than her, at a junior college dance. He was a merchant seaman and came back from America and Hamburg bearing armfuls of tinned ham, chewing gum and nylons. After dating briefly, they moved into a small apartment together on Framnesvegur, on the west side of town, which became the family home.

Her mother enrolled at teacher training college, but had to abandon her studies because of illness, which Vigdís later discovered, after wheedling it out of her father, was related to her 'nerves'. He also mumbled something about a miscarriage, a difficult time, and said that her mother had always been sensitive.

Perhaps her parents' fear of change, or their general inertia, explained Vigdís's late arrival into the world, when her mother was in her late thirties, and her father approaching fifty. She learned that she was neither planned nor 'an accident', and when she asked: 'What, then?' her mother told her, in a rare display of passion: 'Why, it was you of course. *You* wanted to be born', and at that moment Vigdís felt closest to understanding her mother and her mother's philosophy of life, although philosophy was probably too big a word for it.

Her arrival barely disrupted her parents' existence, as they had had plenty of time to settle into their routine. Her father continued to make his little round trips to Hamburg via a shipping canal in the Baltic Sea, and afterwards to Norway before coming home, but he barely spent any time on land during those trips, and besides, as he said himself, by then you could get ham anywhere in Iceland. Following her illness, Vigdís's mother decided to take a correspondence course in shorthand and typing, and after a brief period temping, she found full-time employment as personal secretary to a financial consultant at the head office of the Central Bank of Iceland in Austurstræti.

Vigdís entered the primary school in Vesturbær, moved into her own bedroom, and experienced her first and last tantrum when she set her heart on having a cat, and wouldn't stop crying until her mother procured a kitten from one of the neighbours. After that, nothing of much interest happened. Vigdís did exceptionally well at school, she was quiet, conscientious and had a small group of faithful friends. She only saw her father a few weeks every year, and later suspected that he had accepted as many tours as he could, although she never asked him about it.

Her mother didn't say much, but compensated by taking even greater care of Vigdís; she was more like a quiet, doting grandmother, and this at once confirmed and was an attempt to bridge the peculiar distance between them, a distance Vigdís had never seen observed in other mother–daughter relationships. Perhaps it was simply due to her parents' age and how late they had her. Vigdís's paternal grandparents from the north seldom came to visit; her other grandmother had died, and her grandpa was 'poorly' and lived in a care home in Kjalarnes, which Vigdís later found out was for elderly alcoholics. On the few occasions when her friends came round to her house, they mistook her mother for her grandmother, and for the most part Vigdís didn't disabuse them.

As a teenager she tried to rebel against the mysterious silence and timidity that lay like a weight over their home; the apartment felt as if it were buried deep inside the belly of a silent monster that had swallowed it long ago, as her friend Guðlaug put it. With Guðlaug's help, Vigdís ceased to be the daughter of old parents, learned to act the clown at least once a month, dabbled with smoking and drinking, and lost her virginity at fifteen to a boy three years her senior. He was alone at home in a big house in Skerjafjörður, and before she knew it he had chased her naked and giggling into a hot tub out in the garden. The experience wasn't a total disaster, although she wrote in her diary that she regretted no longer being able to imagine sex as something liberating, something that took her out of herself. Perhaps she simply had difficulty trusting people, giving herself to a stranger.

Shortly after Vigdís started her second year at junior college, her mother was run over. She was walking home from work one Friday, when a car came careering round the corner, close to Landakotskirkja church, hitting her with such force that she was thrown over the railings onto the lawn. She was holding a plastic bag that contained the groceries she had bought for her and Vigdís's evening meal. Three days later, Vigdís found a chocolate bar in the grass near where her mother had lain. For the past few months, her mother had been in the habit of buying chocolate for them to have after dinner on Fridays, and Vigdís became convinced that this chocolate bar was the one her mother had bought for her. She took it home, where her father had returned to arrange the funeral, continued crying herself softly to sleep, and did her best to behave sensibly, then went on a drinking binge after her father had gone back to sea.

She sat down to write an obituary, because the knowledge that no one else would was too painful for her to bear. There had to be some sign that her mother had lived. She wrote down everything she could remember, but had the impression that she was inventing it all, save for the few brief episodes she was able to recall, the times they had spent together in the back garden. The garden was small and they shared it with the other residents in the block, but her mother had obtained permission to take over a corner of it, where she dug a potato patch, sowed carrot and cabbage seeds, and planted a tree. When spring came, Vigdís helped her to plant bulbs and sow seeds, to weed out the dandelions and buttercups. One summer, her father built them a tiny potting shed. She and her mother painted it green, made a curtain for the square window that overlooked the lawn, and put up some shelves where her mother could grow seedlings. Gradually she built up a collection of implements, which she hung on the walls, bags of seeds she had no space to plant yet, and finally she added a table and two stools where she and Vigdís would occasionally sit and chat.

With hindsight, Vigdís found it hard to believe that she had sat there with her mother (who was less able there than in the house to use her domestic chores as a smoke-screen), and that they had been forced to communicate. It was unlike her to make herself so available, and although they didn't say very much to each other, Vigdís glimpsed a more complex side to her mother, which at the time she hadn't the sense or the experience to understand. She remembered the way her mother used to sit and smoke, gazing out of the window in silence, and she knew there was something about her mother's life that she had overlooked, something that encompassed more than she knew, which wasn't overtly knowable but rather remained unspoken . . . Or at least so she allowed herself to hope.

After the funeral, her father went back to sea, and came home even less often than before. Her friend Guðlaug nicknamed her Pippi Longstocking, and started staying over at her house more and more until finally she moved in. Vigdís's father let them have the apartment, refused to take any rent, and would stay at a guesthouse the few times he took shore leave.

Vigdís finished junior college and enrolled at the university to study psychology. Sometimes she would get drunk and have a one-night stand, usually with one of her classmates, but otherwise she spent most of her time in the library. She was good at retaining ideas, and graduated among the top of her year, after which she moved to Copenhagen to take an MA; her thesis was about the link between depression and diabetes.

As part of the course she had to undergo therapy, during which she attempted to gain an understanding of her own life, to break away from herself, from *the silence*. At times she found it all impossible; she was too like her mother and hidden inside her was that something that would one day take over her life, dragging her with it into the silence, if it hadn't already. On her return to Iceland, she opened her own practice on Klapparstígur, where she treated her clients using cognitive behavioural therapy, eschewing Jungian dream interpretation, although occasionally she would give in to temptation. She joined the World Class Gym, along with thousands of other Icelanders, and discovered an afternoon course in Zen Buddhism on Grensásvegur, where she perfected a new form of 'open' silence.

Life was good. Together with Guðlaug, who was now PA to one of the directors of Kaupthing Bank, she joined a society aimed at strengthening networks between women, which included weekly trips to restaurants, monthly golfing, fly-fishing or swimming excursions as well as luxury trips abroad every year. During a trip to Milan, Vigdís, who hadn't had sex for months, allowed an Italian guy to seduce her at a discotheque, and she first heard Hrafn's name mentioned – as one of the most despicable bloodsuckers in Iceland. Shortly afterwards, the man himself walked into her consulting room, his life an incomprehensible mess which she promptly began to untangle with her cognitive behavioural therapy.

She soon formed the impression that he fancied her. One afternoon, after a session, they took a stroll round Tjörnin, the lake in the city centre, dined at a restaurant, and ended up in bed at his place – a big house out on Seltjarnarnes, not unlike the one where she lost her virginity, with a hot tub on the first-floor veranda with a view of Mount Esja, except that the sports car parked outside the garage was black not red. The next day he told her he loved her and wanted to spend the rest of his life with her, showered her with gifts and seemed sincere. She made him promise he wouldn't tell anyone about their relationship (it reflected badly on her as a professional), but soon afterwards she was spending every night at his place. With Hrafn everything moved fast, but above all he was fun: he used more words over one breakfast than her parents had during their entire lives, and he knew the first page of Halldór Laxness's novel *Iceland's Bell* off by heart.

At first, she wasn't too sure what he did for a living, but then she read up about his business on the Internet, met his parents, who lived on Laufásvegur, and spent a week with them at a beach house in Florida, where she watched Hrafn's father grin smugly over his whisky glass, nodding knowingly as his son told amusing anecdotes about him, painting a picture of a friendly sociopath who would order the dissolution of trade unions in the morning, distribute wheelchairs to the needy in the afternoon, and try to rape a waitress at Hotel Holt in the evening. The family reaped their fortune from the sea, which they plundered on behalf of the Icelandic nation, legitimately; and yet, deep down, perhaps there was something immoral about that – it depended on whom you asked.

After Hrafn sold his majority stake in the company to his brother, he started to invest, moving his money all over the world from one account to another, and watching it grow. He insisted it was a difficult, precarious job, but Vigdís didn't think he was particularly stressed or overworked. They would occasionally go to embassy receptions, or cocktail parties thrown by the banks, attended by acquaintances of Hrafn's, and his friends from The Party. He described himself as an apolitical pragmatist, with modest ambitions, who considered himself – and his brother – custodians of the family fortune, whose duty it was, at the very least, to preserve that fortune and hand it down to the next generation. He envisaged having children in the future, and wanted to give them a more loving upbringing than he had received. As for his old age, he would be content with a house on the Grand Canal, where he could paint watercolours on the veranda and read. He was unsure himself whether he was serious or not, but usually had a wry expression on his face when he spoke about it.

Vigdís had no idea what her own feelings were. She hadn't been with many men in her life, and was more preoccupied with what someone like Hrafn might see in her. Although she considered herself charming and cultured enough for him, she was occasionally aware of an *ordinariness* inside her – that inhibited, silent part of her, which didn't know how to, or daren't, break free and demand all the things Hrafn and his family seemed to take for granted. Not that they didn't have problems, only theirs didn't arise from lack of means or excessive humility; they didn't hesitate when they wanted something, or go round apologizing. On the contrary, they seemed to possess a sense of entitlement that enabled them to demand more from others than they did from themselves, which could have been interpreted as a kind of arrogance. Even so, Vigdís was conscious of a distance, a 'class divide' between the two of them, and one evening Hrafn explained it in his own way when he told her that he loved her more than he loved himself; she was independent, and she possessed an inner serenity that radiated from her gaze, ennobling everything around her. Moreover, she was exquisitely beautiful, gentle and incapable of dishonesty – everything his family was not.

She met up with her father three times a year. They would go out for a meal and talk about the past, or whatever was making the news that week. Clearly her father was 'a good man', and yet he was so distant that sometimes she had the impression she was sitting alone at the table, his silence so genuinely profound that it didn't even make her feel awkward . . . Not so much a doting father as a well-meaning uncle. Occasionally Vigdís blamed her problems on her parents, though not in any serious way. Doubtless she could have received a bit more affection as a child, although if that were the sole injustice she had suffered in life, it could safely be considered a minor offence. On the whole, they were good people, mild-mannered, timid, and the only remarkable thing in their lives was that they never married, possibly due to a lack of initiative, and because they shied away from all the fuss associated with weddings.

Perhaps none of this had actually taken place, or in a different way than she thought. Sometimes, she suspected it was guesswork based on photographs from the only family album her mother had made, which Vigdís had pored over after her death. She had no brothers or sisters, so there weren't many people she could ask and, when her father was finally engulfed by silence, there would be no one.

Occasionally she would dream about her mother, hear the thud as she collided with the car, see her float up into the sky, like Mary Poppins, only without the umbrella or the songs, limbs twisted as she hovered above the lawn at Landakotskirkja church, smiling serenely.

Vigdís clasped the back of the seat. The road was getting steadily worse, more compacted, potholed and bumpy. The surrounding sands were more rugged, and strewn with huge boulders.

The jeep was juddering more than before, and Vigdís clenched her teeth to stop them from chattering. Through the window she saw that the road was threading through a rocky, gravelly part of the landscape, between dunes and ridges, which now flanked them. They drove over a few furrows and two or three potholes, until they felt a heavy jolt. There was a loud bang, the engine stalled and the jeep ground to a halt.

'Shit!' said Anna, who had bumped her head against the front seat. 'What's happening now?'

Hrafn didn't reply. He climbed down from the vehicle and the others piled out after him.

The jeep was listing to one side, and the front tyre on the passenger side looked as if it had a puncture.

6
AMONG THE GRAINS

Egill

'Fuck!' said Egill, walking round the jeep shaking his head.

Hrafn lay on his stomach to take a look underneath, while Egill did the same on the other side. Midway under the jeep, on the passenger side, was a big pothole, which they had driven into and out of again. The front edge of the hole was so jagged it had burst the tyre.

'Pile of junk,' muttered Egill, dusting himself off as he rose to his feet.

The stretch of road they were on lay between two stony dunes, and was probably the only place where they couldn't have circumvented the pothole. Trigger stared over at one of the dunes, whimpered softly and tucked his tail between his legs.

'I think the axle is broken,' said Hrafn, standing up. 'Or whatever it's called, the rod that goes between the wheels . . . At least we didn't get stuck in the pothole.'

Anna was sitting a short distance away on the sands, tugging at her earlobe and smoking a cigarette. Egill didn't feel like talking to her.

'We can fix it, can't we?' said Egill.

'Sure, if the old couple have a blowtorch,' replied Hrafn. 'And two spare tyres. Both the front ones have punctures.'

The tyre that hadn't blown completely emitted a low hiss as it slowly deflated.

Hrafn walked over to the girls and told them they should go back to the farm, while Egill pretended to be fixing something on the other side of the jeep. They put on their rucksacks and set off. Egill was glad to be rid of them. He could hear Vigdís trying to reassure Anna, who seemed upset – how typical! – about not being able to get out of there.

'This was only our first attempt,' Vigdís was saying.

Trigger loped oddly ahead of them yapping, before they disappeared into the vastness.

Hrafn rummaged in the boot for the tools and lay down under the jeep again, while Egill sat on top of one of the dunes, opened a can of beer and took a swig of whisky. He had a pre-rolled joint in his shirt pocket.

The weather was brightening up, and soon the breeze dropped and it grew so warm that they took their shirts off and Egill rolled up his trouser legs.

He lit a cigarette. Anna was always trying to control him. She didn't know herself very well – not as well as he knew her, at any rate. Sometimes he felt the need to do absolutely nothing; he would sit blankly, empty his mind, and watch her flap about, desperately trying to connect with him, the same way she channel-hopped, searching for something to take her out of herself, push away the anxiety that flared up in her when she couldn't work out what her surroundings were telling her, when she was confronted with herself.

After tinkering under the jeep for about five minutes, Hrafn seemed to have had enough. He cleaned the rust and oil off his hands and flung the tools into the boot. Then he stood next to Egill, took a swig from his water bottle and looked out at the horizon. Clasped under his arm was a red plastic box he had found in the boot.

'Did it go OK?' asked Egill. 'What were you doing?'

'Seeing whether I could fix the axle.'

'Do you know much about cars?'

'More than you anyway . . . That hole looks recent.'

'What do you mean?'

'The pothole we drove into, I think it has been freshly dug. Or made deeper. The earth at the bottom is darker than the surrounding sand.'

'We drove into it, so it's normal that the ground got churned up. What difference does it make?'

Hrafn shrugged.

'I found some flares in the boot,' he said, fingering the box. 'They might be useful.'

Inside were half a dozen red plastic batons with wooden handles, and the instructions printed on them.

'Encouraging,' said Egill. 'At least they're newer than the jeep.'

They started to make their way back. Hrafn said the rusty axle was probably irreparable, regardless of what tools the old couple might have.

'Are you saying that someone dug the hole?' asked Egill.

'I don't know . . . Who would have done that?' Hrafn shook his head. 'Don't say anything to the girls. We don't want to scare them.'

'What are we going to do if we can't get the jeep going?'

'How should I know? We'll lie down and start rotting away,' said Hrafn, suddenly irritated.

A soft breeze rose from the south. The sands stretched in all directions now, and the skyline was unbroken by hills or mountains. It occurred to Egill that there were few places in the world where they were less likely to meet another human being: Siberia, the Sahara, the Canadian wilderness, the North and South Poles . . .

'We're so tiny,' he said, although he had intended to say something quite different.

'What do you mean! Are you scared, do you want your mummy?'

Hrafn rolled his eyes. His temper continued to flare up, as it had done throughout the trip.

'I don't know.' Egill took a swig from his flask and pulled a face. 'You've changed,' he said, determined not to let Hrafn browbeat him. 'This last year. I realized it the other day when I was thinking about the past. You're more talkative, and yet more distant. More extreme, as if you were . . .' He was about to ask Hrafn whether he was having problems at work, whether he had *lost everything*, but that would be stupid and way too obvious. 'Occasionally it feels like you have a secret, something you don't want to talk about. You do know that you can trust me, right?'

'What do you want me to say? Shall I pour out my life to you in one sentence?'

'Is everything OK between you and Vigdís?'

'Of course everything is OK between us. She's the best thing that ever happened to me, no doubt about it. Why are you asking me about *her*?'

'I'm just asking, my friend. You seem preoccupied.'

They kept walking, saw no sign of the girls, and followed the tyre tracks.

Hrafn came to a halt and apologized for having lost his temper.

'The other day Vigdís suggested I start drinking again, if it would stop me being so prickly.'

He laughed, admitting that he and Vigdís had been going through a bad patch recently, but that it was nothing serious; he spoke about the challenges of running a business these days – given the difficult situation – and Egill had the impression that he was struggling to hold back the tears.

'I don't know,' Egill began, as they set off again. 'Anna and I are all messed up, in any case. Our sex life is dead, over. She wants us to see a counsellor. Everyone I know is all messed up. It's like this nation is a machine that chews people up and spits them out again, glued together any old how – with arseholes for mouths, eyes in their crotches . . .'

They scaled a dune, a minuscule wave amid an otherwise calm ocean, but they couldn't see the house, only the straight line of the road. Hrafn cursed himself for having left his binoculars behind, sat down on the sand and doused his head with water from his bottle.

Egill took a swig from his hip flask, and tossed it onto the sand in front of them, plucked the joint from his shirt pocket, and held it up to his nose as he gave Hrafn a sidelong glance.

'Do you ever think about the days we spent in Árbær?' said Egill. 'We had fun. Wicked fun. Have you ever had *that much* fun since? But perhaps you lived in a different world from me, over there in Selás?' Egill laughed. 'A little bird in a gilded cage.'

Hrafn hadn't grown up in an apartment block. His parents lived in one of the biggest houses on Fjarðarás, where Egill first clapped eyes on a sunbed, an ice dispenser and a cordless telephone. In the games room, next to the Pac-Man, hung a gigantic poster of Val d'Isère in the French Alps, where Hrafn and his family had been going skiing since he was a kid. Apart from that, the members of his family didn't seem to have much to do with one another, unlike Egill's family, but then there were fewer places to hide in his parents' apartment.

They discovered alcohol through Hrafn's brother and his friends, who held a three-week-long party, much to the annoyance of their parents, who were away at the time skiing. Egill and Hrafn's drinking spree had started on the sofa in the sitting room, moved to the games room, the ping-pong and billiard tables, then to the rowing machine which they took turns competing on, before ending in the sauna, where Hrafn threw up over himself, and Egill did the same over the coals. They vowed never to repeat the experience, and collapsed on the bed dead drunk. The smell of vomit pervaded the cellar for months, but the following day some of the girls who were still partying upstairs persuaded them to start all over again. An older girl took Hrafn to bed in nearby Ártúnsholt, where he had sex for the first time, but the only thing he could remember was that her name was Valdís. Egill remarked that the name sounded oddly similar to Val d'Isère, and was convinced ever since that Hrafn had lied about it just so that he could be *first*.

When Egill's parents moved to Vesturbær, he was given the basement all to himself. Hrafn would often sleep over during the week, and he and Egill gave up the petty thieving and hustling they had indulged in at Árbær and in the Kringlan shopping arcade, and began brewing moonshine in a garage on Grandavegur, bottles of which they would deliver by bike to the area between Rauðarárstigur and Seltjarnarnes. In their final year at secondary school they started smoking grass behind the fish huts on Ægisíða, and soon afterwards, almost as if it were destined to happen, Hrafn lost the plot. All the things they had done together for the first time – drinking, smoking dope, taking out their aggression on streetlamps, bus shelters and people – Egill learned to curb, while Hrafn lost control, driven on by something Egill couldn't understand. After Hrafn dropped out of junior college and left home, he started dealing the drugs he himself was taking, and got in so deep he wasn't even aware that anything had changed. Egill could no longer keep up with him, and when the opportunity arose, soon after they both turned eighteen, he broke off their friendship with the help of a girl Hrafn was keen on; and so he got Hrafn out of his life, and never looked back – until ten years later when they bumped into one another at a cocktail party.

Egill rolled the joint between his fingers a couple of times before lighting it. He inhaled the smoke and held it in. After a moment, he passed the joint to Hrafn, who took it, as if there had never been any question of him doing anything else. Egill exhaled, and could tell without looking that Hrafn had taken one, two puffs. They passed the joint between them.

'Did you know that 1.5 per cent of the surface area of the United States is tarmacked?' said Egill, gazing out at the sands.

'Is that a lot?'

Egill giggled, his head felt as if it were swelling up and might explode at any moment, and each time he opened his mouth to speak it swelled up more.

He reached for his mobile phone and switched it on.

'Any signal?'

Egill shook his head, and slipped the phone back in his pocket. Hrafn passed him the joint, and he took a puff, holding in the smoke until he felt his body go limp. The smoke swirled in his lungs, and when he let out a pale grey streak, he knew that every cell in his body was in exactly the right place, and couldn't have been otherwise. When they were younger and drank together, Hrafn had referred to it as boosting the high – not too much, just enough to give them an extra kick. He passed the joint back to Hrafn and said:

'I met a guy at a party once who was writing a book about cows. He maintained that in certain areas of the country where there are no phone signals, no radio waves, none of the crap that clogs up the air in towns, that's where all the spirits come together – imps, ghosts of unwanted babies, elves and fairies, land-wights and ogres. Because they can't exist anywhere else.'

'That makes sense.'

Egill nodded.

'Supposing there are other dimensions and beings that inhabit them, surely they would work on different frequencies, other wavelengths, and some of them might get interference from our little phone signals – which in their world probably feels like the sky is being sprayed with machine-gun fire, nail bombs. Of course they would flee into the mountains. Settle here on the sands, among the grains.'

Egill reached for his hip flask and swilled his mouth with alcohol. He was holding the joint in his other hand, he couldn't remember how long for, and noticed it had almost burned down. He offered it to Hrafn, who waved it away, then rubbed it between his fingers, and gazed at the glowing ember on the sand, like a red squinting eye or a flower from hell. Before Anna met him, she had been unhappy and frustrated. Her sex life had been lousy. He found it exhausting, always having to take the initiative to fuck, putting up with her rejection, occasionally having to look elsewhere; he shouldn't need to do that. He wanted more affection, a burning passion that flowed through his body. Either that or money.

'Anna had never had an orgasm before she met me.'

'Your forehead is bleeding again.'

Egill lifted his hand to his brow. He felt the gauze and the wetness oozing beneath it, and saw the blood on his fingers.

'The heat, I expect.'

He did nothing, had no clue what he should do, and thought in a muddled way about the drops he used to hide the redness in his eyes when he smoked.

'. . . on all fours and ran off into the darkness.' Hrafn was describing something he had seen out of his window the night before.

'Aha . . . Getting paranoid already?'

'I wasn't imagining things. It ran out onto the sands on all fours and disappeared.'

They fell silent. Egill tried to envisage what it would have been like to grow up out there, on the sands . . . in the nineteenth century. Or in the eighteenth, seventeenth or sixteenth centuries.

'I don't understand how people managed to live up here in the old days. Imagine the silence and the *darkness*. No colours, no sounds, no light, apart from maybe a candle end or a fish-oil lamp; nothing to look at, no books, no tasty food. Nothing . . . All day, every day, *your whole life long*. For a thousand years. Skinny little bodies, wizened little souls, like raisins in the sand.'

'At least they had their folk tales,' said Hrafn. 'About other worlds, creatures that live in rocks and boulders, elves, spirits, the ghosts of unwanted babies. Isn't that what you were saying just now?'

'Tales of their own madness.' The conversation was beginning to make Egill uneasy.

'We should head home soon, walk it off,' said Hrafn.

'It'll be fine, we'll manage . . .' Egill was about to add something, but he forgot what it was. As he gazed at the horizon he had the impression that the light was fading, although his watch told him it was much too early. 'Monsters and night trolls,' Egill murmured to himself as he saw before him *the Icelandic nation*: the offices of a trawler owner situated in a huge, lofty corrugated-iron warehouse down by the harbour; a vague smell of fish slime in the air, mixed with pine-scented shit-freshener wafting from the toilet, a computer humming on a desk, a telephone with a shoulder rest; on the wall an Independence Party membership certificate – the diploma of everyone who talked about the *school of life* – the perfect front for those who were against independence and freedom; shelves lined with ring binders containing figures about the catch, local fishing quotas and salaries, and slumped behind the desk the genius himself: a small man with big appetites, a glutton, an avid reader of Arnaldur Indriðason, a 'subscriber' to his work, who *bridled* when he felt Arnaldur wasn't taken seriously, trumpeting his own stubborn opinions about the author's qualities; a staunch advocate of the market economy, freedom of choice, and the virtues of the free market, as well as a staunch advocate of himself and his own desires, equating – as and when it suited him – this and that, culture and money, sexuality and appetite; snoring as he rolled off women; he considered himself efficient, calculating and shrewd, and once he got power he clung to it for as long as possible, for the entire duration of the republic, in fact, through ridicule and scorn, by polarizing all debate, belittling and crushing everyone and everything.

'My father, in other words,' said Hrafn.

Egill realized he had been saying all that out loud, and that Hrafn was right. He was describing his father, Halldór.

'I'm sorry,' said Egill, but he didn't mean it, and didn't know why he had said it. He lit a cigarette. 'I was just going to say, it has no soul . . . The soul is missing, do you see?'

Why couldn't the four of them engage in any real, meaningful conversations when they were together? All their conversations fizzled out; they were banal, polite and sterile, never rising above the lowest common denominator. Were they even friends? Did any of them want to be there with the others? Why not split the group, to mix things up? If he had been sitting there with Vigdís, for example, the graceful Vigdís, he could speak sincerely, make a connection; he yearned for *tenderness and affection*.

'Vigdís is a fine woman,' he said, leaning back on his elbows and gazing up at the scudding clouds. 'She's kind and gentle, unpretentious. I understand exactly what you see in her . . . She makes you a better person, she isn't a narcissist, she doesn't have a spiteful bone in her body and she doesn't turn everything into a *competition*.'

Egill hadn't intended to say any of this out loud, but he seemed unable to stop himself.

'Motherly, even,' he went on. 'Those qualities are rare nowadays. She has a soul. I'd give anything for that, to have what you have. You don't know how lucky you are, you've never known.'

'. . . *sure*.' He heard Hrafn's voice as though from a long way off, echoing against the coldness engulfing them. His voice sounded hard, like an icicle.

'What we need . . .' Egill started to say, but then a wave of drowsiness overcame him, and he decided to close his eyes for a while, let go of all those thoughts and anxieties, that emotional turmoil, everything that was Egill.

'. . . walk,' said Hrafn, and Egill waved his hand, which had gone numb. But his heartbeat was normal – everything would be fine.

'I'm good,' he said with a sigh, and felt the glow from the invisible glacier on his face, felt its coldness spreading over the land – its past and future, penetrating every crevice before bursting forth once more – heard Hrafn's footsteps grow fainter, the sand dissolve, the sand crystals dissolve with each of his movements, and disappear.

7

THE PICTURE OF THE BEAUTIFUL PEOPLE

Anna

Anna woke up as Egill clambered into the bed next to her. After their walk back, she and Vigdís had gone to rest in the bedrooms they had been allotted the night before. He snuggled up to her, and soon they had made up, without really discussing anything.

She and Egill each opened a can of beer and went out to join Hrafn and Vigdís, who were busy prepping for the evening meal, having set up a table and chairs on the sands, close to the house. Vigdís said to Anna in hushed tones that she proposed to spend as little time as possible inside the house.

'I know what you mean,' said Anna.

Fragments of her dream came back to her: a glacier melting to reveal three gravestones lined up in a row, looming like tower blocks; a faint red light shining from the windows, and foxes spilling across the sands like a river of fire.

They divided up the tasks: Hrafn set up the portable barbecue and filled it with coals, wrapped the mushrooms stuffed with blue cheese in tinfoil, and rubbed oil on the steaks; Vigdís peeled the onions and vegetables under the watchful eye of Ása, who was standing by the kitchen window, and Anna fetched the potatoes from the car. Egill, who had a fresh bandage on his head, sat swigging beer and didn't help at all unless he was asked several times. He played with Trigger, patting him and throwing a ball for him to fetch, much to Anna's surprise; he usually couldn't stand 'the dog', complained about his big round eyes when he sat begging at the table, and would preferably have confined Trigger and his hairs to the hallway.

They had bought plenty of food before leaving Mývatn, as they didn't expect to go near any towns for a while. Hrafn had installed an icebox in the boot to prevent the meat from going off, and the lobster Egill was planning to grill when they got to the centre of the country, which was supposed to symbolize a triumph over nature.

Anna couldn't remember how long they had been away. The trip had engulfed her completely, or was it the other way round? She was too impressionable, and after doing something for a few days, she felt she had never done anything else. She reckoned they had been away for about a week; they set off on Sunday, spent the first night at Thingvellir, and the second at a hotel near Geysir, because they couldn't be bothered to put up the tent. After that, they had driven to Hvítárvatn, where they stayed for two nights, and then to Kerlingarfjöll, which she had written in her notebook was Iceland's most picturesque rhyolite mountain range. They climbed up Hánýpur, bathed in

Hveradalir, then drove over Kjölur heading east towards Mývatn, where they stayed at a hotel, relaxed for two nights and stocked up on provisions.

She went into the kitchen to ask Ása if they could speed things up by boiling the potatoes in the kitchen, but saw no sign of her. In the front room, Anna paused to look at a photograph she had noticed earlier, realizing that she hadn't been able to get it out of her head since they arrived. It was black and white, framed behind glass and slightly faded. At first Anna had assumed it was of the old couple when they were young, only now she was convinced that the woman wasn't Ása, but another, more beautiful woman. She was tilting her head and smiling dreamily; in the photograph she looked about thirty, younger than the man, who was broad-shouldered, held himself erect and had the air of a matinée idol: dark, wavy, slicked-back hair, big eyes and a jaw that was prominent without coarsening his features. He wore an immaculately tailored suit, and was staring straight ahead, solemn though not morose, through a pair of spectacles so flimsy they almost didn't show up on the photograph. If Anna hadn't known better, she would have taken him for an educated man from a good family, not a farmer, likewise the woman next to him.

Something troubled her about the picture: perhaps the way the woman was tilting towards the man, one shoulder raised, as if she were holding something that wasn't visible, or was it the composition of the picture, the strange proportions?

On the other hand, why couldn't the old man be educated

or from a good family? Anna had more difficulty imagining the old woman, Ása, as anything but a . . . A what? 'Housewife' was doubtless the word she was looking for. And yet they must *do* some kind of work, or have worked in the past to make money.

She heard the floor upstairs creaking, changed her mind about the potatoes and hurried back outside.

The four of them sat around the table, which was draped with a cloth, and raised their glasses brimming with white wine – all except Hrafn, who was drinking some kind of apple juice. Anna felt sorry for him not being able to drink, but in another way it struck her as childish. Vigdís pulled out the Fotorama instant camera she had inherited from her mother, and took a picture of them.

'To nature!' cried Anna, and they clinked glasses for the camera. The photograph took less than a minute to develop. Anna's eyes were red, her mouth twisted in a grimace, revealing her discoloured tooth which she was planning to have bleached. During the trip Vigdís had used the camera to take photos of flowers and shrubs, and had joked about being the first to discover a new migratory species, transported to the highlands on the soles of foreigners' hiking boots. The new flower would be named Vigdísbloom, after her.

'This is the way women hunt', Anna had jotted down for her article, although it was more likely that Vigdís simply wanted to remember her mother, whom she had clearly loved very much: using the camera she had inherited from her, and discovering the names of plants, which it seemed was one of her mother's favourite hobbies.

Egill emptied yet another glass, and Anna wished he would slow down so he wouldn't end up a liability later on in the evening. Apart from the house to their south, they had a clear view over the sands.

Trigger lay at her feet under the table. Every now and then he would whine softly and rub himself against her, until she gave him one of the bones she had brought with her from Reykjavík. *Tired after running*, she thought. On their way home, he had taken off, reappearing just as she and Vigdís reached the house, panting as if he'd been running the whole time.

After a brief discussion about the weather, Hrafn said he had spoken to the old woman about the jeep.

'They don't have the tools to fix the axle. What's more, both front tyres are punctured and there's only one spare. Nor do they have any glue or patches. But she said we can have the flares.'

'They could come in handy,' said Vigdís.

'So, what now?' said Anna. 'We're not just going to sit here and wait when there's nothing to wait for, are we? How are we going to get out of here?'

Suddenly she had lost her appetite, and she clasped her wine glass, twisting it between her fingers.

'We'll walk,' said Vigdís. 'We can try to get a signal on our mobiles. And if we're lucky, we'll find an emergency shelter with a radio. Otherwise we'll follow the road north to Askja, which isn't very far from here.'

'How far?' asked Anna.

'Half a day's walk, I reckon,' said Vigdís. 'It depends where exactly we are on the map. Considering the time we spent driving round in circles, we shouldn't be more than a few hours away, roughly. We're bound to find a landmark nearby, then we can use the map and the compass.'

It was getting dark, and they were discussing the ambient music playing on the hi-fi. Egill attempted clumsily to explain to them the difference between ambient and minimalist music. Vigdís lit some candles, and lined them up in the middle of the table, making the darkness around them thicken. Hrafn put his arm round Vigdís and kissed her gently on the forehead.

Anna tried to catch Egill's eye, but couldn't. He stared inscrutably into the darkness and carried on drinking. The first time they met he was drunk, but in an attractive way, not like the fat blob he had become, but rather glowing with enthusiasm and self-confidence. His face was tanned, and he wore a white shirt unbuttoned at the neck and a close-fitting jacket. They were at a reception held by the Kaupthing Bank in Borgartún, where Anna was working on a feature about Icelandic businessmen's wives. He introduced himself and said he remembered her from junior college in Reykjavík. She couldn't say the same, although after a brief exchange, she vaguely recollected a rather morose guy in a pullover who ran for office – treasurer no doubt – in a school society called The Future, who went round with his nose buried in a business management handbook, and who was one or two years younger than her.

'I've improved, go on, admit it,' he said with a smile, but his smile didn't light up his eyes. When they got to know each other better, she noticed that his eyes seldom reflected what was going on in his face. Around that time, he had opened his offices on Suðurgata, and he told her that he still wasn't nearly rich enough to stop caring about money. He owned a flat in downtown Reykjavík, two cars, a snow sled and a summer cottage at the foot of the glacier on Snæfellsnes; he invested in gold every month, had a large portfolio of stocks and shares, as well as a speedboat for popping over to the glacier – he hadn't reached thirty yet, but for him that wasn't enough.

For her part, Anna claimed that all she wanted was to be happy, and she was half-hoping to annoy Egill, to shake him off; and yet something in her was drawn to his ruthlessness, his immorality, his naked ambition. She asked no questions, but unlike his parents, she didn't imagine that there were 'no losers', or that his schemes were risk-free. For some reason she felt a strong desire to get to know him, to understand what made him tick. When it seemed she might fail, she did her best to burrow into his life, to make herself indispensable, and at the same time to look out for his biggest weaknesses (his vulnerability and alienation), though only glancingly. And when at last she discovered them, it wasn't due to her own cleverness, but because he gave himself away.

Anna felt uneasy again. She drained her glass, and put on some livelier music. Hrafn and Vigdís soon stood up to dance on their side of the table, twirling on the sands, while Anna had to cajole Egill until he swung her, giggling, round and round in circles. She noticed how he was watching the other couple move – or Vigdís, at any rate. Now that she thought about it she realised this wasn't the first time that evening she'd caught Egill looking at Vigdís in that way. And she wasn't the only one: Hrafn had noticed it too – over the rim of his glass of fruit juice. But Anna didn't figure that out from the way Hrafn was looking at Egill – no, the two men were ignoring each other – but rather from the way he kept stealing glances at *Vigdís*. Anna was sensitive to things like that, too sensitive, and she always had been.

She decided to thrust it aside. A feeling of love welled up inside her, and soon she was oblivious to everything except the rapid, rhythmic beat of her heart, and the stars lighting up one by one in the vaulted sky above their heads.

8

SKIMMI STOKKUR'S CROWN

Anna

Afterwards they sat at the table smoking. The music had stopped and the silence was broken only by Trigger's whimpering.

'He's afraid of the foxes, if they're lurking round here,' said Hrafn.

Egill kept rolling his eyes until finally Anna had had enough. She took Trigger into the house and shut him in the bedroom with his bone.

When she came back, Vigdís suggested they tell each other ghost stories. 'Isn't that what people do when they go camping? We don't really need to light a fire, do we?'

'Vigdís specializes in ghost stories,' said Hrafn.

'And in lost souls,' said Egill.

They demanded a ghost story and Vigdís admitted she had read lots of them when she was younger.

'As well as horror stories and folk tales. I remember one I heard not long ago. It happened at a student residence. I'm not sure I should be telling it to you . . .'

'Go on, for heaven's sake.' Anna shivered. 'I love being scared.'

'This could be classed as a folk tale, although not really, because it's true. It actually happened, and is probably still happening to this day. Don't say I didn't warn you. You made me—'

'Stop! Go on!' said Anna, giggling as she imagined Vigdís on a Girl Guide outing, wearing a red neckerchief and sitting round a campfire in Skorradalur with her fellow Guides, after a day spent learning how to tie knots and administer first aid.

'All right,' said Vigdís, and she started to tell the story. 'Once upon a time there was a young couple who had two children: a three-year-old and a seven-year-old. When the parents began their studies at university, they moved into one of the student residences on Eggertsgata, which are reserved for people with children. Most of the apartments were on the ground floor, overlooking the airport to the south, a few metres away from some rocks, which had apparently been damaged while the block was being built. Not long after the little family moved into one of the apartments, they noticed their daughter behaving strangely. It seemed she had an invisible friend who would materialize whenever she played on her own. Her parents first became aware of this when they saw her walk over to the open balcony doors and wave to something outside. When her mother asked her who was there, the girl instantly replied that it was 'Skimmi Stokkur', her new friend who lived in the rocks opposite the balcony.

'After that, Skimmi Stokkur's visits became more frequent, but the girl's parents weren't unduly worried: their daughter was at an age where children have imaginary friends, and whenever Skimmi was there she was better behaved. As for her little brother, apparently he saw nothing, but one day the girl said that Skimmi had made him a bright-blue, shiny crown with red balls at the front, and that it *wasn't good*. The girl became terribly agitated when she spoke about it, and her parents grew concerned. They questioned her more closely about Skimmi, and the girl described him as being thin or 'bony' and about the same height as her; he wore brightly coloured clothes, and his eyes shone, but were a colour unlike any other. He was always whispering, not with his mouth but with his eyes. She also said he had a funny nose, and from her description the parents understood that he had no nasal septum.'

'Meaning what?' asked Egill.

'That he had one nostril instead of two,' said Anna impatiently. 'What happened next?'

'Well, one day as the mother was washing up, her daughter came out of the bedroom and started tugging at her apron. The girl murmured something about a crown and her little brother and said they must go straight to the bedroom to help him. Her mother told her she had to finish what she was doing, and couldn't understand the girl's insistence until the lights in the apartment started to flicker off and on. Then she knew something was wrong and rushed into the bedroom, where she discovered her son, limbs jerking as he bounced around the room, a plume of black smoke billowing from his head. The fuses blew as the apartment filled with smoke, and the mother ran through the corridors clutching her poor little son, smoke still pouring from his head. But by the time the ambulance arrived he was dead.

'Afterwards, when asked what had happened, the girl told them she was alone in the front room when Skimmi Stokkur came in through the balcony doors and sat down beside her. They started to play, and soon her brother came in and sat down too. Then Skimmi put the crown on the boy's head, whispered something very fast and strange in his ear, and handed him a key that he was supposed to insert into his bedroom wall. At that point, his sister became frightened, and she went to the kitchen to try to alert her mother, but Skimmi tied a magic scarf around her mouth to slow her down. By the time her mother went into the bedroom, the crown on her brother's head was so bright that she was dazzled, and then everything went dark and Skimmi had disappeared.

'After the funeral, the parents left the university and moved to Norway, but people still tell stories about Skimmi. He usually enters the balcony doors of the ground-floor apartments closest to the rocks facing south, but he's been known to go into other apartments where there are children. If there are two children, he becomes the playmate of the older one, and the younger sibling ends up having an accident; if there is one, that child becomes increasingly disturbed and either falls seriously ill, or the parents have an accident.'

'Christ!' said Anna. 'It almost feels like there's some kind of logic to it. How did you hear about the story?'

'I worked with the children's aunt some years later. Their mother never went back to university; she found work as a chambermaid at a hotel in Bergen. After the tragedy, the parents separated and the daughter forgot all about Skimmi Stokkur . . . The aunt had two young children herself, and the moral of the story, she said, was: always listen to your children, and if they see something you can't see, then *be afraid*.'

9

'DON'T FEED THE TROLLS'

Anna

Anna giggled, and then they all burst out laughing without knowing why. Hrafn stood up and vanished into the darkness to take a piss, while Anna lit a cigarette. She was about to ask whether anyone had seen the space station during its orbit round Earth when Hrafn sat down at the table again and said:

'Haven't you noticed something odd about this house?'

They all looked towards the building, which was plunged into darkness, apart from the kitchen windows.

'The ground-floor windows have been walled up,' he went on, 'although you can still see the mouldings. And I'm almost sure the main door was originally at ground level, where the front steps are now. They've been built where the old door was, to raise the entrance.'

'Are there no windows on the ground floor?' asked Vigdís.

'I walked all the way round the house, and couldn't find a single opening on the ground floor, except for where the jeep drove into the wall. The old couple seem to have built themselves a small castle. All they need now is a moat . . .

Which raises the question: *why*? What horrors up here on the sands have forced these good people to take up arms, and driven them into their castle?'

'For heaven's sake . . .' said Anna, relaxing her stomach and feeling the life seep back into her limbs. 'Is this your ghost story?'

Hrafn grinned.

They burst out laughing again, except for Egill, who seemed irritated by the joke, and by the attention Hrafn was getting from the two girls; or perhaps it was the alcohol finally having an effect on him. His eyes were watery and slightly bloodshot, and his jaw was drooping.

'Yeah, I can't wait to get away from this place,' said Egill, as though finishing a thought he hadn't shared with the others. He reached across the table for the bottle and filled his glass. 'We're so *small* here . . .'

Anna vaguely remembered hearing him say this before, although in a completely different situation – in fact, in numerous situations of late. Since he abandoned his moral compass – in her eyes at any rate, and after he predicted that the whole nation would soon follow suit – he had been fumbling around for some kind of philosophical relativism, usually when drunk.

'Is it so bad to feel small?' asked Vigdís, looking up at the sky.

'The Icelandic countryside makes me queasy, always has. It's too barren. The whole middle bit of the country is empty, like a punctured balloon.'

'Perhaps we would feel claustrophobic if it were any other way,' said Vigdís.

'Claustrophobic? In your five thousand square feet on Seltjarnarnes?'

Egill scoffed and seemed to enjoy provoking them. He envied Hrafn's house, his money, his cars, his summer cottage in Thingvellir – at least since he risked losing everything he had hoarded for himself.

'All Icelanders live their lives in terms of this vastness up here, this wasteland,' said Vigdís. 'Even people like us who only come here occasionally.'

'Or never,' added Hrafn.

'Even when we're back in town, sitting in front of our TVs. If anything makes us free in this country it's that, whether we're aware of it or not. The highlands are like a sounding board for all our thoughts—'

'And therefore we mustn't touch anything?' interrupted Egill.

'He's spoiling for a fight,' said Anna, pretending to laugh. 'What's that expression on social media – don't feed the *troll*?'

'I didn't say we mustn't touch anything,' Vigdís retorted. 'But there has to be a balance between what we take out and what we put back. We need to make a pact with nature, to change our attitude towards it. Icelandic nature has always been either idealized and put on a pedestal, or subjugated, enslaved. Made to work. Icelandic nature has always been a woman.'

'Does it matter what gender it is? Besides, isn't it

desirable that women fill the job market? Are you any less hard-working than men?'

'Absolutely not,' said Vigdís, whom Anna had never seen so excited. 'If anything, women work harder. And to give nature its due, people should learn to regard it as a man. Preferably a proud, young, vigorous, sensitive, intelligent man – with a future. The havoc governments wreak during one term in office can be so serious that decades of small victories are nothing in comparison. That means any struggle which doesn't aim to bring about a fundamental change in our attitudes is lost before it even starts. We need to find that balance within ourselves.'

Anna applauded.

'I agree. Yin and yang,' she said, predicting that Egill would snort then roll his eyes, which he did. 'I want the highlands to stay exactly the way they are,' she went on. 'No more harnessing of glacial rivers, no more pylons, no more roads, or shops or hotels. Enough! When I travel to Europe, everywhere I look there are buildings, houses, roads, hoardings, shopping centres. It's depressing. There isn't a single square metre in England that hasn't been measured and valued. Holland, Germany, Belgium and France are no better, and Italy is one long motorway lined with cheap boutiques, football stadiums and hotels—'

'Am I the only man at this table?' cried Egill, throwing up his arms. 'Is there something wrong with being a *man*? I'm quite happy to be part of mankind, in a city, at an airport, or driving down a motorway in Italy. I can sit in a cafe and drink a cup of coffee without bursting into tears!

And isn't there grass in football stadiums? Is the grass outside them any more beautiful? Must there be grass on every mountaintop? Unscaled, untouched, remote?'

'We need nature to survive,' said Hrafn. 'A certain balance between order and chaos, which exists everywhere except where man has plonked himself down. Think of a brick wall, a superstore or a cruise ship – every last inch is planned, excessively ordered. Our brain gets tired of seeing that, it becomes stressed, anxious, weary of its own thoughts. We need nature to renew ourselves, to give us ideas. When we order every bit of the globe, we shut down, our imaginations grow dull, we lose the will to live.'

'Cliché.'

'In America and Britain, when something isn't working they put up a sign,' Vigdís said, grinning. 'Do you know what that sign says? *Out of order*. We are so sick that the moment something isn't rectangular and full of lights and numbers, we assume it needs fixing.'

'Just as well there are other languages than English in the world,' said Egill, straightening up in his chair. 'You're all much too *squeamish* or obsessively perfectionist or something. Besides, I wouldn't call this nature. If nature is supposed to be a balance between order and chaos, then it certainly overstepped the mark up here. It lost control, went into self-destruct mode. What we see around us is nature's corpse, its sand-blown skeleton, and that's what dulls us . . . Black, white, cold and minimalist, like a Manhattan apartment block. Everything else is romanticized drivel, conjured up in our heads.'

'Exactly. Quite right,' said Anna, feeling a sudden wave of resentment towards Egill and his hostile opinions, which were merely a reflection of his emotions at any given moment. 'For heaven's sake, can we please change the subject! Can't we at least agree that the landscape up here is unique, whether in a good way or in a malevolent way—'

'What I have difficulty understanding,' resumed Egill, sounding increasingly angry, 'is why you environmentalists are so keen for everyone to agree that all this is so noble and beautiful. Why? It's not as if nature is self-evidently noble! In fact, it would be much easier to find arguments to the contrary.'

'Stretching it a bit, perhaps,' said Hrafn, looking at Egill and smiling. 'In nature we can see that everything is constantly changing and merging. The only boundaries are in our minds. Which is good. That's the way it should be.'

'Nature teaches us humility,' Anna chimed in, for no particular reason other than to side with Hrafn.

Egill rolled his eyes. 'That sounds like something from the Movement. Therapy-speak, straight from the New Age garbage heap. Everything merges with everything else? No it doesn't. One thing is *eaten* by another, which in turn is eaten by something else, ad nauseam. And so life goes on, everyone in their separate boxes, not joined together, and certainly not noble.'

'So what do you believe in, Egill?' asked Hrafn, who was still smiling, but clearly irritated. 'Do you believe in Gandhi? Something other than yourself?'

Egill pulled out his silver-plated hip flask, took a swig, screwed the lid back on and stood it on the table.

'At least I got where I am on *my own merits,*' he said, and smiled. 'Nothing was given to me.'

'So, you're saying that you are noble, but nature isn't,' said Hrafn, and Anna had the impression that they were arguing about something entirely different. 'You've never stolen anything from anyone, never lied, never broken any of the Ten Commandments—'

'*The Ten Commandments*! That's rich, coming from the guy who broke chairs over people's heads! Who plundered his way through life without a care for anyone, distributing his magic powder all over town . . .'

Egill went quiet. Hrafn gazed at him impassively, even as a smile played on his lips that made Anna shudder.

'No, you've got to be kidding, the lot of you. I don't believe this,' Egill murmured to himself, finally falling silent when a banging noise reached them from the house.

The old woman was standing in the kitchen, rapping on the windowpane, her figure silhouetted against the light. She shouted something they couldn't hear properly through the glass, which sounded like an order to come indoors. Then she stepped away from the window, stopped rapping but continued to stare at them.

'Righty-ho!' yelled Egill, making a thumbs-up gesture at the house and muttering something about a 'fucking owl'. Everything about his face and manner made Anna think of a vulgarian and, no longer able to contain herself, she leaned across the table and hissed at him:

'Will you stop behaving like a child, *I'm ashamed of you*!'

She noticed a look of surprise then remorse in his eyes, before his expression hardened once more.

'I think we should all calm down,' said Vigdís. 'Let's try to be polite to one another, no matter how much pressure we are under. We're all friends here, Egill.'

'I'm not so sure about that, Vigdís dear, but never mind. It's difficult to say . . . Does everyone around this table *truly* feel they have something in common with all the others? You three do. Isn't that enough? You're all *noble*, you all agree and are so well meaning . . .'

The bickering resumed, but Anna didn't take part. She was watching a shadow that had appeared from around the corner of the house and now stood motionless, staring at them. Anna's fingers began to tingle, she felt a lump rise in her throat and a shiver ran up and down her spine, not unlike the sensation she had when she started to climax. Suddenly, she realized that for a long, long time all she had wanted was *to let go*, and at that moment she decided to succumb and gave a loud, frenzied cry. Everyone at the table fell silent, and followed her gaze in the direction of the house.

The shadow stood contemplating them quietly, before slowly making its way towards them. From inside the house they could hear Trigger's loud, incessant barks.

As he stepped into the light from the kitchen they recognized the old man, their host. He paused at one end of the table, eyes bleary, mouth drooping open, almost as if he were drunk.

'Good evening,' one of them said.

The old man moved his lips but no sound emerged. Then all of a sudden he wrinkled his brow angrily and his head began to shake. A renewed rapping came from the kitchen window, and the old woman shouted something then disappeared inside the house.

Before they could stop him, the old man had seized the table and overturned it. The plates, leftover food and glasses were pitched onto the sand or into Egill and Vigdís's laps.

They sprang to their feet. Anna twisted her ankle and nearly fell over, but managed to steady herself by grabbing hold of the table as it lay on its side. Hrafn seized the old man by the shoulders, and shook him hard a couple of times so that his head wobbled.

'What the hell do you think you're doing?' demanded Hrafn.

The old man tried to wriggle free, but Hrafn wouldn't let go of him until Vigdís interceded, stepping between them. She asked the old man if he was all right, but he didn't reply, he simply stood hunched over, arms dangling by his sides, smiling faintly.

'Nature!' declared Egill triumphantly, lighting a cigarette. 'Magnificent nature, turning our brains into mush!'

'Shut up, Egill! Go to bed and shut the fuck up!' Anna yelled, glowering at him as she hopped around on the sand whimpering, before slumping onto a chair.

The old woman emerged from the gloom, walked straight over to the old man, and, stroking his back, asked him what had happened. Anna felt emotionally drained, her foot was throbbing and her ankle was already swollen.

When she looked up again, Ása was apologizing for the old man's behaviour, and Egill had vanished from the table. Trigger had stopped barking.

Finally, Ása insisted they come inside, saying it was too dark to stay out there, and she led the old man away.

'I should probably apologize on behalf of my man too,' said Anna, watching the couple turn the corner as she fumbled for her umpteenth cigarette. Hrafn opened his mouth, but Anna broke in. 'Only I won't. I'm not the slightest bit responsible for what he does or doesn't do . . . I'm going to bed.'

She wanted to say more, but it was all too negative, and she would doubtless regret it the next day. All she wanted right now was to go to sleep.

She stood up, and Vigdís embraced her and assured her everything would be fine in the morning; they were all tired and cranky after a long day.

'But you're right, you know,' said Anna, looking at Hrafn then at the house. 'There is something horrible about this place.'

Then she said goodnight and made her way limping across the sands.

10
THE FENCE

Hrafn

It was light outside when Hrafn woke up. His mouth felt dry, his tongue thick, and when he clenched his teeth they made a gritty sound. He sat up, rubbed his hands vigorously over his face and vaguely remembered the previous day's events as though from a long way off.

He got dressed, brushed his teeth, and went downstairs to the kitchen where the others were sitting in silence. Vigdís was hunched over a detailed map of the area while Anna and Egill smoked and drank coffee. There was no sign of the old couple.

'Good morning, all,' said Hrafn, helping himself to coffee and sitting down. Anna and Egill seemed to have made up after their row the evening before. Egill looked pale and sheepish, and the dark purple shadows under his eyes suggested he had a bigger hangover than usual. After clearing his throat a few times and fiddling nervously with his lighter, he announced that he wanted to apologize.

'Since we're all here . . . I can't remember much of what happened last night, but Anna has filled in the details. I was rude and I'm ashamed of myself. I apologize and I feel bad. I'm a pig.' He grimaced, trying to suppress a smile.

'He wasn't in bed when I woke up. He passed out under the streetlamp out on the sands,' Anna said, shaking her head and giving a slight giggle.

'It was foolish,' said Egill. 'But the weather was fine, and at least now we know they turn it on at night.'

Vigdís became absorbed once more in her map, and soon the conversation turned to their journey home.

'We'll follow the same route as yesterday,' she said. 'Only we'll be on foot instead of driving. And Anna can stay behind to hold the fort. We'll head for Askja and hopefully on the way we'll find a shelter with a satellite telephone we can use. It's still early, so we have plenty of time, enough provisions, a compass and a map.'

'Why is Anna staying behind?' asked Hrafn, sipping his coffee.

'I can't walk.'

She raised her leg and showed her ankle, wrapped in gauze, explaining that she had twisted it the evening before when the old man overturned the table.

'Trigger has gone missing too,' she said. Rising from the table, she hobbled over to the kitchen window and looked out. 'I think I should stay here in case he comes back. If he had a fright and ran off last night, he could still be wandering around out there.'

'When did he go missing?' asked Hrafn.

'I shut him in our room during dinner. When I went up to bed the door was open.'

'Did someone let him out?'

'He sometimes claws at the handle to open a door, but I assumed he had gone out onto the sands with Egill. I should have checked . . . What if the foxes attacked him? They ate that *reindeer—*'

'Darling,' Egill interrupted.

She fell silent and snuggled up to him.

'So, you didn't see him either?' Hrafn asked Egill, who shook his head. 'Strange. But perhaps it'll be just as well if one of us stays behind. I don't trust that old couple to raise the alarm should anything happen. They'll forget about us the moment we leave. If Anna doesn't hear from us within a reasonable time, she can alert anyone passing through.'

'Why should anything happen?' said Vigdís. 'If we don't find a shelter with a satellite telephone we're bound to come across some jeep enthusiasts. Besides, it's only a twelve-hour walk to Askja, a few hours' drive.'

'Exactly,' said Egill. 'The first jeep enthusiast we find can drive us back to fetch cuddle-bunny, here.'

They kissed and Anna giggled.

'You'll be back in no time,' she said, and didn't seem to object to staying behind. 'Don't worry about me. I'll do some writing while you're gone – there's plenty of material here.'

Vigdís had drawn a circle on the map, which she thought was their most likely location. They charted their route according to various landmarks along the way, then packed their things into their rucksacks and got dressed. Hrafn was content to take a scarf, three chocolate bars and some nuts; he slipped the compass in his pocket and brought his new binoculars. They each had a water bottle, and Vigdís packed a couple of flares. She was upset when she couldn't find her mother's camera in the jeep.

A warm southerly breeze had risen and the sky was cloudless. There was no sign of the glacier anywhere. They said their farewells, and Anna gave them each a hug, welling up as she kissed Egill.

They headed north, towards Askja. As they passed the outhouses, they saw the old man standing alone, waving. They waved back. Near him sat the two foxes. One cackled shrilly at them then started scrapping with the other.

At first they kept to the road they had driven along the day before, but veered off when they saw a hill sloping gently up from the sands to the west. Although the hill wasn't on the map, they decided to climb up it to see if they could get a mobile signal, and to have a better view of their surroundings.

They soon realized that the hill was further away than they had thought. They carried on walking in silence, and Vigdís took out her book *Icelandic Flora.* Before they left town, she had bought some guidebooks, with the intention of using the trip to learn about nature, claiming she didn't know what anything was called.

Hrafn was reflecting about space, about how it could expand or contract when there was so *much* of it. Egill strode on ahead, doubtless trying to prove to them that despite his drunkenness the night before he was perfectly capable of walking. He was always trying to prove himself. One of the first things Hrafn had heard about him, when they weren't on speaking terms, was that he was dating the president's daughter. Their engagement was to be announced at a reception, and the president and his family made it very clear that they didn't want any media present. The reception commenced, and the place was crawling with journalists whom Egill had secretly invited. When the truth came out, the engagement was broken off. Next, he was on the news because of a scandalous party at which rising stars from the political and business world drank themselves into a stupor, while in the living room porn movies were projected onto a big screen. Hrafn also heard that he had worked at Landsbanki while still at university and had participated in the sale of shares in deCODE Genetics, the Icelandic genetic decoding company. The share price was high, pending the company's flotation on the New York Stock Exchange, after which the political class, indeed the entire nation, reasonably assumed that their value would only increase. However, not content to sell to willing buyers, Egill came up with the idea of mounting the most aggressive sales drive in the bank's history, organizing cold calls to customers, spreading the net wider to include university students, disabled people, pensioners, anyone with money and even those who had none but were able to take out loans against the shares.

After they patched up their differences, Hrafn had bumped into Egill's parents at Anna's birthday party, and again at a reception in the city, and he did his best to get to know them. Egill had never let his friends anywhere near his family. Egill's parents were social climbers too, in their own small way, although they were too old to have the necessary ruthlessness, and were probably unable to justify it to themselves. Even so, they took their son's advice about how to invest their money, how to make it work for them. Egill's father was a junior college teacher, and his mother was a biologist who did research on shellfish. Hrafn didn't consider them downright stupid or immoral; it was more a case of intellectual laziness, an unshakeable belief in their essential virtuousness, which kept them from questioning their own actions . . . They were good people, who meant well, and 30 per cent interest per annum was an attractive proposition, so they invested their nest egg in well-run companies that paid good dividends, and along came their son with his supreme assurance (or was it a philosophy?), sprayed his sperm over it and a year later the egg hatched. And the beauty of the idea was that there were no losers. Judging from the election results, they weren't alone. The nation voted for the social climbers, supported them, egged them on, watched them climb all over each other, over the ministries, institutions, pension funds and everyone who didn't wish to join in – as well as over the charities, local councils and societies of other nations on far-flung continents.

They reached the hill, and at the foot of it a small mound caught Hrafn's attention. *Man-made,* he reflected as he walked around it. On the north-facing side was a huge, iron door, the same shade of grey as the sand. The door was ten metres wide and almost as high. It had a personnel gate, but no visible lock.

'What the hell is this?' said Egill, who had come up behind him and was pushing against the door, which didn't budge. He hammered on it, but it scarcely made a sound, suggesting the iron was reinforced.

The three of them stood silently contemplating the door.

'I think it's an underground tunnel,' said Vigdís. 'The mound is too small to store anything big inside, but a truck would fit through that door.'

'Why would there be a tunnel here?' asked Egill.

'Perhaps we're about to find out,' said Hrafn, and they set off again.

As they ascended the hill, Vigdís scanned the ground for mountain buttercups, and showed Hrafn a picture of them in her book. Together they searched for the flower, trying to identify the sparse vegetation they glimpsed up there.

From the crest of the hill they had a panoramic view. The smooth black sands stretched away, and the skyline was unbroken, except towards the south-west where the land rose up into a mountain. Hrafn noticed a rounded swelling on either side of the mountain, which gave it the appearance of a cell dividing.

'Shouldn't we be able to see the glacier from here?' asked Hrafn, but no one replied.

All three tried in vain to get a signal on their mobile phones.

'Do you think anyone will miss us?' Egill remarked absent-mindedly, though with a hint of melodrama.

Vigdís asked him what he meant.

'You know, if no one hears from us for a few days. Who do you think will be the first to notice? My mum doesn't expect to hear from me regularly, nor do my friends. None of us have kids, we're all off the radar, officially on holiday – several weeks could go by.'

'Already planning your funeral?' said Hrafn, raising the binoculars and pointing them south across the sands, before swinging west towards the cell-mountain, where he glimpsed something lighter than the surrounding sands.

'That's not a mountain. It's a wall . . . between two hills.'

'*A wall?*' said Vigdís. 'That must be one of the most unlikely things anyone would build here.'

'Long and grey.' Hrafn raised the binoculars once more, scanning the wall as he tried to decipher what he was seeing. 'It looks like a barrage . . . I can't work out how big it is, though.'

'Can you see any people?

'Not a soul.'

The barrage stretched between the two hills, but because they were looking at it from an angle, they couldn't tell how long or tall it was. Hrafn noticed a road running along the top of the barrage, which he homed in on. Spanning the road was a mesh fence with a roll of barbed wire running along the top.

'Interesting . . .' he murmured, lowering the binoculars to a crack at the centre of the barrage stretching downwards.

'I don't remember any barrage around here,' said Vigdís.

'Not according to the map, and certainly not where Ása said we were.'

Hrafn handed her the binoculars.

'Well I never!' she exclaimed after a moment. 'Why is there a fence, and *barbed wire*?'

'Perhaps to keep the sheep out,' said Hrafn, only half-serious, but then it occurred to him that the fence could well have been erected to prevent the spread of infectious diseases among livestock. 'Haven't you heard of disease-prevention borders?' he added.

'Cattle grids on roads, yes, but not fences across barrages,' said Vigdís, passing the binoculars to Egill. 'The barrage looks abandoned to me. Old and full of cracks, sand-blown . . . I doubt anyone's there.'

They took turns looking through the binoculars, and Egill said he'd never heard of such a thing as an abandoned barrage.

'At least it would explain the gate we found,' said Hrafn. 'If there's a barrage, there must be tunnels. The overflow from the reservoir is channelled through tunnels and culverts. There might even be an arterial tunnel used for digging gravel and earth out of the smaller tunnels.'

Before they descended the hill, Vigdís took out the map and studied it.

'Shouldn't there be a river around here somewhere, seeing as there's a barrage?' she said, pointing at the map. 'This line could be a river.'

'Isn't the barrage marked on the map?' asked Hrafn.

'Not that I can see . . . But if the hills either side of the barrage are these ones here, then we're much further south than we thought, closer to the glacier. Which would add several hours onto our journey . . . And if we were that close to the glacier, we should be able to see it.'

Vigdís held up the binoculars, pointing them south. She saw no glint of water, but said she thought there was a gap in the sand about a mile away. They decided to search for the river, and follow it to the barrage to see if anyone was there – some jeep enthusiasts, for example. Otherwise, they would continue along the path heading north from the barrage, which joined up with the road they had just left.

'It'll take too long,' said Egill. 'If we're further south than we thought, we'll need more time, won't we? I'm not spending the night out here.'

'Let's see how far it is to the barrage,' said Vigdís.

They descended the hill, Vigdís leading the way, followed by Egill, then Hrafn, and from there they turned south across the sands. Occasionally, Egill's eye alighted on Vigdís's arse, and his mouth opened slightly, apparently without him realizing. He had always done that, stared just a bit too long, a bit too obviously at girls' arses, tits and crotches, like a fucking *dog*.

11

Hrafn

They walked across the sands until they could hear a low murmur, and a huge ravine opened out before them.

'Aha, finally something's *happening*!' exclaimed Egill, the roar growing steadily louder as they approached. Standing in a line along the edge of the ravine, they gazed solemnly into the yellow-grey meltwater from the glacier as it flowed eastwards from the highlands. The rock face opposite was grey with black blotches, in contrast to the water, which was white where it eddied in the current or frothed against the sides. The frantic movement was dizzying after the calm of the sands.

Hrafn started to feel queasy from staring into the river, and he walked away, rolling up his sleeves, and sat down on a dune close to the ravine. The warm air was almost stifling.

'It's getting hot,' said Egill, sitting down beside him.

'The *föhn*.' Hrafn reached for his cigarettes and offered one to Egill. 'The warm wind cools as it passes over the mountain then heats up again on its way down.'

'What mountain?'

'The glacier. Which should be around here somewhere.'

They smoked together in silence, watching Vigdís, who was still standing at the edge of the ravine. The ground beneath them quaked, just enough so that they could feel it.

Egill fumbled in his pocket and held up a shiny object.

'You haven't lost a key by any chance?' he asked.

Hrafn took the key from him and examined it. It was silver, unmarked, with a red reflector badge on one side.

'I've never seen it before. Where did you find it?'

'Underneath the streetlamp when I woke up this morning. On the ground, right in front of my eyes.'

'Have you asked Anna about it?'

'I didn't want to spook her.'

'Spook her? Why would she be spooked?'

Egill looked uneasy.

'I don't know . . . It wasn't there when I fell asleep. I would have noticed it, on the sand right under my nose, you see?'

'Perhaps you moved during the night and woke up somewhere else.'

The red of the reflector badge grew darker and more intense the longer Hrafn looked at it.

'At least this solves the mystery of the streetlamp,' he said. 'People go there to find the keys they lose in the highlands.'

Hrafn handed the key back to Egill, who waved it away, saying he didn't want it.

Vigdís walked over to them from the ravine, examined the key but said nothing. She seemed distracted, and she asked Hrafn for the binoculars, scanning the ravine with them before setting off along the river. They followed her until she stopped in her tracks and lowered the binoculars.

'There's something over there.'

She pointed to the far side of the ravine. On the opposite bank stood what appeared to be a cluster of long, low dwellings extending across the sands close to the ravine.

'Huts?' said Egill.

'An entire village,' said Hrafn, puzzled as to why they hadn't seen it from the hill. They continued walking along the ravine until they came to a sign with the words: *Beware – Danger* painted on it. A little way ahead, below the edge of the ravine on the far bank, hung a rope bridge, fastened on their side with a cable attached to one of three wooden posts that had been driven into the ground.

To the north-east they could see the old couple's house, grey on black. Apart from the sun glancing off the jeep, which was half-buried in the wall, the house practically merged with the landscape.

'Are we this *close*?' said Hrafn, sensing that the house ought to be much further away; he had the impression that they had walked round in a circle, although without arriving back where they started. When they had stood scouring the landscape from the yard, they hadn't seen the ravine or the container village on the far side. 'How come we didn't see any of this from the house?'

'Perhaps because we weren't looking for it,' said Vigdís.

Hrafn leaned over the cable that hung down into the ravine and started to pull the bridge towards them. It was made of wood and rope, and so relatively light. The three of them seized the end of the cable, and three loops emerged, clearly intended to fit over the three posts, and into specially scored notches.

'Ingenious!' said Egill, excitedly.

Together he and Hrafn straightened out the bridge, which had become twisted, before placing the loops over the posts.

'But why go to such trouble? Why not just leave it across the ravine?'

'To prevent something from coming over,' said Vigdís, gazing absent-mindedly at the far side. 'Like the fence on the barrage, and the barbed wire.'

'What are you talking about?' asked Egill.

'It's a way of controlling the traffic on this side,' said Hrafn. 'Keeping out foxes and reindeer, or whatever they are . . . Preventing sheep from wandering back and forth.'

They finished fastening the bridge, which now hung across the ravine in a V-shape. Cords attached the upper and lower ropes, and a row of wooden planks fastened with double cords lay across the length of the V.

'Why put *Beware – Danger*?' said Egill, tapping the sign. 'Shouldn't it say *Crossing prohibited* unless it's safe? Or does "Beware" mean you're welcome to cross, but it could give way?'

Hrafn clasped one of the bridge ropes and gave it a tug,

as though testing the loops on the far side. The planks were wet and shiny from the river spray.

'I don't like the look of this,' said Vigdís, appearing to recover her senses. 'Or anything else, for that matter.'

'On the contrary,' said Hrafn. 'The fact that the bridge is here is proof enough. If it was unsafe they would have torn it down.'

He took the binoculars from her, and examined the posts on the other side. The village was no longer visible, obscured by a hill between the bridge and the ravine.

'Really?' said Vigdís. 'And who would tear it down – the old couple?'

'If the bridge were dangerous anyone could remove it simply by untying the cable, or cutting through the three—'

'Yes, the three frayed loops! I don't want to play the little woman here, but this is stupid. The planks are flimsy and rotten! Look at the spray coming off the river.'

'I reckon the path to the barrage is on the other side. We'll take a look at those huts and then walk up there.'

'We might find something in them,' declared Egill, tugging on the bridge and making as if to cross. Or *pretending* he was, while secretly hoping Vigdís would try to stop him.

'Like what? An aircraft someone left behind?' shouted Vigdís, addressing Hrafn. 'This is crazy. We need to think about how to get home, not about playing games.'

'What's the problem?' Hrafn shouted back, and felt a strangely intense rage, as if he could rip her head off, and *wanted* to. 'Why are you trying to take control here? It makes no difference to our walk. And if we don't find anything useful, at least we'll have had an adventure! Who knows, there might even be a telephone,' he added, with a grin, trying to needle her.

'Or perhaps we'll get killed,' she said, stepping onto the bridge. 'Let's see who dares.'

Clasping the guide ropes, Vigdís strode out onto the bridge, lost her footing a couple of metres along, but otherwise crossed without incident, before turning and waving.

'Christ almighty!' said Egill, looking aghast at Hrafn. Then the two of them burst into laughter.

12

THE VILLAGE

Hrafn

They left their rucksacks next to a big warehouse at the edge of the village. Vigdís wandered off towards the ravine carrying her book, *Icelandic Flora*. She said she wasn't going into the village, but didn't explain why. Hrafn could tell she was scared, possibly after her sprint across the bridge – he had never seen her lose control like that, never seen her so determined, and the more he thought about it the stranger it seemed.

The wind continued to rise, whipping up the sand in places, but the visibility was still good enough to find their way around.

The warehouse was situated about sixty metres from the ravine; it was taller and longer than the huts in the village and resembled a hangar. On the west-facing side, where an unbroken plain stretched as far as the eye could see, was a massive door with a smaller door set into it.

'A personnel gate,' Egill murmured awkwardly.

From both doors hung a shiny padlock and chain. The warehouse was covered in rust, but the padlock and chain looked relatively new. Hrafn peered through the hole in the door into which the chain disappeared, but it was too dark to see anything. A faint smell seeped through the hole, like damp or mould, with a hint of engine oil.

'I wonder whether it was used to store machinery, bulldozers and tractors,' he said. 'The warehouse must have been emptied when the village was abandoned.'

'And yet it's locked,' said Egill. 'Why bother locking the place if it's empty?'

Hrafn carried on past the hill that rose out of the ravine, pausing at the edge of the village. It resembled a still photograph, a model in a snow globe that hadn't been shaken for a long time.

There were thirty or forty huts in total, made of chipboard, and probably built for workmen to sleep in. They were arranged in two semicircles around a large structure, at the centre of what Hrafn had instantly designated in his head as a village, although 'barracks' or 'camp' might have been a more precise description for the collection of purpose-built huts. They looked much the same in size and appearance; some had been joined together to form an L- or a U-shape.

'Enchanting,' said Egill.

'A quaint little village,' said Hrafn with a sigh. 'Just like any other Icelandic workmen's village. All that's missing is the video rental shop.'

He felt much better for calling it a village; the place was too ugly to remain nameless, and somehow naming it dampened the impression it made on him.

'How long is it since anyone lived here, do you think?' said Egill, taking out his video camera and pointing it towards the huts.

'What makes you so sure no one lives here now?'

At the edge of the village they glimpsed a track coming from the south-west, which turned north past the warehouse and continued until it reached the large central building. Following the track towards the centre, they stopped off outside one of the huts. Along the side were five windows, and at the end a door. The wind and sand had worn away most of the paint, which judging from the remaining streaks had once been blue.

They walked around the outside of the structure, examining it. Hrafn pressed his face to one of the windows and tried to peer inside, but couldn't see past the curtains.

'Why are the curtains drawn across the windows?' said Egill.

Hrafn didn't reply. He tried the handle: the door was locked. He walked over to the next hut, but the door to that was also locked. Then they penetrated further into the village.

Like the workmen's huts, the central building consisted of a single storey, only it was much bigger. The windows were bigger too, and not all of them had curtains. There appeared to be four entrances, one on each side. Hrafn walked over to the door closest to him, which was unlocked. It opened into a light, airy space. Tables and chairs were scattered about the floor, and at the far end was a counter.

'A canteen,' he said, stepping inside. The room was

smaller than he had expected, judging from the outside of the building. They weaved between the tables towards the counter and peered into the kitchen, which was empty apart from an enormous fridge with an icemaker that had been abandoned. In the sink they found a mouldy-looking plate and a pint-sized beer glass with dried black streaks on the inside. The fridge was empty.

Stepping back outside, they walked round the corner and came to another door leading into a room the same size as the canteen. All the furniture had been removed – except for a desk and in one corner a battered grey filing cabinet, which suggested this had been an office.

One of the inside walls had a window overlooking a square garden or sandpit with some benches and clay pots – ashtrays, probably. From the outside the building looked like a single structure, but in fact it was made up of four separate huts arranged in a square with an opening in the middle.

Strolling round the room, Hrafn noticed some brown splodges on one of the walls near to a half-open door that led into a small room. The doorframe, at the level of the lock, was splintered, as if someone had kicked it in. Hrafn gingerly pushed the door open and peered inside. In the half-light he glimpsed the outline of another desk, a filing cabinet and some shelves lined with ring binders. The light inside was dark blue and filtered through the curtains. An intense, musty odour pervaded the room.

He started to pull back the curtains. The window had been smashed and the parquet floor below was stained and swollen, although he couldn't see any broken glass. The floor was awash with papers and ring binders that had fallen off the shelves. The drawers of the desk had been pulled open, and were crammed with still more papers showing rows of figures and symbols – some kind of obscure calculations that made no sense to him.

Hrafn had the vague impression that the disorder in the room wasn't entirely random, as if someone had gone in there looking for valuables . . . No, as if a traveller in distress had broken the door down to look for food, or matches or candles, and had holed up in this enclosed space to try to get warm. But then why smash the window? The fact that there was no glass on the floor suggested it had been broken from the inside. *Someone ran into the room, slammed the door and locked it, and when the door was being kicked in, they tried to escape through the window . . .*

He walked out of the room and back through the main door to where Egill stood smoking. The village seemed almost quieter than the surrounding desert, where at least they could hear the whistling sands. Perhaps it was all those curtains and gloomy rooms that made him uneasy.

'So, are we looking for something in particular?' asked Egill.

'Not as far as I know. Are you looking for something?' Hrafn felt a sudden urge to whisper, as if he were afraid of waking someone.

'It seems like we're searching for clues.'

'Clues? What are you talking about?'

'Or rather, you're searching and I'm tagging along . . .'

'Searching!' said Hrafn and burst out laughing. '*You* seemed pretty busy in there yourself!'

'It's probably just the landscape . . . The sands,' said Egill, hawking and spitting on the ground.

Hrafn was tired of having him around – all day every day since the trip began, and he realized that Vigdís felt the same, regardless of the glances she and Egill had exchanged the evening before.

Hrafn walked over to the window he had just been examining. Below it lay shards of glass, supporting his theory that the window had been broken from the inside – which could mean anything. He stooped to pick one up, but his eye was instantly drawn to another object: a tiny, bleached skeleton lying on the sand. Leaning forward, he prodded it with his fingertip. It felt fragile.

Egill crouched beside him, and Hrafn showed him the skeleton. Close by they saw another, and a little further away another.

'Do you see that?' said Hrafn, and Egill grunted.

Strewn on the sand, the entire length of the building, were tens or hundreds of tiny skeletons. Hrafn held one of them up. It was so light he could scarcely feel its weight, and when he let it fall it practically floated to the ground.

'Birds, don't you think?'

'I guess so, yeah. Not that I'm an expert on the subject.'

'Of course they're birds – the bones are so light. They're hollow inside.'

Making his way along the wall, Hrafn held up a beak

the size of his nose, and considered that passing birds might have flown into the window and got killed.

'Sunset would be the riskiest time, I suppose, when the light reflects off the glass.'

They walked in a circle round the building. From a certain angle, where both the inner and outer walls had windows, you could see straight through, and the majority of the skeletons lay beneath those windows. Along the wall of the canteen, which had fewer windows, there weren't as many bones, which seemed to support Hrafn's theory.

And yet it wasn't that simple. He remembered something about *white sand*, which he had noticed before but ignored.

Returning to the office, he found the entrance to the garden and paused in the doorway. The sand was covered in skeletons, so thickly in places that they seemed to be piled on top of one another, both alongside and away from the surrounding wall.

He walked out onto the sand and stepped carefully around the skeletons, or trod on them and heard them crack and turn to dust. Egill followed, and the two of them moved silently about the garden. Some of the bones appeared to belong to creatures larger than birds; they weren't very long, but were too thick and heavy to be bird bones.

'Look at this. Antlers, wouldn't you say?' said Egill, pointing down at a mound of bones, sheared off in places, but resembling reindeer antlers. Other bones nearby could have been ribs, and what looked like a large femur belonging to a mammal was split down the middle and ended in a ball joint shaped to slot into the pelvis.

'Are those reindeer bones? How did they get broken like that?'

Hrafn's eye alighted on one of the benches, and he leaned against it before sitting down. Beside the bench was a clay pot. It was empty.

Looking up once more, he noticed a cigarette between his fingers that had burned down to the filter. He flung it into the pot, felt a wave of nausea, and couldn't understand what they were doing in there.

'I can scarcely tell whether we're inside or outside . . . What is this place? An elephants' graveyard? Where do all these skeletons come from? It's as if these creatures came here to die.'

'Maybe this is what the old couple feed to the foxes?' said Egill.

Hrafn scoffed.

'Yes, hordes of foxes. Legions of them! And they dragged it all the way *inside* just to impress those sophisticated foxes. And the reason why there's no meat left on the bones, and no teeth marks, is because the foxes used knifes and forks.'

'It was only an idea,' said Egill, raising his hip flask to his mouth and taking a swig. 'Maybe some fugitives set up camp here for a few months, and they went out foraging. I wouldn't mind being a fugitive, going to ground up here in the highlands . . .'

'They're called outlaws,' said Hrafn, glancing up at the grey scudding clouds, which he hadn't noticed before. The weather was changing. 'Men who were outlawed from society, and became miserable wretches who could be killed with impunity.'

He rose from the bench.

'It sounds better than insider trading or breaching the Companies Act, at any rate.'

Hrafn walked slowly around the garden, doing his best not to step on any bones; he couldn't stand the sound they made. He was aware of his own weight, his stiffness and strength – which in some sense kept him upright, pulling this way and that through a complex synergy of joints, muscles and nerve impulses. If he lay down for long enough, he would eventually die, and his body would dissolve and merge with the earth. With that second death all trace of his existence in the world would disappear, turn to dust and scatter across the sands.

'Among the grains,' he muttered to himself as he saw Egill crouching over something in the centre of the garden.

'What are you doing?' Hrafn asked, walking towards him.

Egill glanced over his shoulder.

'Nothing,' he said, straightening up. As he wheeled round, he reached behind his back and slipped something into his pocket.

'Yes you were. What were you doing?' Hrafn insisted, drawing level with him.

'This is crazy . . . total fucking bullshit. I think we should go home.'

'Did you find something there?' said Hrafn, gesturing

with his head towards the place where Egill had been rummaging.

On the sand was a mound of bones, too high for the wind to have blown them into a pile.

'I know nothing about it,' said Egill. 'It was like that when I found it.'

Hrafn contemplated the bones, which had been shaped into a crude pyramid rising from the sand, although the ground around it was bare. The bones were the size of fingers. As if to confirm that they hadn't drifted randomly together, near the base of the mound was an opening, like a small door.

'What was inside it?' asked Hrafn, convinced that Egill had stuffed something in his back pocket. 'What are you hiding?'

Egill hesitated, glancing first at the mound then at Hrafn. He wore an expression that Hrafn had never seen before, a mixture of fear, confusion and something else which he couldn't identify.

'I'm not hiding anything. What makes you think that?'

'You're lying. I saw you stuff something in your back pocket. Show it to me!'

'I was just looking at the mound—'

'Stop bullshitting me! I know you're lying. Do you think I'll be scared? Did you find an old Viking axe? An Egyptian death mask? What was it?'

Egill shook his head.

'I think it's best we forget it.'

Hrafn extended his hand, holding it still until Egill fumbled for the object he had slipped into his pocket.

'I don't know anything about this,' he said. 'I saw the mound and I found this inside it . . . in the opening.'

He passed him a photograph. Hrafn saw instantly that it was from the camera Vigdís had inherited from her mother – the same size, the same paper. The image was dark and grainy, although it was unmistakably a picture of Vigdís herself. Her eyes were closed, and one side of her face was in shadow, the other dimly lit. Her lips were parted slightly, showing her teeth, and halfway down the photograph he saw her pale, round, naked breasts and her dark nipples. She was lying on her back, asleep, or so he thought at first.

'This . . .' he began, but forgot what he was going to say. He turned the photograph over and examined the back, as though expecting to find the explanation there.

'I have no idea what it was doing there,' said Egill. 'When was it taken?'

'When was *what* taken?'

'The photo . . . That's Vigdís in the picture, isn't it?'

'Of course it's Vigdís. Isn't that obvious? I've never seen this photo before.'

'You mean you didn't take it?'

'Of course *I* didn't take it. I've never seen it before. And I've never taken a photo with that camera, or of Vigdís . . . not just so that I could stuff it inside a pile of bones, anyway! Why were you trying to hide it?'

'Because I knew you'd be shocked or angry, I guess. I

needed time to think . . . I'm as bewildered by this as you are.'

Hrafn fell silent. His thoughts were churning. Her breasts and nipples, erect, standing out against the paleness, Egill wandering alone on the sands at night, arranging the bones in a mound, Vigdís's half-open mouth, her serene expression, the long-drawn-out sigh escaping from her lips . . .

Egill turned on his heel and left the building. Hrafn stood for a long time contemplating the photograph then gazed down at the sand between two small bones, which could have belonged to a bird, but also to a mouse, a rat, a fox or anything for that matter.

They had to get out of there.

IT HAS NO SOUL

13

ICELANDIC JOURNALISM

Anna

After the others had left, Anna shut herself in her room, flung herself on the bed and flicked through her notebook. She had bought three new ones especially for the trip and had already filled half of the first.

'Icelandic nature is unique', she had written during their first day in the highlands, after they had left the Golden Circle tourist trail. Of course that wasn't enough – she needed to define exactly what that uniqueness entailed – and yet she had lost interest the moment they penetrated the wilderness: height-wise, Icelandic mountains weren't particularly impressive, and even the fascination of glaciers palled relatively quickly. She knew this was her own fault. And yet she found it difficult to see how she might change, what would need to happen in order for her to take interest in these trivial things, to find them breathtaking even.

'Delirious, breathtaking. Insolence?' she scrawled in the middle of the page. 'Is landscape the same as nature?' she added.

She jotted down her ideas and uncertainties about the

old couple and the house. She began with a physical description of the old man: 'He has the squint of one who has spent his whole life struggling with the wind and cold, his skin is leathery from the harsh summer sun in the highlands . . .' and all at once she felt a burning curiosity about the couple, what had brought them here, and what eventful lives they might have led prior to settling here. They were shrouded in mystery and would make the perfect subject for her article, but she had no context. Did she need one? Or was there no place for hermits in the new nationalistic ideology? Could she jazz them up a bit, if necessary? Or perhaps they didn't even count as hermits because they had each other. A hermit couple? A contradiction in terms? Were they actually married? If so, how did they meet? How did the reindeer that the foxes ate die?

Yawning, she closed the notebook, rolled over onto her back, and leafed through a play about the outlaw Fjalla-Eyvindur and his wife Halla, but couldn't concentrate. She had noticed the odour for the first time when she came back into the house, and wondered why she hadn't smelled it before: an odour of overcoats, old shoes, cooking fat, damp and something else redolent of iron or copper; less overpowering but pungent all the same – like the smell of blood.

Anna's first memory was of the sun peeping over the mountaintops in Ísafjörður, in late winter. It frightened her and she cried out 'evil eye' – something her mother would later tease her about. Next she remembered her parents screaming at each other in the kitchen. She lay down behind the sofa in the living room, and peered round the corner in time to see her mother receive a blow to the face, doubtless from her father – no one else was there. And yet in her memory she didn't see this, she only heard the sound. Afterwards, beneath the duvet, the pain came; the world spun slowly around little Anna, who could hear her mother's sobs inside her head, and this made her so overwhelmingly afraid and sad. Ever since then, when the light fell at a certain angle, Anna imagined she could see the imprint of a hand on her mother's cheek, and she only understood why when, aged twenty, she halted at a junction in London: what looked like a red hand appeared on the traffic light, and she remembered the scene in the kitchen for the first time.

Her father was a newcomer to the region. He had taught for a few years at the local junior college, but after the divorce he moved away, never to be seen again. Later on, Anna's mother would sometimes refer to him mockingly as 'the intellectual'. Mother and daughter moved into the basement of Anna's grandparents' house; the four of them ate breakfast and dinner together, and occasionally they would all drive out to Flateyri or Bolungarvík. Sometimes her mother and grandfather would drink strong liquor together, always upstairs, and she could hear them quarrelling through the basement ceiling.

She remembered her grandfather, a tall man with red hair, standing in her room and stooping to kiss her. He once gave her a rose, after her mother had spent the entire day sobbing in the living room. Soon afterwards, they left Ísafjörður. Anna's mother picked her up from school, having packed their things in the trunk of the car, and she sobbed nearly all the way to Sauðárkrókur, where they stayed with a friend of hers. Anna started at a new school; she never saw her grandparents again, and her mother tore up all the photographs of them.

Next she remembered making a cheese sandwich in their new apartment, listening to the Pixies and writing a letter to Ye Mimi, her penfriend in Taiwan, who had advertised in the magazine *Youth*. Both girls wanted to practise their English and get to know other cultures, both had asked their mothers if they could visit each other, assuring them it would be fine, and both had been refused. At the time, Anna's mother was seeing a man who drank a more sophisticated brand of alcohol than her father and grandfather – and in bigger quantities, and Anna knew it wouldn't be long before her mother – or she herself – lay weeping on the floor. The 'Ye' in her penfriend's name meant 'leaf', and 'Mimi' meant 'searching for something'.

When it came to her memories, Anna had no friends to back them up. During that period she changed schools a lot, and followed her mother from town to town. Her mother did her best, but sometimes there was no food in the house – at least not until Anna reminded her mother that she needed to eat. She made friends easily, but when joining a new class soon learned not to make herself look too pretty or be too amusing so the other girls wouldn't become jealous of her; she mustn't be too talkative or shy, too intelligent or stupid – in fact she mustn't be too anything. It was a matter of just biding her time. She liked to write about her everyday life in her diary, to change it at whim even, and to speculate about other people – those who would suddenly appear in her or her mother's life, only to disappear equally quickly. She enjoyed writing essays, and seemed to have more of a flair for it than most, but she kept that to herself too, until she reached junior college where she started to contribute short stories and an occasional poem to the school magazine.

As a teenager she lived in Reykjavík and made her first real friend, Heiða, with whom she met up everyday, regardless of which side of town they were living in. Heiða had moved a lot as well – all over the country in fact – as her parents were travelling schoolteachers and hippies of a sort. She and Heiða both adored literature, and could spend long hours together reading in silence. They started smoking and hanging out at coffee shops like Mokka or Hressó, and as soon as they were old enough they moved into a basement flat together in Ránargata. At the time, Anna's mother was moving to Akureyri, to be with a man she claimed was different to all the others, although Anna begged to disagree. She had never understood exactly why her mother was the way she was, and yet for as long as she could remember, she had known that something wasn't right: her mother either fretted over practically everything, or was completely indifferent; she laughed louder than anyone else at gatherings and cried her eyes out during films, even when they weren't weepies; she either chattered incessantly about everything that happened to her or everything that went on in her head, or she shut herself in her room in the dark. Sooner or later her behaviour would inevitably exasperate the men she was with, or so Anna supposed, most of whom started out trying to change her or to solve her problems. But when they realized that was impossible, they would quarrel with her or beat her up, or storm out calling her a bitch and a whore. Anna never got used to this. Once she asked her mother why she was so changeable, and her mother said there was nothing she could do about it:

'Don't worry, my love,' she said. 'You'll be a much better person than me.' Occasionally she would threaten to kill herself, shout at her men, or hurl things at them and smash the furniture. Once she went missing for several days, and Anna moved in with her mother's brother and his wife, who was tidy and knew how to behave. Anna's mother always wanted what was best for her daughter, and yet she was impossible to live with; everything revolved around her and how she felt, and although she occasionally apologized for being so difficult, this didn't help much. When Anna became a teenager, she felt a burning desire to save her mother, just like the men who came and went, even though she knew it was impossible.

The best years of her life were when she lived with Heiða. They had lots of friends, and for years all they did was party, although they were capable of easing off when they had to study or get up to go to work. Anna started at the junior college in Reykjavík, where she majored in languages.

During term time and over the summer holidays she worked at the checkout in the Hagkaup supermarket on Eiðistorg, writing in her spare time. She also went hiking and jogging with her friends, sang in a band, won a short-story writing competition in the school magazine, and during their final year at junior college she and Heiða took part in a weekly radio programme for Rás 2. During all that time Anna felt that she was burning with energy, a mysterious *excitement* that seemed to be constantly searching for new outlets, and if she didn't use that energy, it seemed to turn against her, morphing into a deep, dizzying despair – not unlike her conviction that her mother could never be saved.

The summer of her graduation from junior college, she found a job as a temp on a daily newspaper where she wrote minor news items, and did brief interviews, which she obtained by ringing up this or that celebrity and asking them what was in their pockets, or their opinion on various matters. After an office party, which ended in debauchery, she started seeing the editor, and would fuck him in his office after work, or at one of several hotels in town. He was a married father of three, who lived in the posh neighbourhood of Hlíðar, a staunch member of the centre-right Independence Party and a frequent guest on the news and on TV talk shows. Anna wasn't in love but found sex with him exciting. He whipped her with a belt, clipped clothes pegs all over her, and occasionally choked her during sex, as well as sodomizing her, which she had never tried before. Sometimes, he would send her commands, brief messages about what she should do the next time they met, or how she should dress, which for a while she found quite amusing.

Through the editor, she did several assignments for a glossy magazine, which then offered her a full-time post. She gave up studying literature at the university, which had never been more than a stopgap (she hadn't wanted to do Icelandic studies because she thought it too lame, even though her written Icelandic was excellent), and started to do feature interviews for the magazine. This was both more and less of an achievement than she had anticipated; *less* because, besides interviewing the nation's prominent women, she was expected to translate a string of advertorials for beauty products, which wholesalers paid the magazine to publish.

However, that was reality, and in the end she always felt best when rooted in it, or at least when she knew that she was hovering just above it. After she stopped seeing the editor, she slept with as many as fifteen men during a single summer in downtown Reykjavík – ranging from one-night stands through hour-long assignations to trysts lasting several days. She tried sleeping with a woman, which she found intriguing. At the end of the summer, she dated a wealthy man from Garðabær for a few months. He was about ten years older than her, and liked her to tie him up and humiliate him, to sit on his face and suffocate him; once she peed in his mouth and watched him greedily swallowing her urine. She had a talent for sex, enjoyed equally giving and receiving, dominating or being submissive, and she discovered that the excitement raging in her since she was a teenager was to a large extent her libido. She had masturbated regularly from the age of twelve, more so the older she got; she still hadn't met a man who liked fucking as much as she did, or who enjoyed doing it in such a variety of ways. She wrote articles about sex for the magazine she worked on, interviewed women about their sexual behaviour, and after a discussion on self-stimulation ended up taking part in a group masturbation session with four women from the business, art, and media world in the sauna room at a spa facility, where she lost count of how many times she climaxed.

As a rule, she kept these things secret from the men she was with; she was convinced that if they knew the extent of her sexual desire, which was becoming more voracious as she grew older, it would scare them off. The myth about women's frigidity had always been precisely that: male fear of the insatiable, all-consuming hunger between a woman's thighs, which could devour legions of limp dicks before spitting them out flaccid and bewildered, and which, in the end, was both more impersonal and *masculine* than their own. She fell in love easily, but found it equally easy to change partners; she liked making men work hard to please her, but also had a strong urge to please the men she was with – and to please men in general. She was unsure of her own abilities, but felt good when she brought out her recording device, armed herself with a pen and took the lead in discussions, and she felt closest to being a distinct individual when she saw her name in print.

Her reputation continued to flourish, and she was offered

a job on a popular magazine with wider pretensions, which barely extended to social criticism but consisted mainly of off-the-cuff interviews, pre-selected topics and image repair – the same as any other Icelandic journalistic publication of that time, although its readers were more discriminating than the average suburbanite dupe. She moved into a downtown apartment in Bergstaðastræti, which was small but overlooked Tjörnin, and started receiving invitations to openings, and premieres, went out for cocktails with her friends who worked in finance, fucked her first politician, her first stockbroker, tried cocaine, contributed to the right-wing feminist magazine *Bitch*, interviewed big businessman Björgólfur Thor in Cannes, flew from Oslo to London with financier Olafur Olafson in a private jet, gave a lecture on Icelandic journalism at Bifröst University, declared that Greens were out and garden gnomes were in, and became a consultant on recapitalization, currency baskets and real estate, about which she knew nothing.

Things were going smoothly, except that at the beginning of every month, almost like clockwork, her mother would call (after seeing Anna's name in print) and alternately weep or berate her daughter, for any number of reasons – usually for not loving her any more, and for never coming to see her. Her mother worked at the checkout in a hypermarket in Akureyri and was oblivious to what was happening in the rest of society or in the countryside, or in Akureyri, or anywhere. Anna didn't let this get in her way. She arranged to be sent on assignments in northern Europe, which was easy thanks to Iceland's growing role on the international stage, and secured a residency in Berlin, then in Paris. There she met Gísli Marteinn, a prominent member of the Independence Party, at a reception at the Icelandic embassy, and they lived together for a while in Edinburgh.

After they split up, she moved back home, where she felt that something had changed. She was approaching thirty, had no children, had forged her own path in life, and her job was relatively rewarding but not too demanding or time-consuming. And yet the tempo of her life was slowing down; fewer things astonished her, filled her with awe or fear. Even her libido seemed to have stabilized, acquiring a sort of *mildness* it hadn't possessed before. She began to put out feelers about a possible editorial post on the magazine, but doubtless came across as too eager, overstepped herself, and was put in her place by the existing editor – a woman who had gone to a sanatorium in Switzerland (for a facelift) paid for by an investment company.

Her first realizations about her *mistakes* came as a shock, and showed her how truly vulnerable she was: she had put all her eggs in one basket, and always allowed herself to be so naive and immature. Why hadn't she got a better education, saved up more money? She was a journalist, but if one day she ceased to be that – if she lost the trust of those around her – then she was *nothing*. She was afraid others might consider her needy, see inside her soul, find out how ignorant she really was, and gradually she began to lose confidence in herself, and the people around her seemed to sense that.

But what saddened her most was the discovery that for

nearly ten years she hadn't written one sentence for herself, no fiction, no short stories, not a single line of poetry. She had stopped chronicling her life in her diary, save for the occasional comment about the weather or how she was feeling, and then she stopped doing that too. For nearly ten years she had produced nothing creative except what conformed to the magazine's sales requirements, column requirements or interview length. Her writing, the one thing that never let her down had been employed by a bunch of money men to help raise the profile of the Independence Party in the eyes of middle-aged women, or to make Finnur Ingólfsson, the ex-minister of the centre-right Progressive Party, come across as interesting, or the businessman Hannes Smárason as human, or the first ever female Icelandic doctor Kristín Ólafsdóttir as creative, or the prime minister Geir Haarde as amusing. She could no longer even justify herself with politics.

She split up with a man she loved and took longer than usual to find a new one; she started to take pleasure in pulling her hair out, she pinched her nipples and labia until she wept, and one night she stormed into the kitchen and slashed her elbows, knees and calves with a knife. She was filled with intense, profound guilt, and couldn't fall asleep until almost twelve o'clock the next day, when she picked up the receiver to call for help, but didn't.

Around that time, her grandfather got in touch. He rang her at midnight, drunk, told her he had just come back from sea, that he hadn't 'long to go' and wanted to see her. She pictured before her a clichéd scene from a song by

Gylfa Ægisson, and, not wishing to complicate her life even further, asked him to leave her alone – the way he always had – adding that he could go eat shit. After she hung up she instantly burst into tears and couldn't stop crying; she tried knocking herself out with a rolling pin, clipped clothes pegs all over her face until she felt safe, then curled up next to a red-painted wall. The next day, Heiða, who had just finished her PhD in Sweden, came round and took her to the psychiatric ward at Landspítali where she was admitted for a few days' 'rest'.

Anna had a vague suspicion that she was on the ward instead of her mother, but she didn't care. She had always been good at adapting and soon got her bearings. In less than a week she had been discharged with a prescription for some tablets, and after that she saw a shrink every week. She prohibited her mother from reducing her to tears over the telephone, and realized how much she enjoyed suffering, up to a point anyway, how she equated it with being alive, and certainly with being interesting.

Afterwards, she seemed to rediscover her equilibrium. She continued to work for the magazine, although word soon spread about her 'illness' and her admission to a psychiatric ward, which, however interesting it made her, ended once and for all her chances of obtaining the editorial post. She continued to do interviews, write opinion articles about this and that, and accepted that she had reached the limits of her ability: in short, her ascent had been relatively swift but far from meteoric. It was the people around her, the subjects of her interviews, who had accomplished the exploits.

She was a mere chronicler, a satisfactory wordsmith, but she knew deep down that she would never be enough of a scoundrel or an idiot to amount to anything more. She was a simple journalist, a simple person even, and because of that her life would doubtless remain basically unchanged.

14

Anna

The house was quiet apart from an occasional creak and the howling wind, which was steadily growing stronger. Out on the horizon, a dark mist rose from the sand, moving sometimes closer then further away from the house.

Anna glanced towards the outhouses, but could see no sign of the old couple. If she wasn't mistaken, she was alone in the house. This realization awakened in her a burning *curiosity* – not unlike her desire for sex – which occasionally seized her, but which hadn't shown itself for a long time.

She thought of her friends out there in the mist, but decided not to worry; she trusted Hrafn and Vigdís to find their way, and besides it was warm outside.

She stepped out into the corridor. Apart from Hrafn and Vigdís's room, there was a bathroom in the corridor. It had no hot running water, and they were obliged to flush the toilet using a bucket. On the other side of the stairwell was a closed door. The part they were staying in barely spanned a third of the length of the house, so whatever lay behind that door had to be enormous.

Creeping past the stairwell, she paused in front of it. A greyish light seeped through the keyhole into the dimly lit corridor. Placing her eye to it, she glimpsed rows of books. She felt an overwhelming desire to scurry back to bed, squealing as she buried herself under the covers, but instead she turned the handle. Such is the nature of curiosity.

The door opened with a gentle click.

She found herself confronted by what appeared to be an office. Books lined the shelves that covered the walls from floor to ceiling; next to one of the two windows stood a large oak desk, and on the wall above it hung several black-and-white photographs. In the centre of the room were two freestanding bookcases filled with newspapers, magazines and ring binders. On another wall was a red-brick fireplace.

Her first thought was that the old couple must be wealthy, or that they had been in the past; many of the books had leather bindings and looked antique and valuable, the cornices on the floor and ceiling were carved, and the curtains at the windows were made of red silk.

On closer inspection, she saw that the walls and floors were damp and raised in places, a thin dusting of sand had settled on the shelves, in between the books, and the musty odour in the room suggested they were liable to be damaged by the humidity. If the house had been built in times of prosperity, clearly circumstances had changed – either that or the owners had allowed it to fall into disrepair out of inertia. The ceiling in the room was higher than anywhere else in the house, and rotten beams propped up the corrugated iron roof. Between the two central bookcases stood a bucket containing a residue of water from a leak in the roof. There was no sand on the floor, which meant that someone went in there to clean, and she glimpsed traces of soot in front of the fireplace, suggesting it had been recently used. She crouched beside the grate, trailed her finger through the soot, then peered up the chimney, but saw only blackness.

Walking over to the desk, she cast her eyes over the photographs on the wall above. In the centre hung a framed diploma. The old boy had been around, even if he had ended up there; the diploma was from Princeton University and stated that Kjartan Aðalsteinsson had been awarded the degree Doctor of Medicine with Distinction, while another university in Boston acknowledged his excellent exam results. In addition, a certificate from the junior college in Reykjavík congratulated him on coming top of his year in mathematics, and further down the wall a tiny, yellowing document attested to his having come first in his lower secondary school exams.

Anna had difficulty equating this with the grinning, twitching old man, although it confirmed her suspicion that he was no farmer. One of the photos, probably taken when he was about thirty, showed him receiving a scroll (another diploma most likely) from a man whom Anna thought had once been prime minister of Iceland. In another, Kjartan was sitting at a table with the industrialist Björgólfur Guðmundsson and his wife Thóra, a member of the Thor dynasty, smoking a fat cigar, and laughing so hard that his back teeth were visible. In one photograph, which (from its composition) could have come from a newspaper, Kjartan was on a podium, fist raised, possibly after winning a debating competition; and in yet another he was about twenty years old, dressed in a black suit and standing on a quayside with an ocean-going liner behind him, clearly about to embark for America.

It struck her that the old woman wasn't with him in any of the photographs, although clearly in many of them he was on holiday: wearing short trousers in a forest, a pair of binoculars round his neck; smiling next to a llama, on skis in front of a log cabin. He looked relatively youthful in all the photographs, younger than forty, which meant that during the last thirty or so years no snapshots had been taken of him, or at any rate none he wanted to hang on his wall.

She turned away and glanced about the room before sitting down at the desk. On the desktop was a framed photograph – the only one with children in it. A boy and a girl about ten years old sat bolt upright on chairs, and standing behind them, respectively, were a man and a woman, apparently their parents. The man was resting one hand on the boy's shoulder, while in the other he clasped a cane; his expression was stern in contrast to the woman's face, which appeared kindly, despite being almost completely obscured by the white film shrouding the photograph. She wore a long dress, her dark hair was plaited, and jewellery glinted about her neck and wrists.

The little boy was Kjartan when he was young, and Anna instantly recognized the girl next to him as the woman from the photograph downstairs. If she wasn't mistaken, this meant they were brother and sister, and indeed there was no denying they were strikingly similar: exceptionally beautiful, flaxen-haired and graceful, the children of a wealthy, upper-class family, which was evident from their parents' clothing, the father's cane and the mother's jewellery. Once again Anna asked herself what the old man was doing up there in the highlands.

She riffled through a sheaf of papers in the desk drawer: pages torn from a notebook, which she couldn't find. Most were blank, but a few words had been scrawled on one page in cursive script that was almost illegible. Anna read falteringly: 'The Ice Lands' and after that a series of numbers. Other words included 'cellar' and 'key', and further down she made out 'cowshed', 'streetlamp' and 'front door'. The words were written separately, sometimes only one word to each line. It looked like a kind of memo, possibly something the old man was writing before he became ill. She reread the words at the bottom of the page: 'It has no soul.' The sentence had been underlined twice.

A few of the other pages included descriptions of the weather, written in the same hand. She was tempted to take them, but didn't see the point.

What had no soul?

She closed the drawer and rose to her feet, aware of the house creaking as the weather worsened. She moved along the shelves reading the spines of the books. Most were volumes on science, biology, geology, chemistry and physics, as well as medicine – the old man's speciality. The majority were in English, but a few were in German, French or one of the Nordic languages. Many of the shelves were numbered, presumably to classify them by subject.

On one she found some Icelandic books by Dr Helgi Pjeturss, Sigurður Nordal and Alexander Jóhanesson, as well as translations of Homer and novels by Einar H. Kvaran and Gunnar Gunnarsson. She slid her eyes over the titles, pausing when she came to a series in three volumes entitled *Icelandic Businessmen*. Plucking out the first volume, which was published in 1955, she scanned the index looking for Kjartan Aðalsteinsson.

She found his name in the third volume. According to the book, he belonged to one of the country's most privileged families, which stretched back generations: they had started off as landowners and county sheriffs, before apparently changing direction, their ranks filling with politicians and businessmen – principally in the fishing industry. Kjartan's paternal grandfather was a minister, whom Anna had never heard of, and his father had outlets and wholesale businesses in Reykjavík and Akureyri; he was reputedly 'a bold entrepreneur', his name linked to the Thor dynasty ('a close friend of Richard Thor'), who had made his fortune on the currency markets. Kjartan had a sister, whom the book didn't mention by name, and both she and her mother were designated as housewives.

Kjartan himself was described as an excellent student, who had shown an early interest in science. The summary of his academic career mirrored the diplomas on the wall, and there was a reference to his medical research at the Boston University Hospital, where he had begun to develop his ideas about a 'life-force', a form of electrical energy inherent in all living beings, which, among other things, could be harnessed to control growth and cure cancer. Following his 'sudden departure' from America, as the book described it, Kjartan returned to Iceland and set up his own research laboratory in the port area of Grandi in Reykjavík. However, there was some controversy about the laws passed which allowed Kjartan to set up such a company, not least because of his personal links to members of the political class: the story was that he had exploited access to databases at the National Hospital, Landspítali, including the medical histories of tens of thousands of Icelanders, and in addition had participated in medical research on people which contravened 'medical ethics'. Later on, the company was liquidated, the Icelandic state assumed the debt, and immediately afterwards Kjartan found himself facing further difficulties: he was charged at the Reykjavík district court for violating 'public morals', and the book referred to his 'libertine lifestyle'. Finally he was said to have had a son, who, along with the child's mother, wasn't mentioned by name.

And that was all. Anna browsed a few other entries before returning the book to the shelf. What most intrigued her was the bit about Kjartan violating public morals, and that his son and wife weren't named, unlike those of others in the book. Perhaps the explanation for both was simply that he was a philanderer and a cad and had sired at least one child out of wedlock, although she thought it unlikely – that sort of behaviour wasn't uncommon enough to be deemed scandalous.

And why wasn't his sister named either?

She was about to leave the room when she glimpsed a familiar phrase on the shelf in front of her, the same phrase she had seen scrawled on the notepaper in the desk drawer: *The Ice Lands.* It was the title of one of the books. Anna tried in vain to pull the volume out of the shelf, although as it tilted towards her she heard a click coming from behind the shelves and the bookcase began to move away from the wall with a low, scraping sound.

15

THE MAN WITH FEELERS GROWING OUT OF HIS HEAD

Anna

Anna took a step backwards, disconcerted, assuming that the bookcase was about to topple over, before realizing that it was pivoting on hinges.

Magic, she thought, as the bookcase came to a halt. She hesitated for a moment, and then decided to peep through the open door that had appeared behind it, but saw only blackness. A cold, musty smell emanated from within, and a silence that was filled with tension, as if at any moment it might give way to commotion.

She hovered in the doorway, before fetching a candle from the desk, which she lit, pointing it towards the darkness. The tall, steady flame enabled Anna to make out the shape of a bed, a small desk and a bookcase. The room was no more than two or three metres long and roughly the same width.

Just inside the door, she noticed a switch on the wall. Above it, written in large capital letters, were the words: 'See me'. There was nothing unusual about the switch, so what was she was being invited to look at – the room's occupant? She reached out to see whether it turned on an overhead light, but withdrew her hand at the last moment. There was something fishy going on here.

She scanned the room until she was sure no one was hiding there, edged her way across the floor, and came to a halt beside the bed. Spread over it was a musty brown blanket. She tugged idly at one corner of the blanket, instantly letting go as a sickening stench arose from it that made her retch, reminding her of rotting fish or the smell of the homeless man who had sat down next to her on the New York subway.

The darkness above the bedhead was slightly paler, and on closer inspection Anna made out the shape of a window, the same size as the ones in the study. The glass had been coated with a thick layer of black paint that almost completely shut out the daylight, save for where a single scratch let in a thin shaft of light.

As she put her eye up to the scratch, Anna could see thick clouds of sand drifting across the ground, amid which she glimpsed the outhouse, and remembered the old couple. Although there was no sign of them, Anna was suddenly afraid of being caught red-handed, and she cast around for an object she could take with her, something that might reveal the secret of the house on the sands.

Close to the desk hung a framed photograph, which Anna assumed at first was Ása, but then she began to have her doubts. The figure was middle-aged, with dark hair that rose straight up as though underwater. Moving the candle closer, Anna changed her mind again as she realized this was no photograph, but rather a photorealistic image of a man with squinting eyes, and what looked like tentacles or feelers growing out of his head.

On top of the desk, which was lower and smaller than the one in the study, sat a candleholder containing a candle stub, and a plain, polished wooden box. Hurriedly (before she lost her nerve), Anna unhooked the clasp and opened the box, removing a piece of dark silk to reveal a gun. It was small, but had a long barrel that gleamed in the candle-light. She reached out and touched the gun, sliding her finger carefully along the barrel. After hesitating for a moment, she picked it up, turned the cylinder and saw that four of the six chambers contained bullets.

She put the gun down again and contemplated it on the desk. She couldn't leave it behind – this was evidence, not simply that they had been there, but of something that had yet to be disclosed. Why were two bullets missing? Had they been fired at someone? She had a friend in the police force who could help her look into this.

She wound the piece of silk around the gun, tucked it into the waistband of her trousers and closed the box on the desk.

On her way out, Anna turned in the doorway, casting a backward glance at the room, and at the wall bearing the words 'See me'. She was overlooking something. Seizing the candle in her left hand, she reached out with her right hand and flicked the switch up. There was a blinding flash of light as the current shot up her arm and coursed through her entire body. Her jaw clenched and she felt herself stiffen and go numb, as she heard the candle drop to the floor far off in the distance, and, staring wide-eyed into the centre of the room, she *saw*. She stood trembling next to the wall for a few seconds or for an eternity, before shrinking away from it.

She took a couple of paces, resting her hands on her thighs, before slumping to her knees and finally onto all fours. Her head was spinning and she could feel her heart thumping erratically in her chest. She did her best not to throw up, swallowing the saliva that filled her mouth, and shook her hands to try to get the blood flowing. She shuddered at the thought that she might be dying, or already dead, that something inside her had broken, but then the numbness subsided, her heartbeat slowed and she looked up from the floor.

The door was a white frame in the wall. Someone had come home and was walking around downstairs. She was aware of every inch of the house, the slightest movement or sound it made. She was alone in the darkness with whatever it was she had seen amid the flash, a being so unfathomably cold and vast that Anna curled up in its presence, becoming a cringing animal before her master; it possessed a terrible cruelty, devoid of understanding or compassion, and probably wasn't human, although it had appeared to her as *a man with a large, clumsy head, a gaping mouth and narrow eyes, with skin that sagged as if it had been slung over him. Rising from its head were squirming black feelers that reached out towards her . . .*

She went on all fours out of the room, and managed to

give the bookcase a shove, pressing her back against it until she heard it click shut. Then she crawled out of the study and along the corridor. She felt the gun digging into her thigh, but kept going until she reached the bedroom, where she retched before throwing up on the floor. Finally she heaved herself onto the bed and went out like a light.

16

'DID YOU THINK YOU'D GOT AWAY?'

Egill

'In other words, an underground passageway . . .' said Egill, although he had intended to say something quite different, something about the sands and the village.

The three of them sat leaning against the warehouse at the edge of the village. Egill felt a strong urge to get as far away from the village as possible, but the sandstorm was too fierce. They could barely see the poles on their side of the bridge, which meant that visibility was less than fifty metres and diminishing.

Vigdís had discovered another door in the hill between the village and the ravine – another underground passageway, assuming the barrage theory was correct. The door was locked from the inside.

Hrafn had his eyes closed, while Vigdís studied the map. She seemed uneasy about something. If she only *knew.* They hadn't told her about what they had seen in the village.

The heat was so still stifling that Egill was perspiring freely under his shirt. The water level in the ravine had risen and its now-thunderous roar merged with the howling wind. Egill held up his camera, pointing it at the ravine, but then lost interest. He rose to his feet and said he was going for a piss. Neither Hrafn nor Vigdís looked up.

He rounded the corner of the warehouse, where there was less shelter from the wind, but enough to light the 'secret weapon' he fished out of his shirt pocket. While he was relieving himself he inhaled the smoke, holding it in before exhaling a thin, bluish streak.

He had the distinct impression that the hairs on his body were standing on end; he felt like a wounded veteran who hears the whistle of the bullet as it hits him in the head, feels the pain in his frontal lobe, who almost loses control, but keeps shooting at everything around him. Yes, now he reflected about it, that would be the likely outcome of such a *brainstorm*.

He zipped up his flies, leaned against the wall, and smoked some more. He watched as the sandstorm started to die down, taking on a reddish hue, the grains of sand spinning around one another, confiding their secrets about the sun at the Earth's core, the plates colliding like restless dragons. When he re-joined them, Hrafn would look probingly at him, detect the signs – and envy him; he would doubtless drift even further into himself, lose control. It was unavoidable.

After he graduated, Egill worked at a lawyer's office in downtown Reykjavík, until he gained enough experience to branch out on his own. He and two friends from university went into partnership, rented an office space on Suðurgata and started building up a client base. At one of the first cocktail parties they gave he met Hrafn; during all that time they had avoided bumping into each other, although Egill had heard his former friend's name mentioned increasingly in connection with the business world.

'Did you think you'd got away?' said Hrafn, extending his arm. They shook hands, and he told Egill that it was his brother – a lawyer – who had been invited to the reception, but was unable to come, and had sent Hrafn in his place.

Hrafn claimed not to know that Egill was one of the partners in the firm, but Egill didn't believe him (absurd though that sounded), although he couldn't understand why Hrafn would lie about it. They talked about meeting up again soon to 'renew their old acquaintanceship', and although, given Hrafn's rapid ascent up the social ladder, Egill felt relatively enthusiastic about the prospect, he had no intention of taking the initiative.

Not long afterwards, they met at a mutual friend's stag party, a gathering they both claimed they hadn't wanted to attend, but couldn't get out of. They ended the evening together drunk at Vegas, a strip club on Laugarvegur, where Hrafn admitted to Egill that his girlfriend had thrown him out the week before for being unfaithful and that he was currently living at a hotel, had no idea what was next on the cards but regretted everything. He introduced Egill to an acquaintance as his oldest and dearest friend; later that night he told Egill he loved him and wanted to forgive him for what had happened between them 'way back'. Egill didn't remember what he had replied, but somehow they ended up back at his and Anna's – she had moved in around that time – where Hrafn crashed out on the sofa.

Over the next few months they would meet, just the two of them, without their respective partners, usually on a Thursday. They would walk out to Grótta, chat and smoke cigars, and afterwards go out for a meal, occasionally sending a few drinks to some girls at another table, before ending the evening at the Rex, where they topped up with whisky until they were dead drunk.

Over time, Egill managed to build up some idea of what had happened to Hrafn after they had stopped speaking. Following his first stay in rehab, when he was about twenty, Hrafn left the ugly world he had inhabited and crept back into the bosom of his family, where he sank deep into their safety net. He promised to be a good boy, and was forgiven everything, on certain conditions. He had never finished school, which was unfortunate, although certainly not unheard of in his family, but his experience as a coke dealer gave him a better understanding than most of the new market-oriented way of thinking that was consuming the nation at the time. With his father's help, he was given the opportunity to work his way up in the fishing company, and he started to wear a suit, met his father's friends and their sons at parties, got to know his own family network, became reacquainted with the *ruling families*, and after that things happened fast.

By the time he was twenty-six, Hrafn was more or less

responsible for the day-to-day running of a business with an annual turnover of billions of krónur, and although his father was still the director in name, he had more or less renounced his management role. Hrafn's older brother Geir returned to Iceland after finishing his law studies in Boston, became the company lawyer and attended committee meetings with ministers and bankers; and when their father signed the business over to his sons, and started to spend more time in Florida, Geir was responsible for drawing up all the legal documents.

Although the two brothers didn't get along, the business thrived, and they began to consort with those of their class, attending meetings at the Icelandic Chamber of Commerce, Promote Iceland, the Federation of Icelandic Fishing Vessel Owners, and Business Iceland, as well as the Independence Party's national convention, and although they wouldn't turn up drunk like their father, they had no objection to smoke-filled backrooms, and Geir had been known to take the occasional cognac, thus fulfilling one of the main prerequisites of being an Icelandic businessman.

Considering what the other men in his family were like, this came as no surprise to Egill. Yet one evening, almost a year after they had started meeting again, when he was particularly drunk, Hrafn confided to Egill that something in him remained alert, detached, that he wasn't completely consumed by his job. He said he had never doubted himself, and knew he could be happy doing something other than business or finance; part of him questioned money, despised it even, and he felt a sort of spiritual restlessness. Occasionally it occurred to him – as it had in the past, in Ægisíða – that he could have become an artist.

'Haven't you simply forgotten something?' Egill had jested, clapping him on the back. 'Isn't that the problem? Don't you need to sail out to sea, cast your line on the water and reel in a fish? Stay in touch with reality.'

But those were different times; never at any moment in the history of the world had it been easier to take out a loan, and Hrafn had plenty of ideas about how to make money grow. He had long been aware of how much his father paid annually in interest alone, and the amount he could borrow against relatively little collateral was astonishing. And perhaps the fact that Icelanders had the same word for loan and luck emphasized their unique situation. In consultation with auditors and special financial advisors, he and Geir started selling off the company assets, using future fishing quotas, or rather the actual trawlers, as collateral, because the other way would have been illegal. They invested their money in Icelandic banks and holding companies, in real estate in the old Eastern Bloc countries, in transportation, telecommunications and in the energy market. They set up their own holding companies, and glimpsed the shape of something they did not yet fully grasp, but which made the *new market-oriented thinking* look like a toaster beside a stealth aircraft. They learned to increase the value of their money simply by shifting it from one place to another, between accounts, buying and selling shares; it was like mixing money-dough and watching it rise, and it worked like a charm – providing no one slammed the door.

Around that time, Egill also grew rich, but no matter how much money he had, Hrafn always seemed to have ten times more; he claimed he was weighed down by all his money, had lost count of his *accounts,* said he dreamed about forests of gold, that his name was Scrooge McDuck, and he had a red ruby cap and a diamond-studded deer hitched to his bumper. And then one day he stopped talking about it, unless Egill pressed him. All of a sudden he had lost interest in money. He said he had met a woman, whose identity he must keep secret for the time being, but who was the love of his life. And then one Thursday evening, he announced to Egill that he was going back into rehab – on the advice of this mystery woman.

'I'm an alcoholic, a chronic alcoholic,' he drawled over a cocktail in 101 Hotel, having come straight from a reception at the Canadian Embassy. He told Egill he had woken up drunk, and couldn't remember which shares he had bought and sold in New York that morning, but he probably should have gone straight back to bed.

'Never trust me, never . . . *trust* me,' he had added. Then he informed Egill that he was on his way to rehab in Sweden.

When Hrafn came back, everything had changed. He started seeing Vigdís, whom Egill assumed was the mystery woman from before, and Grótta and the Rex were out of bounds for the time being. However, because Egill was keen to go on meeting his friend – indeed, he had never needed him as much – he suggested they go hiking. Hrafn accepted. They walked up Mount Esja, took their girlfriends, and on one of their hikes Hrafn brought up the idea of a trip to the highlands. He was a shareholder in a company that had the lease of a proper mountain jeep, and he suggested they go on a trip together; they could take provisions, tents and sleeping bags, relax and recoup after the winter, which had been difficult for everyone.

Egill's first instinct was to say he was too busy; he felt nervous about Hrafn and Anna becoming better acquainted, and he also found the timing odd. Everything in his life had suddenly changed, not least his and Hrafn's relationship. Not long before, Egill had asked Hrafn to lend him some money to get him out of a tight spot, prevent him being investigated on various counts, and to tide him over, for a while at least. When Hrafn refused, Egill assumed that he was right in his suspicions, which had strengthened since Hrafn went into rehab: he too had lost everything. They were in the same boat, only Hrafn was better at hiding it. On the other hand, it was quite possible that Hrafn had just as much money as before, and had only ever wanted one thing: *revenge*.

Anna insisted they go. She said she was fed up with the way they isolated themselves, fed up with his envy of Hrafn and of anyone who hadn't screwed up their lives, fed up with his self-destructiveness, his inertia, his drinking, until Egill became increasingly convinced that there was something fated about the whole thing. A month later, they drove out of town, even though they all knew that the trip was a bad idea.

17

Egill

He crushed the joint between his fingers and watched the ember blow away across the sand. The storm had grown darker again, but inside his own chest it was warm and soft, his heartbeat strong but steady.

On his way past the smaller door into the warehouse – the personnel gate – Egill had the impression that something was different. He paused for a long time in front of the door then pushed it and watched as the chain slipped through the hole and fell onto the ground. Or perhaps he was mistaken.

Having resolved not to say anything, he walked back to Hrafn and Vigdís and instantly blurted it out.

'The warehouse is unlocked,' he said, assuring them he wasn't mistaken.

They stood up and followed him to the door, which was indeed open. Hrafn scarcely glanced at the open door, stooping instead over the chain that lay on the sand.

'What did you do to it?' he asked, inspecting the padlock, which was attached to one end of the chain, not both as they had thought earlier. 'I examined the chain and I'm positive it wasn't like this.'

Egill raised his hands, and said he knew nothing about it.

Vigdís entered the shed and Egill followed her.

'Are we trespassing?' she said, and Egill heard himself air what he considered a sensible opinion (regardless of how much it clashed with his fundamental views on life): that the idea of private property seemed absurd, or at any rate unrealistic, up there in the highlands; of course anyone in extremis should be allowed to take shelter inside a building, especially if the alternative was to die of exposure outside the door, which would doubtless be far more distressing to the owner than any damage incurred from wilful breaking and entering. He was puzzled by his own attitude: it had a *humane* quality that made him smile.

The warehouse was dark inside, save for a glimmer of light seeping through a window high up on one wall. Above them they could see heavy timber beams, but not the ceiling. The floor was made of the same sand that was billowing against the walls. Egill strode into the centre of the warehouse, which seemed empty. At least, he hadn't tripped over anything yet, or banged his head against an aircraft, or a tractor or a hundred-foot, pitch-black speed-boat. He giggled softly.

Thanks to Hrafn's labours they discovered that the main door was also open, and, as with the smaller door, the padlock was only attached to one end of the chain. They all helped push it open, letting in more light, although close to the walls it remained dark. After making doubly sure the warehouse was empty, that no one else was in there besides them, they sat inside the doorway waiting for the storm to die down. They would never make it to Askja before dark, and had decided to postpone their journey until the morning.

'This will ease off soon,' said Egill, kicking off his shoes and massaging his toes. 'At the latest by this evening, right? The weather always quietens down in the evenings.'

Vigdís nodded.

'If not, we should be able to find our way back using the compass and the clock,' she said. 'Whatever happens, I'm not spending the night here.'

She took the flares out of her bag, and she and Egill wondered whether they worked or not.

Hrafn walked off and lay down in the shadow alongside the wall. He muttered something about taking a nap, but looked as if he was sulking.

Vigdís took out her provisions and made herself a snack. Egill felt uneasy sitting this close to her, surrounded by the whistling wind, which evoked a kind of *intimacy*. Not for the first time, he found himself wondering what Vigdís was like in bed; she was more self-possessed than that little butterfly Anna, she had breasts, *full* breasts, as someone had put it, and probably cried after she climaxed, deep, heart-rending, choking, sobs, maybe she even *gushed* when she came . . . or squirted.

He couldn't remember when squirting had first appeared on the scene: he usually only noticed the different types of Internet porn after he became bored of them. Perhaps everyone was like that, and doubtless it said something about their libido. There was something rather elegant about squirting. He remembered first reading about it in an English, nineteenth-century erotic novel: *Fanny Hill*, when he was about twenty, and once when he was drunk he had slept with a woman who ejaculated like that. Up until then he hadn't quite believed it was physically possible, and didn't dare broach the subject with anyone. He read a book called *A Delicate Subject*, by Sigrún Daviðsdóttir, a correspondent with the Icelandic state radio in London. It was about a young Icelandic photographer in New York who falls for an older woman, a widow. Egill wasn't usually interested in contemporary Icelandic literature, and he couldn't remember how he had come across the book, but the main character ejaculated, or 'squirted' as it was described in the book. He couldn't figure out where the liquid came from. Was it something that accumulated in the ovaries and was then released through the cervix and the vagina during orgasm? Did women have a secret pouch which scientists had kept quiet about, or had simply overlooked – an uncharted Shangri-La that lay buried inside every humdrum situation only to be utterly exposed at *the pinnacle of pleasure*?

Vigdís finished eating, packed her provisions away and said she was going to 'lie down' for a bit. She sat propped against the doorpost, eyes closed, but her top button was undone and Egill glimpsed the shadow between her breasts. Beads of sweat glistened on her brow and chest.

Egill rose to his feet, stepped outside the warehouse and glanced about him at the area surrounding the warehouse, at the hill that sheltered the village from the cold north wind in winter, and the edge of the ravine, which he glimpsed every now and then through the storm. He noticed there was no sign this side saying *Beware – Danger*, and wondered why not.

And who had arranged the bones into a pyramid? The answer was easy: the same people who had killed the geese, swans, reindeer, mice, birds and rats – or whatever they were. The outlaws. After killing the animals, they had removed the bones, made them into a pyramid the way you stack coal in a grill – except there was nowhere for them to get coal – and that's how they had cooked the meat.

Cooking meat with bones?

He shuddered. He didn't like shuddering but did so all the same. Looking down, he realized he was barefoot and turned back to the warehouse to fetch his camera from his rucksack. He stole a glance at Vigdís's tits before wandering inside the warehouse.

'Let's see,' he murmured to himself with a grin, as he pressed the record button, reflecting about the possibility, the faint possibility that this might be of some interest one day in the future, when this was all over, consigned to memory like a *bad dream*.

He penetrated as far into the warehouse as he could, leaned against the back wall and felt how stoned he still was after the joint. He pointed the camera at the doorway, where Vigdís's outline was just visible.

'I'm standing in a warehouse at the northern edge of Vatnajökull,' he whispered into the machine, 'one of the most inhuman, desolate places on the planet. And yes, unique. We all know words like *sour*, which are sometimes used to describe our traditional winter fare, or the stench of brothels where nobody has seen hot water in years. But why do we always shun the other end of the pH scale – Icelandic nature is alkaline, the equivalent of forcing Grettir the Strong down your throat.'

He saw something shoot across the floor then come to a halt nearby. A mouse. It sniffed suspiciously in his direction.

He zoomed away from Vigdís and onto the mouse.

'And yet despite everything, here we see a little mouse . . .' he resumed, but couldn't think of a punchline, his voice taking on a childlike wonderment that made him cringe.

The mouse vanished, and Egill walked back towards the door, where Vigdís had given up trying to fall asleep and was browsing *Icelandic Flora*.

'And here she sits, unable to fall asleep. What do you say to a brief interview for future reference, for posterity? Tell me, Vigdís, how do you reconcile your work as a therapist with belonging to Friends of Nature, the members of which have sparked controversy by travelling naked around the highlands, and because of their permissive behaviour during the evening entertainments?'

Vigdís glanced up from her book.

'We're all good friends, of course.' She smiled. 'Here in the desert we're free, au naturel. We can all be the way we are supposed to be: wild and free.'

'I sense a trace of irony in the therapist's voice, possibly even a repressed aversion towards nature. Which comes as a surprise, since repression itself is inimical to the Friends of Nature, is it not?'

They both giggled, and Egill was surprised by how playful she was, flirtatious almost. Perhaps it was the camera.

'Tell me, I sometimes wonder what is the matter with this nation. What do you think? What is wrong with it?'

'I don't know.' She closed her book and became pensive. 'I read some figures once about how many Icelandic women visit crisis centres each year because they have been raped. Approximately one hundred and fifty. Out of a population of three hundred thousand, that's about three times more proportionately than in the other Nordic countries. And in a UN survey of unprovoked public violence, Reykjavík came third, behind two other port cities in the developing world.'

'I understand. In fact, I know about this, about why our society is broken, why women here are raped the way they are in the worst port cities, and why no one, including the politicians and the media, bats an eyelid. Do you want to know why?'

Vigdís nodded.

'I never understood either, until I went out for a stroll one night. Take a walk down Laugarvegur late on a

Saturday night, and you'll see the reason for everything that goes on in Iceland – binge drinking. Stand on the corner of Laugarvegur and Skólavörðustígur at 3 a.m. on a Sunday morning and look around you; it's like a zoo where all the animals have been let out of their cages, whipped on the backsides and encouraged to create mischief – they have no idea how, but you can tell from their faces they are determined to find out.'

'I've been there myself,' she said, and grinned, revealing a row of even white teeth. 'What were you doing there, simply taking a stroll?'

'Well, I certainly wasn't raping anyone! In any civilized society they'd treat it like a riot: station cops on every corner, use water cannon and tear gas to clear the streets. The Icelandic nation is full of drunks: from civil servants and bankers to politicians and petrol pump attendants; everyone is either hung-over or about to go on a drinking binge. The checkout woman at Bónus, the sales rep, your lawyer, the checkout guy at BYKO, the guy who serves hotdogs at the Bæjarins Bestu stall, the young female assistant at Eymundsson's bookshop, all of them are either pissed or about to get pissed. The few that *aren't* are either plotting to take over the world, blogging on the Eyjan website, or attending debates at young conservative or socialist clubs. Then there are two or three who live in Mosfellsbær and are just laid-back, into handicrafts and painting stones and things. And they'll never have anything to say about this society.'

Vigdís laughed and asked him whether he was talking about himself.

'Do you know what the difference is between men and women?' she added. 'When a man drops a glass on the floor, he blames the glass, and when a woman drops a glass she blames herself.'

'Yeah, go figure.'

They heard a rustle from inside the warehouse, and a moment later Hrafn emerged from the gloom. Egill moved the camera off from Vigdís, considered turning it off but pointed it at Hrafn instead.

'Good morning,' said Vigdís.

Hrafn didn't reply, he walked over to them and gazed out at the storm.

'Shouldn't we make a move?' he said, taking out a packet of cigarettes.

'The visibility isn't good enough,' said Vigdís. 'As I'm sure you can see for yourself . . . Did you have a good nap?'

Hrafn shook his head, nudging with his toe the bag in which Vigdís kept the flares.

'I couldn't fall asleep.'

He lit a cigarette and Egill zoomed in on him, for no particular reason, perhaps simply because he wanted to annoy him.

'Take that fucking camera out of my face,' said Hrafn, without looking at Egill.

'Don't be so rude, Hrafn,' said Vigdís, and Egill swung the camera onto her. 'Are you OK?'

'I'm absolutely fine, thanks. Shouldn't we try one of those

flares to make sure they work? It would be good to know,' said Hrafn, making a visible effort to contain himself. But the old hatred was still simmering, as Egill had always suspected – only it was better hidden after being channelled by the twelve steps, or the higher power, or whatever it was called.

'To see if the old woman comes to our aid?' said Egill, and Vigdís grinned. Clearly she had chosen to side with him.

'How *tiresome* you two are,' said Hrafn. 'At least I want to *do* something, not just sit here staring into space. I want to go back—'

'Then *go* back,' said Vigdís with a flash of anger. She stood up. 'We'll follow later! Or do you expect us to go with you after you just told us how tiresome we are?'

'Didn't you say I was rude? I couldn't fall sleep. And it was tiresome listening to you two. Giggling like a couple of kids, high on their own imaginations.'

Egill glanced at them furtively, taking care to hold the camera still. Their words echoed softly off the roof of the warehouse.

'Didn't we talk about this before we came on the trip?' said Vigdís. 'You feel irritable and you're trying to blame it on us. You're a grown man, stop behaving like a child.'

Hrafn walked deeper inside the warehouse, gritted his teeth then stormed back.

'*I'm* behaving like a child? I'm not the one sitting here flirting with your friend right under your nose! It's been like that the whole fucking journey! What do you expect, how did you two think I would react?'

'My love—' Vigdís started to say, but Hrafn cut across her.

'I'm exhausted, I know. I can't tell any more whether it's all in my head, but I don't think it is. Not in your case, at any rate,' he said, rounding on Egill. 'Why do you *look* at her in that way? Do you think I don't see? Is your brain so numb from self-pity, from worrying about your own pathetic life—'

'What are you talking about?' said Egill, lowering the camera, but Hrafn grabbed it and flung it through the door, where it disappeared noiselessly into the storm.

'And stop talking about my girlfriend as if you want to go out with her. As if you know how to appreciate her more than I, as if you *deserve* her and I don't! Stop sniffing around her and harping on about her as if she were the mother you never had, stop abusing everything that comes near you—'

'Now you've lost me completely, my friend.'

Egill raised his hands in a gesture of surrender even as he thought about the mouse safe in her little nest.

'You know exactly what I'm talking about. But isn't that just typical of you to pretend you don't. Or rather, not to give a damn. You are so self-pitying you don't even understand that other people can suffer or have problems.'

'Of course I give a *damn*. If you don't know that, then you don't know me very well. Look, I'm sorry about what happened with that girl. I already apologized to you about that. And I'm sorry if I've done anything, or – how should I put it? – talked too much with your girlfriend. What do you want me to do?'

'What are you two on about?' asked Vigdís, looking from one to the other.

'*Talked too much* with my girlfriend?' Hrafn scoffed, staring straight at Egill. 'When did I say that? You don't understand a thing. You're incapable of communicating with other people. You mooch around the countryside for a week, snivelling about yourself, wallowing in despair, trampling over everyone around you, or lording it over us with your pompous self-satisfaction—'

'Clearly you have strong feelings about all this. But I'll tell you one thing I've never done: I've never said such ugly things about anyone as the things you're saying to me now. Not anyone. It isn't very nice to hear you speak like this about your oldest, though clearly not your dearest, friend.'

Hrafn howled with laughter.

'Poor Egill, everyone says such nasty things about him. Who insulted his friends last night at dinner and then fell asleep under a streetlamp? Who behaved like an idiot yesterday? And the day before, and the day before that? Surely not good little Egill!'

'You're losing it, Hrafn, you're really losing it,' Egill started to say, and his anger felt like a mask on his face, a flame threatening to burst out and shoot down into his fists.

'And what did you get up to last night? Where's the camera, Egill? Did you find it in the jeep when you went there to crash out? Perhaps you took a photo of her – did you want to get your hands on something you knew you could never have unless you stole it?'

'I don't know anything about that photo. This is bullshit and you know it!'

'Why were you trying to hide it, then?'

'To protect you! And because I knew you wouldn't believe me.'

'You're lying. Who else could have taken it? There's no one here like you,' said Hrafn, lifting his finger and prodding Egill's chest hard, once, twice. 'No one as pathetic. You're pathetic, Egill, that's all you've ever been—'

'You're one to talk,' said Egill, recoiling, aware that his anger had gone numb, his muscles were heavy, and his skin felt thick and clammy. 'It wasn't me who wrecked the car. And while we're on the subject, I wasn't the only one who lost the plot yesterday. How much grass did you smoke? You sound fucking paranoid enough anyhow. And you say *I* behave badly towards my friends. At least I apologize when I make a mistake. *And I don't lie to my girlfriend.*'

'I think you should both calm down,' said Vigdís, her voice sounding a long way off.

'Not another word, you bastard,' hissed Hrafn, seizing Egill by the throat, and twisting the collars of his shirt together. 'How dare you say that, how dare you use that against me with her, you fucking coward!'

Egill groped for Hrafn's hands, pulling and clawing at them, although with each movement he felt increasingly numb. Vigdís tried to separate them, and Egill caught a whiff of her soft, womanly scent, saw Hrafn's lips move, the sounds he was emitting at once shrill and booming, and everything turned white and shimmering. He should get in better shape, he thought, he had let himself go lately, his body was flaccid . . .

Then Hrafn released his grip. Egill retched, his throat rattling as he gasped for breath, and he could hear once more, the echo from the roof, the wind. Vigdís clasped his shoulders and asked him if he was all right. He stood up straight and started to laugh – he always laughed when things went wrong, and yet he had no recollection of ever having laughed about anything, at least not the way he was now, a whole-hearted belly laugh. He watched Hrafn leave the warehouse, through the main door, not the personnel door. Vigdís shouted something after him, before turning to Egill to ask if he would be OK on his own for a while. Egill nodded and watched her disappear into the sandstorm, in the direction of the bridge.

Egill slumped to the floor and lit a cigarette. He was overwhelmed by a deep, inner hatred of being who he was, of being stuck inside a character he no longer understood, and which he couldn't fix. And yet wasn't there something rather noble about it all, something courageous, Vikingesque? Being bogged down in weakness together, knowing too much about one another to be able to blab, having too much to lose. Until a moment ago, at least.

Egill sprawled on his back, closed his eyes and heard the flap of some unimaginably huge object wheeling above the sands, watching them and waiting.

18

THE MINOTAUR

Vigdís

She felt her way along the bridge, the wind behind her, then ran headlong into the storm. She glimpsed Hrafn a dozen metres ahead of her, where the sand became a black wall. Every now and then he merged with or was half-immersed in the wall.

'Hrafn! Wait!'

The sand whistled in her ears, blowing and swirling all around her. She was catching up fast, but even from a few metres away, Hrafn seemed deaf to her calls, and his outline was still blurry.

She ran the final stretch, reaching out to touch him when he dissolved and vanished.

'Tsk, tsk,' she murmured, and came to a halt, clutching her head with her hands as though making sure she was still there herself. She reflected for a moment, but decided not to turn back to the warehouse, although that would have been relatively easy: if she headed into the wind she would arrive at the ravine, and after pacing up and down it for a few minutes she would find the bridge and after that the warehouse. But she didn't want to be alone with Egill.

She rummaged in her rucksack for her sunglasses and wound her scarf tightly about her nose and mouth. Without the sunglasses the sand flew into her eyes, making it impossible to see further than ten metres.

Based on her observations earlier that day she guessed it must be roughly half an hour from the house to the ravine; if she timed herself and kept walking north-east she should be able to find the house, and with any luck she would bump into Hrafn along the way – either to give him a piece of her mind or rescue him, she hadn't quite decided which.

She set off once more, marching in step, and tried not to think about anything. The sand slid down her neck, up her sleeves and trouser legs, and rubbed against the sore patch on her thighs, the result of her attempt to use the toilet the day before.

Fragments of the quarrel floated around inside her head. If Hrafn had been smoking, then he had relapsed – which didn't exactly surprise her given the problems at home during the past few months. Egill's mention of 'the girl' no doubt referred to something that had happened when they were young. Hrafn had once spoken to her about his first love, a girl he had started seeing when he was seventeen or eighteen. She was used to the men she came across in her practice regarding their *first love* as one might a fluffy lapdog, as a pretext to justify finding fault with their current partner, wallowing in self-pity, their nostalgia wagging its tail and yapping, shrilly but prettily: the girl became increasingly pure, and their love, which took on mythical proportions, less tainted, more beautiful. And the role of their current partner, like Vigdís herself, was to be a carbon copy, which although not bad, was still inferior, more down-to-earth, more motherly. Hrafn had hinted that the relationship with the girl had been serious, but then it ended, according to him because he was unable to sleep with her; he responded to his shame by consuming more drugs and alcohol, and ended by forgetting her name. He never mentioned Egill in connection with the girl.

Through the sand, Vigdís glimpsed a grey, streamlined object, which as she drew near she realised was a car. It felt like a relief to be able to fix her gaze on something that wasn't constantly moving. She ran her fingers over the body, which was sand-blown metal stripped of paint, although the shape was familiar. The windows all appeared intact.

She peered through the driver's window, but saw nothing of interest, then opened the door, climbing in quickly so the car wouldn't fill with sand, before slamming it shut. She was out of breath from walking, and her loud gasps filled the silent vehicle. She took off her sunglasses, loosened the scarf from around her face, unbuttoned her shirt and managed to brush most of the sand off her. Her eyes searched for the rear-view mirror, as though out of age-old habit, but the mount where it should have been was empty, as were both the wing mirror casings.

She lit a cigarette and opened the glove compartment,

to dispel the idea that there might be something inside it. Apart from a logbook, which had no entries, it was empty. The wind buffeted the front of the vehicle, rocking it gently. Outside, the visibility was no better, and when she looked straight into the wind, she no longer saw the sand grains, only the *traces* they left. Each time she moved her mouth she found herself crunching sand.

She smoked the cigarette down to the filter and placed it on the dashboard. The car had done fifteen thousand kilometres, which wasn't a lot. Scarcely enough to warrant abandoning it on the sands, was it?

Most of what she knew about Hrafn, about his inner life, she learned during the first months of their relationship, while he was still undergoing treatment with her. He told her he was an alcoholic, that he had recently started drinking again and couldn't sleep. Drinking made everything in his life worse, but there was more: deep down inside he felt a kind of sickness or chaos that had been dogging him for years, the key to which he suspected was hidden in a memory he didn't know how to unlock, something that had happened to him a long time ago.

'And which could be dangerous to get close to, on your own?' Vigdís had ventured, and they had started to meet once a week. Afterwards, he told her all about his life: how since he was a kid he had suffered from fits of rage, how he used to hurl the remote control against the wall, smash electrical appliances, tear up books, kick the wing mirrors off cars, and how when he became a drug dealer he sometimes beat people up quite badly: he once smashed a beer glass in a boy's face, disfiguring him for life; he stamped on people's heads, broke their bones, punched their lights out, cut them up. He had calmed down over the years, but suspected he had simply become better at directing his rage against himself or at concealing it. Occasionally he would angrily vent his political views about the incompetent Icelandic elite, their greed and immorality – not just the traditional kind, but what he described as the new, much more destructive kind, and sometimes, when he admitted to being part of it, his anger and shame about what he did would become as one.

He appeared to have a phobia about confined spaces, and would often complain of feeling closed in when he was on her couch. All of a sudden, he would leap to his feet and tear off his tie, and once he hurled it on the floor and ripped the top button off his shirt. A month into his therapy, he had an intense experience when he remembered that shortly after his eleventh birthday he had started wetting the bed. This had gone on for some time, and he recalled how ashamed he felt, how he would wake up in the middle of the night, take the sheets off his bed and carry them to the laundry room, and his father's rage when he found out, an oddly *intense* rage, which Hrafn assumed was because of the bedwetting, although he wasn't sure.

Vigdís was convinced they were making headway, and that Hrafn was probably right: something buried deep inside him was polluting him, and nowhere was it more evident than in his sex life, which had been a disaster from the beginning. His first experience was in a 'cramped, dark room', as he described it, and although he was drunk, he felt overwhelmed by anxiety and claustrophobia, with the result that he lost his erection. Indeed, despite various attempts, it seemed he hadn't had an orgasm with a girl until he was nearly twenty. Sex awoke in him a deep dread, which he was convinced was common among men, and he referred to it as 'performance anxiety'. It turned out that before seeking help he had been in numerous relationships with women, which ended after a few weeks when he started to feel obliged to sleep with them. He said he couldn't imagine having sex with the same person in an ongoing relationship; he hated having sex in the dark, in bright light, in the morning, or late at night, or just after the evening news, in a bed that was too small or too big, in a basement or on the ground floor, in a windowless room or an attic, with women whose breasts were too big or too small, who were too eager or too frigid. Sometimes when he slept with a woman he was seized by an almost intolerable dread, as if he were all alone in the world, the walls closing in on him, folding above his head. He said that sex had always alienated him from people, from everyone he loved.

Although his impotence had diminished over the years, it was never 'far away', and he found himself making up excuses before going to bed with a woman, inventing the most ludicrous stories about how he had just jerked off in the toilet of the bar where they met, or had slept with his ex-girlfriend that morning, or was physically burned-out after a heavy sports session earlier that day, and it didn't bother him if the woman he was with each time abandoned him as a result.

During these revelations, Hrafn would become extremely agitated and burst into tears, before flying into a rage, and the remainder of the session would be spent calming him down. At the beginning of their next session, he said he had been 'thinking about things', about why his life had been so 'full of fear', why it had 'failed'. He spoke in a cold voice and would avoid looking Vigdís in the eye, as though afraid he might break down again. He told her about his epileptic fits which started when he was eleven, although he had no idea why. His parents had no memory of them, but a doctor he met at a party told him that children sometimes responded this way to physical trauma. The fits went on for a year or two until he started drinking, and the alcohol seemed to put a stop to them. After he gave up drinking the fits didn't come back, as if they had got lost somewhere inside him; at one point he compared them to the Minotaur, half-man half-beast, trapped in a labyrinth which King Minos had built to contain his shame.

However, it turned out that talking about his fits was simply a preamble to the visit he had made a few days earlier to Stígamót, an organization for the victims of sexual abuse. He said he had stumbled across their booklet while browsing through the magazine rack at a coffee shop, and before he knew it he'd dialled the number and made an appointment to talk to someone. The night before the interview, he fell ill, started vomiting and ran a temperature;

he felt too sick to drive down to Stígamót, so he bundled himself into a taxi. As he approached the entrance his muscles went slack and it was all he could do to shuffle forward, as if he (or some other he) were incapable of walking through the door. In the second-floor office, he found himself confronted by a woman of about fifty who was 'ordinary in every way', and yet Hrafn felt that she was an adult while he was a child, or a poor wretch. He told her he wasn't sure why he had made the appointment, adding vague references to 'something that had happened'. The woman reassured him that this was perfectly normal and that there was no hurry, at which point he interrupted her to insist that he wasn't there to *accuse* anyone. She said she understood, and asked him to try to remember what had happened, and if he had difficulty he should simply guess, which was often the first step – for some reason he found that amusing, although he didn't laugh out loud.

Vigdís quickly realized that this wasn't part of the story, but rather the framework to it, an introduction that appeared to play a key role. Adopting the same proviso Hrafn had used with 'the other woman' – that this was all hypothetical, nothing more than guesswork – Vigdís asked him to tell her what had happened.

Hrafn was eleven years old. One day after school, he said goodbye to his friends and headed for Skalli, the shop where he sometimes went to buy sweets. Then he set off home along Hraunbær, where he bumped into two older boys – known to him and the younger kids in the neighbourhood as local 'thugs'. They were hanging around at the bus stop, smoking. When they were younger, one of them had punched him and stolen his cap, but now he walked up to Hrafn smiling as if they were friends. The other boy had an ugly, scowling face and was notorious for having once stubbed a cigarette out on the back of someone's hand. He didn't talk much, but when he did Hrafn felt uneasy, because he discussed Hrafn without looking at him, always addressing his friend and laughing, as if he found something hysterically funny, something Hrafn couldn't see.

The first boy, whose name was Hjalti, asked Hrafn if he would follow them further into the neighbourhood, to help them with something – Hrafn didn't remember what – and in exchange for this they would give him money. Hrafn hesitated but then gave up trying to resist, and off they went. Hjalti talked a lot while the other boy kept sniggering and using words that Hrafn didn't understand. Eventually he must have let on that he was frightened, because Hjalti seized him by the shoulders and explained (not in an unfriendly way) something about what the ugly boy was saying.

They came to a courtyard, beyond the shop, and walked across it. Hrafn saw a boy from his class kicking a football with a younger lad, and had the impression he was seeing them from a long way off and could never reach them, no matter how hard he tried. Hrafn wanted to turn back, but they assured him it wasn't far now. The next courtyard was deserted, with no football court in the middle. They headed towards a corner of the quad, where there was an open stairwell, and they climbed the stairs. Hjalti walked ahead of him, with the other boy behind. At this point, Hrafn was terrified, but he didn't want them to know that, because they would only laugh at him and then something bad would happen; instead he decided to do what they asked in the hope they'd let him go home. They came to an open door, possibly on the first floor, which they entered and shut behind them. Instantly Hrafn started to whimper softly, and said he wanted to leave, but the boys started laughing and blocked his way to the door.

The apartment was deserted and silent. The nasty boy called out something behind him, and led Hrafn towards a door at the end of a passageway. From behind the door came a deep, continuous drone, like a bass guitar, and the sound of approaching footsteps.

The story ended there. Hrafn had apologized to the woman, told her he had no idea what happened next, and didn't want to waste her time with pointless speculation. Then he left the building, walked down Hverfisgata, and the next thing he knew he was sitting on the rocks next to the sculpture of the Viking ship, *Sólfarið*, watching the waves wash back and forth on the shore with a soothing murmur.

Over the weeks that followed, Hrafn repeated the story during his sessions with Vigdís, but always on the understanding that this was what he would have told the 'other woman'. Despite her assurance that she accepted his provisos about the recollections being nothing more than guesswork, Hrafn's story scarcely changed, as if from the beginning it had been carved in stone. Vigdís tried prodding him to go on, but they never broke through the door at the end of the story. In context, it seemed as if this closed door was the reason for his visit to Stígamót, and Hrafn suspected that his sexual problems, his fears and his 'shame' had its origins behind that door. She put him under hypnosis, but got little out of him, apart from some vague murmurings about darkness and a red glow, which never developed any further. Nothing took shape, nothing was added, and when Vigdís put even more pressure on him, Hrafn's last defence was always the same: he wasn't sure in the end whether any of it had actually happened.

In any event, dredging it up seemed to have a positive effect on him: he had fewer mood swings, and he booked himself into rehab. But Vigdís wasn't convinced; something underneath all this worried her. They started seeing each other, and the therapy ended, but from time to time she would reflect on the things they had discussed. During all her years of practice, she had never encountered defences strong enough to keep the floodgates from finally bursting, the memories from unfurling, like a plant pushing through the soil, taking on a definitive shape before finally blossoming. A lot of people had difficulty knowing *exactly* what had happened in their past, but by and large the memories they recounted had a definite beginning and end. In Hrafn's case, his story was complete from the outset, its veracity highlighted and placed in question, and it didn't change one iota as time went by; it was spherical and slippery, impossible to get hold of, or do anything with except go round in circles.

Vigdís also found it suspicious that the story always started at Stígamót. At first she thought this must be Hrafn's way of distancing himself from what had happened, while at the same time lending his tale more credibility. It occurred to her that 'the thing that happened' in Árbær was made up, not because Hrafn wished to deceive her or anyone else, but rather himself; it was a lie he wasn't even aware he was telling, born of an inner contradiction he could no longer ignore. He was attempting through the story to restrain the forces that threatened to tear his life apart, and when he found himself unable to control them on his own, he had sought help.

She formulated her own theory: after a series of sexual failures in adolescence – the result of his indifference to the girls in question, his father's bullying attitude towards his performance, and his mother's unpredictability, which gave him an aversion to women who showed their emotions – Hrafn became caught in a vicious circle that had an increasingly negative effect on his relationships with women. He confessed that he had never understood, then or now, how he could be so 'messed-up' inside when his life was otherwise happy, defined by his enterprising, competitive spirit, and an almost ceaseless resolve; it had never occurred to him to think of himself as a *victim* until that 'memory' came to him.

So, what role did it play? Everything that couldn't be accommodated in his daily life was stored in a single, partial memory: his shame, his self-loathing, his gentleness – his inner feminine side – were justified and contained in this one story. And although the story worked, thought Vigdís, that didn't make it true.

19

MARY POPPINS

Vigdís

She ground her cigarette underfoot and placed the stub on the dashboard. Four cigarette butts – the only measure of how long she'd been sitting there, since she had lost all sense of time.

Her eye was drawn to a familiar logo at the front of the bonnet, the *Mercedes* emblem, which always reminded her of a rifle sight. She was sitting in a five-door, leather-upholstered automatic Mercedes, which someone had abandoned – with fifteen thousand kilometres on the clock. She looked over at the back seat, then again at the bonnet, and felt sure she hadn't seen the emblem when she first sat in the car.

Glancing sideways at the wing-mirror casings, she saw they were still empty. She had the impression the car was tilting. She moved over to the passenger side, which seemed lower down, and peered out of the window. The front tyre had either burst or had sunk into a hole in the sand, she thought; not a deep hole, though possibly deep enough to have brought the car to a halt – just like the jeep the old couple had lent them. She didn't dare get out to take a closer look.

A Mercedes car had played a part in her life once before. She couldn't recall how, only that it had been brief and rather unhappy.

Daren't she get out?

She was breathing more rapidly, without knowing why. Nothing outside the car daunted her. She had a watch, a compass and a map. She disliked not having wing mirrors, and being unable to see properly out of the back of the car – a gust of wind or the whipping sands might have shattered them, but that wouldn't explain the missing rear-view mirror.

The car windows were electric so she couldn't open them to let in any air. Instead she closed her eyes, concentrated on the top of her head, then scanned down her body, relaxing her muscles, relaxing her thoughts until she felt her breathing begin to slow. She listened to the murmur of the sand buffeting the Mercedes and imagined she was on her way to work, sitting in her own car in Reykjavík in the early morning, a file of identical vehicles (engineered in wind tunnels in Germany, as Hrafn had put it) stretching in front and behind, full of people like her, also on their way to work, waiting at the lights, engines idling as they stared straight ahead through the windscreen listening to the purring machines.

Looking back, she was astonished at how much she had struggled in life, how much importance she had given her sufferings and joys. Why? Images from the past that had caused her untold anguish at the time flashed through her mind, but she no longer let them undermine her, she no longer took them as personally as before. Where did this continual defensiveness against the world spring from? A wave of calm swept over her. She was in the garden at her parents' house, after her mother died. The lawn hadn't been mown for years, the vegetable patch was a riot of weeds, there wasn't a flower in sight, and the window in the potting shed was broken. She was sitting in the shed, face buried in her hands, weeping, sensing the presence of a person whom she didn't understand.

'Vigdís . . .' she said, opening her eyes. She looked down at her hands to find them clasping the steering wheel. She felt at once that she wanted to let go but didn't want to. The steering wheel had a brown leather cover with tiny holes that allowed the leather to breathe, and made for a firmer grip.

She closed her eyes. Somewhere behind her she heard the click of a door opening, the sound of the wind howling and then the door slamming shut. Her thoughts jostled one another in her head, and something slithered between them only to merge with them once more. On reflection, it was as if she had changed – in some fundamental way; she didn't understand how, only that this had happened relatively recently. What she referred to as her self was both vaguer and more defined; she was able to glimpse her own outline, everything that was her, almost as if she were a *character* in her own life, at once inside and outside herself.

That hadn't been true before, when she first sat in the car; this was happening too quickly. Her fear started to creep back, and, opening her eyes, she knew that she was no longer alone in the car. She had realized this just now, but it didn't seem to matter then. Someone was sitting in the seat behind her, only she couldn't see because the mirrors weren't where they were supposed to be, and she didn't dare look; if she turned around she would die, her heart would crumple up and stiffen into a hard red dot.

The man was sitting behind her and the car was moving; she felt the steering wheel turn between her hands and the car sway from side to side. She looked through the windscreen at the grains of sand rushing towards her, as the car cut through the storm swiftly and inexorably. Her hands gripped the wheel, and to the sides she made out the shapes of buildings. Lights she hadn't noticed before were flickering on the dashboard, and the radio emitted a low murmur. Although the car was speeding along, the man behind sat motionless, still as a shadow, his eyes boring into the back of her neck. A tall building loomed ahead, and on either side familiar houses flew past, the stucco apartment blocks near Hringbraut, and Vigdís knew what was coming. Soon she would reach a bend in the road, and right where the road straightened out again was where it would happen, there was no way she could prevent it, and all her attempts to do so had failed. She tried in vain to close her eyes, to wrench her hands from the wheel, but they only held on more tightly.

She took the bend too fast, heard the screech of tyres

and saw the church on her right looming out of the grass – silhouetted against the sky. A person with black hair and a sprinkling of grey on top appeared in the middle of the road carrying a bag of groceries in each hand, eyes wide with astonishment: her mother. Something heavy collided with the vehicle, and Vigdís was thrown forward onto the steering wheel even as she saw her mother float up from the ground in a long, rolling arch. She screamed, fumbled for the door handle and flung herself out of the car.

The storm had abated. The sand lay calm on the ground as though it had never done anything else. Vigdís stood up and looked about her. Over on the horizon she could see the house, dark against the grey sky.

20

THE KITCHEN DOOR

Anna

Anna slept late into the afternoon and awoke with a headache and a dry mouth. Remembering where she was, she buried herself beneath the covers, sighed gently and wished Egill were there to comfort her and give her a cuddle.

Soon she felt so thirsty that she couldn't put off getting up any longer. She grabbed her sponge bag and went out to the bathroom; her skin was beginning to stiffen like a shell, and there was no chance of her having a shower any time soon. The tap was rusty and spewed out a brownish jet. She waited for the water to run clear, and sipped hesitantly at it before guzzling it down, then applied a dab of face cream and some deodorant, took her tablets and decided that would have to do for now.

Replacing her sponge bag in her room, she noticed a small pool of dried vomit on the floor beside the bed. Instantly she remembered the old man's study, and something that had happened in there – an electric shock she received from touching a switch or turning on a lamp. She couldn't think about it; in short, she hadn't a clue what had happened, but she hurriedly cleaned up the vomit with a towel she moistened in the bathroom.

It was almost seven o'clock. She decided to see about some food, went outside to the jeep and rummaged in the freezer until she found a four-cheese pizza, which she felt a sudden craving for – something hot that didn't need much preparation. While she was there she grabbed half a bottle of red wine.

Ása was standing in the kitchen.

'You're here!' cried Anna.

'And where else should I be?'

The old lady was stooped over a bowl on the table, kneading dough.

'I didn't see you when I went out,' said Anna. 'It's blowing a gale,' she added, turning the frozen pizza over in her hands.

'The wind is dropping,' said the old woman.

'That's good. I hope my friends haven't got into any difficulties.'

The old woman didn't reply. Anna held up the pizza and asked if she could heat it.

'Of course, my dear. I'll see to that,' the old woman said, glancing up from her kneading. 'Have a seat in the front room, and then we can chat afterwards.'

Anna sat in the front room, plucked a bottle of blue nail varnish from her pocket and began to paint her nails. Every now and then she took a swig of wine, preferring the bottle to the tumbler the old woman had handed her, which had sand in the bottom. She decided her toes were too dirty for her to bother painting them, even though it calmed her.

Her ankle was better. Examining it, she saw that the swelling had disappeared. Perhaps she had made the whole thing up, because she hadn't wanted to walk. Unless the electric shock had caused the swelling to go down? It was the switch on the wall not the lamp that had thrown her onto the floor, and there had been something written above it. She remembered the window in the room too, the one that had been painted over, and the gun. Had she taken the gun? If she wasn't mistaken, it was lying in its silk covering under the bed, or even under the pillow. She should put it back, immediately.

Dizzy from the wine, she went out onto the steps to get a breath of fresh air. The wind had dropped. She glimpsed dust devils moving on the horizon, and the sand floated like a veil obscuring the line between earth and sky.

Something shot across the yard. Her first thought was that Trigger had come back, but then she saw that it was one of the foxes. Repulsive creatures.

Why did the old woman want to *chat afterwards*? If they had discovered her visit to the library, she would say she had a vomiting bug, and that stumbling about in a daze in search of the toilet she had opened the wrong door. If the conversation turned to what she did for a living, she would say she was a teacher – she had the feeling they wouldn't take kindly to journalists.

She heard Ása calling to her from the kitchen, something that sounded like: 'Girl!' She fetched a fresh bottle of red wine from the boot, and vowed to herself as she returned to the house that she wouldn't go back into the study while it was dark. Perhaps she should simply forget about the gun, and let the old woman find it under their bed after they were gone.

Ása had stopped kneading, and was brewing some coffee while she let the dough prove in the bowl. Pointing to a plate on the table, she told Anna that her food was ready. For a moment Anna didn't recognize the steaming plastic bag filled with brown sludge: it was the pizza, which the old woman had apparently boiled in the bag.

'Great,' she said, nodding her head so abruptly that she felt her neck crack. 'Excellent.'

She sat down, and Ása asked whether she wanted scissors or a knife. Anna didn't understand the question at first, then envisaged cutting the corner of the plastic packaging and pouring out the contents onto the plate. The thought made her queasy and she snatched the pizza off the plate, placing it on the chair next to her.

'I think I'll wait a while,' she said, rubbing her hands over her face as she stifled a giggle that was bubbling up in her.

'Have you lost your appetite?' asked Ása, seemingly surprised.

'I'll be hungry soon.'

She refused the offer of coffee, then changed her mind:

'On second thoughts, a coffee would do me good. I need perking up.'

Ása poured them both a cup, shut the kitchen door then

sat down opposite Anna, and asked whether she had slept well that day.

'You did sleep today, didn't you?'

Anna nodded.

'Yes. I slept very well. I was only planning to have a rest, but I slept far too long. You must think me terribly lazy.'

Anna glanced at the door, wondering why the old woman had shut it.

'I have no thoughts about you whatsoever,' said the old woman rather brusquely, shaking her head. 'Although you do look a bit pale. Are you sickening for something?'

'I feel absolutely fine . . . I saw a fox out in the yard just now,' she said, changing the subject. The coffee tasted bitter and smelled of manure.

'The poor things catch mice for us. They're very efficient.'

'I see. Where do the foxes come from?'

The old woman avoided her gaze, and Anna interpreted this as a form of old-fashioned courtesy, rather than downright aloofness.

'From the earth, I suppose, like the rest of us. Then they just come out of each other.'

The old woman glanced furtively at Anna, as if to gauge her reaction. *Interesting choice of words*, reflected Anna, *'from the earth'*, and she made a mental note of it.

'Silly question,' she said, smiling. 'I guess what I meant to ask is whether they are tame or completely wild. Do you think they might have attacked my dog? He's gone missing.'

'I'm sorry to hear that.'

'Oh no, Trigger can take care of himself. I'm not in the

slightest bit worried about him.' Anna noticed that she sounded as if she were speaking to a child or a halfwit. She decided to turn the conversation to Kjartan, mindful of what she had read earlier that day. 'Is your husband outside somewhere?'

'Don't worry about him. He knows his way around here.'

The old woman seemed unfazed by her question.

'I couldn't help noticing the photograph in the front room. Of Kjartan and the woman . . . They are a handsome couple. They could be—'

She broke off. She had been about to say film stars, but realized the old woman might find that awkward, hurtful even, given her own looks. There was no getting round the fact that she wasn't particularly pretty.

'What photograph would that be, then?'

'The one in the front room. Of Kjartan and the woman next to him. I was wondering who she was.'

'I know very little about that . . .' The old woman muttered something which Anna couldn't hear properly, but which sounded like the word 'servant'.

'Is the woman in the photograph his servant?'

'It's possible.' Ása nodded, gazing out of the window and smiling faintly.

'I see . . . Perhaps she's the wife of the man who kills the reindeer for you? The ones you feed to the foxes?'

The old woman didn't reply. Anna smiled to herself at the idea of a landowner having his photograph taken with his servant, and then hanging it in his front room. The old woman wasn't a very good liar, but that didn't mean she gave much away.

'So, how long have you and Kjartan been married?'

Anna was convinced by now that their hosts weren't a couple, but she wanted to hear the old woman say it, in order to find out her true position in the house. Most likely she herself was a servant, and that might explain why she was attributing that role to someone else connected to the household. But why lie about it?

'You must have met many years ago,' Anna went on.

'What's your job?' asked the old woman, finally looking straight at her. In the corners of her eyes, two prominent red lines, not unlike scars, extended to the corners of her mouth; their shiny texture reminded Anna of a blown-up photograph of a clitoris she had come across once, and she thrust the image from her mind.

'I'm a teacher. I teach Icelandic at a primary school in Reykjavík.'

Anna suddenly noticed that there was no handle on the kitchen door, only a small, square hole. She couldn't stop herself from blurting out:

'Why hasn't the kitchen door got a handle?'

'Why do you ask?' said the old woman, still staring at her.

'Out of curiosity.'

'Curiosity, yes. No one could accuse you of not being curious, my girl. That I know for a fact. You have a way of looking at things. And you ask questions. Too much curiosity can be dangerous.'

'What do you mean?'

'Exactly what I say.'

'I take an interest in my surroundings.'

As she sipped her coffee, Anna glanced about the kitchen until her eye alighted on a second door in the corner, which she hadn't noticed before. Although she was more concerned about the one with no handle, and about getting *out*, it occurred to her that this other door might lead to the ground floor, where the windows had been bricked up.

'There are lots of doors here,' said the old woman, as if reading her thoughts. 'And I can satisfy your curiosity, tell you everything you want to know. If you answer one question for me first.'

Their eyes met.

'What?' said Anna, forcing herself to hold the old woman's gaze.

'Did you go into the room on the top floor today, when you claim you were sleeping?'

'What room?'

'What room?' the old woman echoed. 'Perhaps you went into several rooms, and you're not sure which one I'm talking about?'

Anna smiled.

'I didn't go anywhere. I stayed in my room reading, slept for a while then read some more.'

'I know what you did,' the old woman whispered, leaning across the table and narrowing her eyes. 'You went into the room and you took something. I don't know what it was, and I have no way of knowing. You must tell me that yourself. What did you take from the room?'

'I didn't take anything from any room!'

'It's important that you tell me, I need to know so that I can—'

'And it's important that you let me out,' said Anna, standing up, unable to bear staying in there a moment longer. She strode across the room and pushed against the door. It didn't open.

'Where's the handle? Give it to me.'

She walked over to the old woman and thrust out her hand.

'If you answer my question,' the old woman said without moving.

'I don't have to answer any of your questions!' yelled Anna, seized by a sudden panic. 'I'm a guest here. Not out of choice, but because I'm *forced* to be! What's more, I have no interest in knowing what is or isn't inside this house, I want to get out . . .'

As she said these last words, Anna saw something move outside the window: a shadow crossing the courtyard in the gloom.

They had come back.

'My friends are here. Open the door!' she shouted, and the old woman fumbled in her pocket for the handle. Anna snatched it, thrust it into the hole and opened the door, hurrying down the steps to where Egill was standing in the courtyard. She flung her arms around his neck, so overcome with emotion that she was unable speak. His face was covered in sand, but she smothered him in kisses all the same, clinging to him as she realized she had never expected to see him again.

21

THE OLD MAN DIGS

Anna

Egill, it turned out, was alone. He said that Hrafn and Vigdís had set off home ahead of him.

'They aren't back yet,' said Anna. 'What's going on? Why are you carrying two rucksacks?'

'Vigdís left hers behind.'

He said he would explain everything later. He seemed exhausted, and almost stumbled up the steps. She helped him up to their room, undressed him and put him to bed.

Fifteen minutes later Hrafn appeared, immediately followed by Vigdís. Anna was heating some water in the kitchen when Hrafn walked through the door and disappeared upstairs. Vigdís explained that they had got lost in the storm on the way back. She looked dishevelled and was covered in sand. She told Anna that she would be down shortly, and went up after Hrafn.

Anna carried a bucket of steaming-hot water up to Egill, and wiped him down with a damp towel. Black streaks clung to every moist area of his face: the corners of his eyes and mouth, below his nostrils, his belly and all the way up his arms were covered in a thick grey coating of sand, even though all his shirt buttons were fastened.

'I want to go home . . . home, home,' he murmured, eyes closed, as he leaned forward over the edge of the bed.

Anna asked about the expedition, and he told her they had become stormbound on the outskirts of a village, which was probably connected to the barrage they had glimpsed further to the west.

'We had to turn back because of the wind. It seems Askja is also further north than we thought, according to Vigdís anyway.'

'Why did they get back after you? I thought you said they left first?'

'They must have got lost . . . I decided to wait there until the wind died down a bit more.'

'What was in this village?'

'Nothing special, some empty huts. An old fridge.'

He clasped his head, leaning further forward, and she stroked his back.

'Don't you want to take off your scarf?'

'I'm cold.'

'We'll go home tomorrow, my love,' said Anna, dipping the towel in the water a few times before wringing a light brown out of it. She repeated the action then wiped his shoulders and massaged them. 'First thing in the morning.'

'I'm not sure I'll be able to wake up.'

'Of course you will.'

He lay sprawled on the bed, swigging from the bottle that Anna had fetched for him from the jeep. Despite all her efforts, he still had a greyish tinge, and the sheet was covered in sand that came off him each time he moved. She thought about enticing him into having sex, but didn't want to get sand inside her. When they first met Egill had been passionate in bed, and for a long time he did his best to pleasure her, and yet she had never really known what excited him, and he'd never talked about it. In fact, he didn't seem all that interested in sex; most of his energy went into his work.

'Why don't we set off now, just the two of us?' he said, gazing up at the ceiling. 'There'll be no wind at night. We'll reach Askja by morning.'

'We're not going anywhere now, Egill. What's got into you?'

'I'm fed up with this . . . I want to be alone with you.'

She asked whether something had happened between him and Hrafn, but he didn't reply. Nor did he thank her for her ministrations, or enquire about her ankle, or tell her he loved her, which wouldn't have been that difficult, would it? To say a few nice words to her, despite how tired he was, the selfish wretch.

Clenching her fists, she was overwhelmed by an anger so intense, so lucid that it was as if she were waking up for the first time: this man had ruined her life, taken away from her the only thing that mattered to a journalist: *her reputation*. That was all she knew. Unlike him, she had no savings, nothing put aside in some dodgy deposit box on one of the world's dodgy islands, in spite of his denials. She had become his accomplice, if not in the eyes of the law, at least in those of society, and the newspapers would have a field day with them, her name would be dragged through the mud on the Internet, in the press, on the lunchtime news, in coffeehouses, canteens, confirmation parties, in emails and texts: everywhere. He had forced his greed upon her. When things started to fall apart, she had allowed him to register as many assets as possible in her name; she had given in, even as – in the throes of the crisis – she had fantasized about going off on her own, back-packing, staying in three-star hotels and reading Eckhart Tolle, and when she came back he would be in jail, where he deserved to be. But of course she would do no such thing. She was a coward. And her cowardice threatened to destroy everything she had built up.

'I saw the old man, the old loony,' said Egill, continuing to swig from the bottle without sitting up.

'What was he doing?'

'You don't want to know.'

He grinned stupidly as she sat down beside him on the edge of the bed and took a sip from his bottle.

'I was near the house when I saw him by the streetlamp. He had a spade, and was standing in a hole shovelling sand out of it.

'In the storm? Digging a hole in the sand?'

'It was dying down by then. But the hole reached up to his midriff, so yeah, he probably started when it was still windy.'

'Did he see you?'

'I don't think so. I was in a hurry and I couldn't be bothered to talk to him.'

'You couldn't be bothered! Aren't you curious as to why the man is digging a hole in the ground? Perhaps you ought to have stopped him. What if it's a grave?' Egill didn't reply. 'What business has he digging a hole there?'

'How should *I* know? Maybe he knows he's dying.'

'Was the streetlamp on?'

'Yes. It's a bit difficult to dig a hole in the dark.'

'Something fishy is going on here . . .'

Anna took another sip from the bottle and resolved at last to come clean and show Egill the gun. There was nothing to be gained from concealing it. She reached under the bed, and without any explanation tossed it over to him, declaring she had found it in one of the other rooms.

'What is it?' he said, without stirring.

'I think it belongs to the old man . . .'

Since Egill didn't move, she unwrapped the silk cloth and placed the gun between them on the bed.

'It's loaded,' she said.

'Are you *nuts*, Anna?' he said, sitting up. 'What are you doing with a loaded gun? Where did you find it?'

'I told you, in one of the other rooms, in the old man's study. I daren't put it back now. Should we take it with us? I'd like to keep it, but I'm not sure if that's such a good idea . . .'

'I want nothing to do with it,' he said, taking another swig from the bottle before lying back down on the bed.

'What do you mean? Aren't you going to help me?'

'I've had enough, Anna. I don't understand this. I can't be bothered to think about it . . .'

'Oh, you poor thing, just close your eyes then, and relax,' she said, snatching the gun and wrapping it once more in the piece of silk before replacing it under the bed. Then she stood up and told Egill she was leaving the room, and Egill mumbled something about going to sleep.

She bumped into Vigdís outside the toilet and handed her the bucket. Vigdís seemed almost more exhausted than when she had first arrived, and Anna asked her if everything was all right.

'Are you sure nothing's the matter, sweetheart?' she said.

Vigdís nodded and suggested they meet afterwards for 'a nightcap'.

'I have to get away, I can't stay in there,' she said, and Anna assumed she was referring to the bedroom she shared with Hrafn.

'Of course,' said Anna, perking up. 'A nightcap, or two.'

They arranged to meet downstairs in the front room, and Anna went out to the jeep again to fetch more booze. Passing through the hallway she glimpsed a box at the bottom of Vigdís's rucksack, containing what looked like flares. She contemplated one of them – a red plastic tube with a narrow wooden handle. Printed on the plastic were instructions about how to flip the safety catch, hold the flare away from the face and gently pull the string hanging from the plastic.

Pull, she thought and shuddered without knowing why. She had to get rid of the gun before she went to bed.

22

The child

Anna

While she waited for Vigdís downstairs, Anna studied the photograph on the wall, of the old man and the woman. The beautiful people. She paced around the room contemplating it from different angles, and started to realize what it was that troubled her.

'Not her,' she said walking right up to the photograph, then stepping back and shaking her head. 'Their child . . .'

She lit a cigarette, casting her mind back to the book *Icelandic Businessmen*, the study, and the secret room, which she saw in a different light now, and finally she felt as if the puzzle was coming together.

Anna hadn't seen the old woman since the 'incident' in the kitchen. Perhaps she ought to have felt ashamed for screaming at her like that, but the old woman had no right to shut her in – even if she had been snooping.

Vigdís came down the stairs, and Anna indicated the bottles she had lined up on the table with a sweep of her hand:

'Would you like red or white?'

'Amber would be good,' said Vigdís, pointing at the whisky. 'One shot. And then some red?'

'No problem.'

Anna gestured to her to take a seat on the sofa, filled a shot glass, which Vigdís downed in one, then handed her a glass brimming with red wine. She had cleaned the glass herself, or disinfected it rather, while she was heating the water in the kitchen.

Vigdís sighed and settled deeper into the sofa.

'This is good,' she said.

Anna caught a strong scent of shampoo, and saw that Vigdís's face was glistening, as if she had rubbed moisturizer into her skin.

'You smell great.'

'Thanks. I did my best to scrub down, but I couldn't be bothered to heat any water. I didn't realize *hot water* was such a necessary part of life. My skin is beginning to feel like a shell.'

'Tell me about it. I was thinking exactly the same earlier.'

Anna peered through to the kitchen to make sure they were alone, and asked Vigdís if anything had happened during the excursion.

'You all look so dazed.'

'I don't know . . . Didn't Egill say anything?'

'He mentioned a barrage and some village, and a bridge. He was even weirder than usual. What was in the village? Is the American army dumping radioactive waste there? Or carrying out research in underground bunkers?'

'I didn't go with them into the village. Didn't he say anything?'

'Such as?'

Vigdís hesitated, and then told her that Hrafn and Egill had quarrelled about something that she didn't understand, something from their past. Afterwards she had got into an argument with Hrafn, who had run out of the warehouse, with her in pursuit.

'That's why we all came back separately . . . That's why I sat in an abandoned car somewhere, waiting for the storm to die down . . . I have no idea what's going on here.'

She drained her glass, which Anna promptly refilled.

'Sweetheart. And where was Hrafn while you were in the car?'

'I don't know – he said he took shelter behind a hill. I don't feel like talking to him right now. I just hope we can go home tomorrow, and then we'll be able to discuss this like two civilized people.'

'You don't know what their row was about?'

Vigdís shook her head, staring impassively into space, as if she hadn't heard the question. This wasn't the alert, observant Vigdís, Anna knew. In fact, all three of them seemed slightly changed: emptier, duller, more distant. And, now that she thought about it, couldn't the same be said about her? For example, shouldn't she have felt more afraid to be there after what had happened earlier that evening? *Like a zombie*, she thought, recalling the line by the old poet. How did it go: *I am rocking a changeling*. Her friends went out onto the sands and came back changed – isn't that what happened in one of those folk tales?

She resolved to rouse Vigdís from her stupor.

'I've had a few adventures myself,' she said, with a shiver of excitement, the thrill of the *game*, which was doubtless more intense because the men weren't there – as if they could enjoy themselves more easily without them, at least when it came to secret rooms in old houses. The more she thought about it, the more dubious it seemed, like something out of a boy's annual. 'Which the old couple mustn't get wind of,' she added, in hushed tones.

'What are you talking about?' asked Vigdís, her eyes finally lighting up.

Anna began at the beginning: she told Vigdís about being left alone in the house, about her burning curiosity and the door at the end of the passageway; she described the old man's study, his books, his diplomas, the photographs of him on the wall in the company of wealthy people, ministers, Björgólfur Guðmundsson and Thóra Hallgrimsson, what she had read about Kjartan in *Icelandic Businessmen*.

'This guy is no farmer and never was. Back in the day, he carried out experiments on humans; I can't remember the exact wording, but they were illegal. Perhaps he paid vagrants or mentally challenged people so he could test drugs or perform surgery on them – poverty was more widespread in those days. But there's more. While I was browsing the books on the shelves, I went to take a volume out, and I heard a click.'

She described how the bookcase had moved away from the wall, the small, dimly lit room behind, the desk, the bed and the note that said 'See me'.

'See me?' said Vigdís, as she sat motionless on the sofa, her eyes like saucers.

Anna explained about the switch and what had happened when she touched it, how she fell to the floor, went numb all over, but managed to escape and close the secret door behind her.

'Then I crawled out into the corridor and back to my room, where I threw up on the floor.'

'*You threw up*? I don't believe it. Do you have a headache? Are your fingers numb?'

'I feel fine now. But what was that writing above the switch? It's creepy, kind of like a *trap*, don't you think?'

'This is serious. Electric shocks can be dangerous. You must see someone about it the moment we get back to town.'

Vigdís was getting agitated and Anna told her to lower her voice.

'I had no business being there. I went in without asking.'

She topped up their glasses.

'And there was no one in the room?'

Anna shook her head.

'I couldn't understand who would live in a room like that. With a bed, a desk, blacked-out windows. It made no sense. Until a moment ago, when I was standing here waiting for you, and suddenly everything seemed to fall into place.'

She stood up and beckoned Vigdís over to the photograph on the wall.

'I noticed this picture when we first arrived,' said Anna. 'A few things about it struck me as odd, the more so the longer I looked at it.'

They contemplated the photograph. It was behind glass, which gleamed.

'Do you notice anything in particular?'

Vigdís shook her head. 'I'm not sure. Could it be Ása and the old man? I recognize him at any rate, although he's a lot younger here.'

'Right.' Anna nodded. 'But the woman isn't Ása. This woman isn't just young, she's . . . how shall I put it? *Beautiful*,' she whispered. 'They both are. Their bone structure is similar too, the wavy hair, the eyes. They look nothing like the old woman.'

Vigdís nodded, and carried on contemplating the photograph.

'I see what you mean. But why is there a photograph of him here, with another woman?'

'Because he and the old woman aren't married – we just assumed they were. I don't know what Ása's position here is; she's probably his housekeeper . . . No, I think the woman in the photograph is the old man's sister. Which explains why they look so alike.'

'I see, brother and sister . . . But couldn't they have grown to resemble one another, the way married people do? If, as you say, Ása and the old man aren't a couple, then couldn't this woman simply be his wife?'

'Perhaps. If I hadn't seen another photograph of these two upstairs today – an old family portrait from the fifties. First I recognized the old man, then I saw the resemblance between him and the grown-ups – and the little girl next to him.'

'This woman here?'

Anna nodded.

'Let's assume they are brother and sister,' Anna went on. 'Now take a closer look at the photo. Do you see the man's proud expression, his raised chin, narrowed eyes, as if he were staking his claim, challenging someone to a duel? In contrast to the woman, who is in another world, distracted, not defying anyone – she's oblivious to other people. She radiates beauty, joy. And look at the way she's standing; the man's posture is distant, on the defensive or poised to attack, whereas hers is open and *insinuating* . . . Yes, what is she insinuating?'

Vigdís peered at the photograph, and said she could see something, but wasn't quite sure what.

'Is it the way they are standing, or the way she's leaning over? They both seem rather low down in the—'

'The picture has been tampered with,' Anna said abruptly, looking at Vigdís. 'Someone has been cut out of it. I realized it just now, when I was pacing round the room; I was sort of looking sideways at the photo and all at once it became clear. Then I remembered what I read today, about the old man . . . And I saw what was missing from the photo. The reason why the woman is standing like that, holding out her hand, and her expression, and why the proportions are skewed, why the wall behind them looks so high – they are too low down in the photo, as if the bottom of it has been cut off . . . What's missing is a cradle – and in the cradle is a child.'

'*A child*?' said Vigdís, scrutinizing the photograph.

'That explains why the woman is tilting her head with that motherly air of: "Oh, look", and reaching out her hand. She's touching the cradle, or her child's head, and if it were old enough, the child might even be standing in front of them. When I recalled what I'd read about Kjartan having a child, I knew I was right . . . There was a child in this photo.'

'But why cut it out—'

'*Their* child,' interrupted Anna. '*The brother and sister's* child.'

Vigdís's eyes opened wide, but she said nothing.

Anna went on:

'It struck me that there was no mention in *Icelandic Businessmen* of the old man being married. Why not? On the other hand, there were references to his violating "public morals" and to his "libertine lifestyle". Are they saying he was a womanizer? Would anyone describe a mere womanizer in such strong terms? I doubt it. The book goes on to say that Kjartan had a son, and yet there is no mention of either the son's name or that of his mother. This might make sense if the child was illegitimate and some shame was attached to him. But then why mention him at all? They don't with the others in the book. And why is Kjartan's "sister" mentioned without being named? For the simple reason that the child's mother and Kjartan's sister are *one and the same person*. In trying so hard to conceal this fact, the book gives itself away; it betrays their secret. And what better way to violate public morals than by having a child with your own sister?'

'I don't believe it.'

'And when was this picture taken? When the old man was nearly forty, his sister slightly younger. Doubtless soon after he arrived back from the States, where for ten or fifteen years he had been trying to escape from their shameful relationship. But when he came home he couldn't help himself, he lost control – they both did. One day the child was born – shortly before they decamped up here, and before this photograph was taken of them together, *as a family* . . . There aren't any more photographs after this, and there was no need, because this one tells the whole story: it's clear from the old man's defiance, his air of rebellious pride, that he had resolved to fly in the face of society and acknowledge his family. No doubt he insisted on having the photograph taken to please the child's mother, before he gave up . . .'

'*If* indeed there is a child in the picture,' Vigdís broke in, stepping away from the photograph.

'There's a child, all right. If *not*, why would the old man be living up here? Why would anyone live up here unless they had to?'

'Then where is his sister? The one who bore the child?'

'Dead, buried out there somewhere. Either that or she was banished, murdered by the old man, and now she haunts the sands in a tattered robe; a restless spirit, moaning outside the windows at night! How should I know?'

Vigdís shook her head and lit a cigarette, seemingly in an effort to shake off the spell.

'You've got a screw loose,' she said, grinning. 'What about the child? Where's the child?'

'I don't know where it is *now*, but I know where it was. Aren't you're forgetting something?'

'What?'

'I'm convinced the child was here – for reasons that have nothing to do with the photograph. Who else do you think they kept locked in the secret room next to the old man's study? Hidden away like a pariah?'

23

Anna

Anna sipped her drink. Vigdís was shaking her head, and her face had assumed the same vacant expression as before.

'Oh, the stories one invents,' said Anna, sitting down on the sofa again. She was aware of feeling giddy, slightly drunk too, although not enough to cloud her thoughts.

'At least we don't have to think about our own lives in the meantime,' said Vigdís, sitting down beside her. 'But aren't you forgetting something? We could just ask them.'

'I already did. The old woman lied.'

Vigdís announced that she was tired, and Anna felt a wave of drowsiness mixed with embarrassment, as if she had said too much.

But there was one other thing. She reached into the plastic bag next to her, pulled out the silky bundle, and started to unwrap it, suddenly not caring whether the old people saw what she had taken. She waited for Vigdís to raise her eyes and stare at it, before explaining where she had found it.

'It's an antique . . . Or, I don't know. Something the old

man bought as a souvenir of his stay in Boston or Princeton or wherever it was, one of those New England campuses.'

'Is it loaded?'

Anna nodded.

'I think the old woman knows I took it. They've locked the study door since I went in there.'

'Why did you take it?'

'I don't know. I suppose I wanted to have something with me to show . . . To prove we were here.'

Anna wrapped the gun in the silk cloth again and put it back in the bag.

'How does this fit with your theory?'

'What do you mean?'

'Why have a loaded gun in a room where someone was being held against their will?'

Anna didn't reply.

'I'll keep it,' said Vigdís, after a brief silence, standing up and reaching across to pick up the bag.

'Are you sure?'

'Isn't that what you were going to ask me to do?'

'Just for tonight . . . Egill is drinking. You can't keep a gun in the same room as a drunk.' She giggled. 'And there are four bullets in it, you see . . .'

'We'll get rid of it,' said Vigdís. 'When we leave tomorrow. In the meantime, let's call it a day. We need to sleep.'

They decided to clean up after themselves the next morning, and went into the kitchen where they each filled a glass of water to have during the night. As they were leaving the room, Anna glanced at the door in the corner, which she had noticed earlier. She hurried over to it while Vigdís wasn't looking, and tried the handle. Locked.

She followed Vigdís up the stairs, said goodnight and watched her go into her room carrying the plastic bag. Anna searched the inside of their door for a lock or bolt, but found none. Instead she jammed a chair under the handle and decided that would have to do. She got undressed, and gave a little squeal as she leapt across the floor and under the duvet. She snuggled up close to Egill, who grunted then carried on snoring.

They could have taken the photo out of the frame to see if it had been tampered with. Doubtless they spent too much time in front of *monitors*. Soon she became aware of the whole house creaking and groaning, especially the roof, as though transparent, ghost-like giants were cavorting on top of it, clambering onto it, howling as they bowled through it, light and heavy as the wind.

It was a strange notion, and other images followed, obscure sentences swimming round in her head as though urging her to grasp something, only to be forgotten a moment later; or were they mere swirling shapes rousing in her a vague anxiety, a flurry of chattering thoughts: that someone was hanging upside down outside the window looking in, or waiting for her out in the darkness, in the distant darkness, whispering her name . . .

She reached for a sleeping tablet, which she swallowed, burrowed down into the semi-gloom beneath the duvet, clasped one hand between her thighs and let it lie there motionless. Occasionally, at the exact moment of falling asleep, Anna had the impression that somehow everything was *wrong*, that she had overlooked something at the centre of her being, or had neglected to cultivate it, and because of that everything in her life was founded on a misunderstanding. Sometimes, this made her so upset that she couldn't fall asleep, and she would stay up all night chain-smoking, or read, or go for a walk and mull over how she might organize her life better, and find a lasting inner peace.

She considered masturbating, despite Egill lying right next to her. He never woke up. She had done it several times recently, after they stopped having sex. There had always been this imbalance between them, her wanting it more.

She saw Egill before her, sitting in front of his computer in the middle of the night, staring at the screen, open-mouthed, leaning forward, shoulders oddly hunched, like a ski-jumper hurtling down a ramp. She had woken up alone in the bed, and had got up to see where he was – and he was there. The floor creaked when she got back to the bedroom, and he came after her, pausing in the doorway to ask her what she was doing. She was standing at the foot of the bed facing away from him, and she told him she was looking for her slippers. He asked her if she had come into the living room, but she didn't reply. After a while, she turned round and saw him leaning against the doorframe staring at the floor; she saw his inner suffering, saw what an anxious, needy soul he was, and how she pitied him.

From then on she started to spy on him. Not that she

had any real appetite for it, although it had a kind of sordid attraction. Around that time, Egill had stopped going into the office, and Anna knew the password to his laptop. He would often leave it at home, and when she got back from work in the early evening, she would check what he had been browsing that day before he went out to meet one of his friends at a restaurant or bar. He would start off looking at news websites and an occasional blog, and then he would look at porn. As time went by, the list of porn websites grew longer and longer, and Anna began to recognize a pattern; tracking his browsing history over a few days, she could see that he was looking at certain types of porn – stills rather than videos, perhaps because he needed time to focus on each image. She discovered that the porn pages were divided into categories, with as many as a hundred different topics, like a menu – a kind of chronicle of her boyfriend's unconscious, from *arses, legs, anal-licking, knickers*, through *young girls, Asian, young Asian, Indonesian, Italian, French*, to *sleeping, stockings, transgender, animals*.

However sad it made her, she couldn't stop looking, but after glimpsing a poodle licking a young girl, both in pigtails, she gave up. She lay on the bed and wept until she felt numb, then took a long walk along Ægisíða and tried to pluck up the courage to call him, to scream and cry and tell him she wanted to finish their relationship.

In the end she said nothing, because she didn't want to admit to breaking into his computer. She spared him most of her anger, directing her rage instead against a world that proposed such abominations as viable choices, as if it were perfectly normal – not merely dog porn, but all those images that had more in common with anatomical studies or the aberrations of serial killers than anything she thought of as *porn*. She brought the subject up in conversation with her friends and discovered that the majority suspected their men of looking at porn, and even of giving it priority over their sex life. She didn't mention Egill or his categories, but decided to do some research on the subject. Finally she wrote an article called 'The Silent Epidemic', about the growing use of porn among Western men, to the point where it was affecting research on the subject itself. In Canada, for example, scientists looking for a comparison group of young men between the ages of eighteen and twenty-five couldn't find a single one who didn't masturbate over web porn images. And few people seemed to care: the debate was stuck in the same old rut of sexual politics instead of being looked at as an issue of addictive behaviour. She concluded that this epidemic was undermining the majority of relationships between young people, not just in terms of their sex lives and mutual trust, but because of its effect on dopamine production and the nervous system, which could provoke serious mood swings in users that had been well documented by the medical profession.

Soon afterwards, Egill gave up porn, either because he had drowned whatever was left of his libido in drink or he had read her article and been impressed by her arguments. She toyed with the idea of publishing a book called *The Final Image*, a collection of the last images in each category

Egill had browsed and pleasured himself over, and dedicating it to her man. She felt bitterly angry towards him sometimes, for no apparent reason, and had to bite her lip hard to stop herself from punching him. Instead she let him sign his filthy lucre over to her, and continued to fantasize about leaving him, while at the same time feeling a mawkish sympathy, so analogous to love, superior even – a sublime, dizzying benevolence welling up from the depths of her being.

Or was this about something completely different? Did a man not have the right to masturbate? She could feel the sleeping tablet beginning to take effect; everything was becoming soft and warm and luminous. That wasn't the first time she had discovered people doing things they shouldn't in the middle of the night. When she was a little girl living in the basement at her grandma and grandpa's house in Ísafjörður, she was woken by a noise one night. She climbed out of bed, peered into the shadowy living room and switched on the light. Her mother and grandfather were on the floor, she was lying on top of him, and when the light went on her mother sprang to her feet.

Anna closed her eyes.

24

NO FUR

Egill

He stood over Anna, shaking her until she woke up.

'You have to wake up . . . Wake up now, Anna,' he said.

She opened her eyes, startled, and gasped, her face glistening with sweat.

'We need to talk.'

'What are you doing?' she groaned, sitting up in bed.

He laid her clothes on the edge of the bed and told her he would explain when she came down to the kitchen, then hurried out of the room.

On the way downstairs he went back into the bathroom, took off his scarf and studied his neck in the mirror: there was a dark blue line where his shirt had cut into him, and a circular bruise below his Adam's apple.

'That fucking loser . . .' he muttered, although he wasn't sure to whom he was referring. He couldn't work out whether it was anger he was feeling, or shame; perhaps they complemented one another. If Anna refused to go with him, he would show her the marks on his throat.

His first impulse when he woke up had been to get out

of there, as fast as possible, before the wind started to pick up. He made breakfast, brewed some coffee and packed a rucksack for both of them, more focused than he had been in a long time.

'What time is it?' said Anna, entering the kitchen. She sat down at the table, and he pushed her breakfast over to her: toast with sliced cheese, and a bowl of yoghurt. 'Why are you up so early?'

'I went easy on the whisky yesterday, I guess, and I was awake by dawn.'

He told her he had done their packing.

'Everything's ready. We can leave as soon as you've finished breakfast. I've packed our clothes, your fig biscuits, nuts, water, a compass, a map, a torch—'

'Where are Hrafn and Vigdís?'

'They're still asleep. My love . . .' He paused. 'We need to get away from here. Everything's fine with Vigdís, but I'm not walking home with him. It's over.'

He recounted their quarrel in the warehouse, how Hrafn had attacked him verbally, then grabbed his neck and tried to throttle him, but Egill had managed to fight him off.

'Then he stormed off and Vigdís ran after him. He went berserk—'

'Why didn't you tell me this yesterday?'

'I don't know.' He shook his head. 'I wasn't thinking straight. I didn't realize how serious it was until I woke up.'

'My love,' said Anna.

She rose, came round the table and sat down beside him, placed her hand on his thigh and gave him a kiss.

'I don't need friends like him, people don't talk to their friends like that . . . We'll walk to Askja as arranged. But just the two of us. We'll start off at the barrage we saw, and follow the road north from there. We can say goodbye to Vigdís in Askja, if we haven't already hitched a lift to town. Otherwise we'll get in touch with her once we're home, and I'll explain everything better.'

'What about Trigger?'

'Trigger will have reached the nearest town by now. He's probably waiting for us, either at the local police station, or with a farmer somewhere in Egilsstaðir. He's a clever dog. We can't stay here any longer.'

He stood up and paced around the kitchen.

'But shouldn't we let them know? I'll tell her now, and then she can go back to sleep . . .'

'We'll leave them a note. I'm not talking to Hrafn ever again.'

'Are you scared of him? Was it really that serious?'

'Of course I'm not *scared* of him, Anna. I'm not scared of anything, except that he's made me lose my grip like this. I don't know what he's been getting up to here . . . But I'm certainly not going on a half-day trek with him across the sands.'

Anna lit a cigarette. After a moment's reflection, she said she'd be glad to get away from this place as soon as possible. Egill found a pen and paper, and wrote a note explaining that they had woken up early and decided to set off for Askja, and that perhaps they would meet up there. *Perhaps*. He signed both their names, but Anna insisted he mention the reason why they were going on ahead, and so he made a brief reference to their 'disagreement' the day before.

While Anna went to the toilet, Egill carried their rucksacks outside, propped them against the front of the house and forced himself to relax. A deep silence reigned over the sands, and that bright light which was at once so mild.

He decided to take a joint with him, and rummaged in the boot for his fishing-tackle box. His weed was hidden in the bait box. He had lied to Hrafn about finding a joint in his fishing jacket. Anyone could have figured that out: the joint they'd smoked wasn't bone-dry, it was freshly rolled that morning. And yet Hrafn had chosen to ignore this, as Egill knew he would – because it suited him, because he craved it too much.

He took a pinch of weed, mixed it with some tobacco in his palm, and rolled a joint, which he slipped into his pocket for later.

Closing the boot, he noticed that the fishing rods had vanished from the roof rack, and the elastic cords holding the boxes in place were dangling loose. He searched on the back seat, and underneath the jeep, but couldn't find them. The two rods belonged to him, and were probably the only thing he valued out of the stuff he had taken with him.

'I'm ready,' said Anna, appearing at the top of the steps. They put on their rucksacks and set off.

They walked in silence across the sands, heading for the hill that Egill remembered from the day before. They could see the barrage from there. Anna chewed her bottom lip as if mulling something over.

'I had the feeling Vigdís was keeping something back yesterday,' she said at last. 'Why did you and Hrafn start arguing?'

'He couldn't sleep and was generally irritable. He took it out on us.'

'On you and Vigdís? Were you doing anything in particular?'

Egill knew what was coming next.

'Nothing like that, my love . . . It was all in his head. He can't cope with being out here in nature. Let's not get drawn into his bullshit.'

'I was only asking.'

'It'll all be fine,' he went on. 'They'll see the note and make their own way back to town. There's nothing more I can do for him.'

By the time they reached the hill, Anna had seemingly forgotten all about Vigdís and Hrafn, and insisted they walk along the ravine.

'I'd like to see the glacial river. Do you know what it's called?'

She was holding the map, having tried unsuccessfully to locate the hill.

'There are lines all over this map, which must indicate rivers. We seem to be in the middle of a basin.'

They heard the roar of the water, and saw it tumbling through the ravine. Tossed about by the current were random grey and white chunks of ice that had broken off the glacier in the warm weather, and swirls of spray reached them from the abyss. Anna clapped her hands and rubbed the spray into her face.

They made their way along the edge of the ravine without speaking; indeed, it was difficult to hear anything above the roar, which Egill thought resembled the sound of traffic. Noise was good, he reflected; the whistling sands could give you the jitters, and the silence was almost worse.

Hrafn had always been crazy. Now that he thought about it, Egill felt he should have ended their friendship long ago. He was too nice, as well as being weak, he knew that – it was why he had never been top dog; Hrafn had set the trap, and he'd walked into it.

Gradually the barrage loomed out of the plain ahead of them. Stretched between the two hills, it was bigger than Egill recalled, a hundred metres high and several times wider. They kept following the ravine, which soon curved southwards in a long, sweeping arc, before straightening out as it turned towards the barrage.

Where the ravine levelled out they glimpsed a large hole halfway down the rock face, and a path leading diagonally into the abyss.

'It's probably something to do with the barrage,' said Egill. 'A drainage tunnel or whatever they're called.'

They soon reached the top of path, and Anna walked down it a few paces before stooping over something on the gravel.

'The collar . . . What's this doing here?' said Anna, holding up a blue collar, the sort people put on their pets to identify them. She lifted the plastic tab at the front of the collar: on it was printed 'Trigger', in her own writing, and their address.

Egill glanced about. Further along the path, a few metres from where the collar had lain, he noticed some pebbles arranged in the shape of an arrow.

'Did you put those stones there?' he asked. The arrow was pointing down the path. 'Am I seeing things? Talk to me, will you!'

'It's telling us to go down there, isn't it?' said Anna. 'Did you hear Hrafn and Vigdís go out last night after we went to bed? Perhaps they saw Trigger and followed him here . . . Were they in their room when we left?'

'Of course they were *in their room* when we left,' he said, puzzled by her question.

'Did you see them?'

'This has nothing to do with Hrafn and Vigdís.'

Egill looked along the path, which appeared to plunge into the water.

'Who else could it have been? I think something has happened.'

She set off down the path, then turned around and looked at him pleadingly.

Egill shook his head and gave a mock laugh.

'They haven't been down there!'

'Well someone has, Egill! And they left the collar and an *arrow* for us to find. In any case, I can't think where *else* Trigger could be. I'm going to check it out.'

She took off her rucksack and started to walk down the

path. Egill paused, and then followed her, after grabbing the torch to light their way in the tunnel.

The roar quickly grew louder, and Egill felt a pang of fear, even though he found it hypnotic and fascinating on some primitive level, like the rapid drumming of bongos or a male choir chanting mantras.

The path led all the way down to the opening, where it became rutted before dropping steeply into the water. The opening was circular, several metres wide and looked like one end of a pipe sloping upwards to the barrage.

Egill whistled softly, but the roar of the river drowned out every sound now. The water was less than a metre below the edge of the path, and resembled wet cement; it tumbled past them, ripping and clawing at the earth beneath their feet, exuding a smell he didn't understand – a grey desert flowing from one place to another.

Anna kept as far away from the river as possible, and, flattening her body against the rocky wall glistening with spray, she looked smaller and more forlorn than ever. But then everything appeared minuscule in comparison with the roaring water.

All of a sudden Egill had an urge to laugh, and he felt a kind of strange recklessness as he walked over to the opening. Down the centre of the pipe a stream of reddish-brown water trickled out of the darkness. Either side of the stream was caked with mud, but the walls were dry. Egill was aware of a faint draught, indicating that the pipe opened out somewhere at the other end. He saw no foot-prints in the mud.

He turned round and called out to Anna that he was going to take a look inside the tunnel. She shook her head, mouthing something he couldn't hear, and gestured for him to follow her as she set off back up the path.

'Two minutes!' he shouted, raising two fingers, before scrambling into the tunnel, avoiding the sheer drop in front of it. The roar started to fade almost instantaneously, and after a few more paces stopped completely. Egill switched on his torch and penetrated the darkness, one step at a time. The tunnel sloped gently upwards. He carried on walking even as the light from outside disappeared, and he had no idea what he was doing there. Anna had wanted them to descend the path, and then she wanted to go back up – which was probably a good idea. All the same, he pressed on.

The pipe ended, giving way to glistening black rock, a metallic smell and the sound of dripping water. Egill hummed softly, sensing rather than hearing the echo within. The tunnel was still more or less circular, carved out with a drill that bored through rock a trillion times faster than water could – even a seething, pounding river like the one outside.

He shone the torch far ahead into the darkness, moving its silent beam erratically from side to side. Surely if he could no longer see the opening there must have been a bend in the tunnel?

Further along the tunnel he glimpsed something lying on the ground.

His mouth tasted metallic, and he shivered inside as he

inhaled a breath of cold air. A long way off, he thought he could hear Anna's voice calling his name, but he wasn't sure which direction it was coming from.

Egill reached whatever was lying on the ground and aimed his torch at it. The first thing he noticed was the tail, and the shining white folds on the torso, which reminded him of glazed chicken. The tail stood erect like a phallus, stiff and ridiculous.

No fur, he thought, as he gazed into the imploring black eyes and knew that this was Trigger. The dog's little tongue was lolling out of his mouth, and he took rapid, shuddering breaths as he struggled in vain to stand up. Droplets of blood the size of pinpricks glistened all over his hairless body, and his tail moved in circles before standing erect once more. He had been flayed.

Egill shuddered, recoiling from the animal, and shone his torch quickly over the walls, heard a rustle behind him and wheeled round.

THE HOUSE

25

IN COMPETITION

Hrafn

Vigdís put down the note, drumming her fingers briskly on the table the way she did when she was agitated.

'What is it?' said Hrafn.

'They've gone on ahead.'

He reached for the note and read it.

'I don't believe this . . . He doesn't dare come near me, so he's dragged her with him. *The moron.*'

'Hasn't he good reason to be afraid?'

Hrafn didn't answer. He went over to the stove to put some water on for the coffee, then stood rubbing his eyes, which were puffy with sleep.

'How long since they left, do you reckon? Dawn?' she said.

He turned towards Vigdís.

'Egill went to bed early last night, didn't he?' All of a sudden he found it so funny that he could barely contain himself. 'He woke up full of energy and couldn't wait to get going!'

'You should have apologized to him the moment you got

home,' said Vigdís. 'But you're right, this was a stupid decision. Let's just hope they wait for us somewhere, if Anna can persuade him to stop for a while. Or that they turn back.'

The water came to a boil and they drank their coffee. Vigdís buttered some slices of bread from their small breakfast hamper, and they munched in silence. There was no sign of the old folks. Doubtless they were tending their invisible cows or sheep or hens, thought Hrafn. The foxes were the only animals they had seen there. Perhaps they were milking them.

They finished their breakfast and Hrafn lit a cigarette. The evening before, when Vigdís came upstairs to bed, he had apologized to her for what happened in the warehouse. She asked him whether he had smoked a joint, like Egill said, but he denied it, said he had held one and sniffed it – for old time's sake – insisting that Egill had been imagining things. After all, the guy had been stoned since the day they left. She said she didn't want to talk about it, turned over onto her side and instantly fell asleep, the way she always did. He hadn't mentioned the photograph and the bones in the village; she wouldn't be able to handle that, at least not until they were back in town. For his part, he'd lain awake most of the night.

They cleared away the dishes and the food, and Vigdís wrote a note to the old woman thanking her for letting them stay. Meanwhile, Hrafn removed all non-essential items from their rucksacks to make them lighter, but took along a few packets of cigarettes, and added three flares apiece. Then they walked outside.

There was a mild, southerly breeze, which meant the wind could rise at any moment. They walked across the yard until they picked up Anna and Egill's tracks, heading west.

'The barrage,' said Vigdís, and took out her map, where she had marked the route they decided on the day before. 'After that they'll follow the road north.'

'Do they have a map?'

'Anna had a map and a compass.'

'She doesn't know how to use a compass. And neither does he, regardless of what he might have told you, or pretended to Anna.'

'Even so, they must be going in more or less the right direction. If we hurry, we'll catch up with them.'

'Do we really want to?'

'*Of course we do,* Hrafn. We're travelling together, whether you two are on speaking terms or not. It's safer for all of us that way.'

He set the compass bearing to the hill from which they had glimpsed the barrage, and they set off. Vigdís borrowed his binoculars and scanned the surrounding area. When Hrafn asked, she said she was looking for the car she had sheltered in the day before.

'I'm sure it was around here somewhere. When the storm died down I could see the house.'

'If it's the same colour as the sand, we could be standing on it without knowing.'

'How odd,' she said after a brief silence.

'What?'

'My friend Ólöf used to take tourist groups across Sprengisandur onto Langjökull Glacier. She said that people's first response to the sands was awe and amazement at their beauty and stillness, and after that they'd start asking questions about distances, heights, lengths, breadths. They wanted facts about the area – about everything they could see, because we no longer see or hear anything – our thoughts are starved. It's impossible to *think* about this sort of nature, it makes us dizzy; we go round in circles.'

'Don't most people just relax? Rid themselves of their Parisian stress?'

'Yes, of course . . . But which group do you think we belong to?'

The wind began to rise but without whipping up the sand. Vigdís continued furtively scanning their surroundings, and when Hrafn asked her what the matter was, she told him there were a few things from the day before that puzzled her.

'Why didn't Egill mention your quarrel to Anna?' she asked. 'When I spoke to her last night, she knew nothing about it.'

'Well, he certainly told her something this morning. Maybe he didn't want to upset her . . . In any case, Egill never talks about personal stuff like that. Anything to do with the past is too personal for him; he sees it as a weapon to be used against people. Besides, he's too proud to whinge about me.'

'And isn't there something you're too proud to talk about?'

'What do you mean?'

'Egill mentioned a girl. He said he had apologized to you over "the girl". What did he mean?'

'I already told you about her.'

'About the girl, yes, if she's the one I think she is. But not about Egill . . . I want to know, Hrafn. You owe it to me after yesterday.'

'I *owe* it to you . . . ? OK.'

He reflected for a moment, then started to tell her about the evening after he had failed his exams at the junior college in Reykjavík for the second time. On his way to a party he stopped off at home to fetch something, and ended up getting into a fight with his father, who knocked him to the floor.

'We were both drunk. Later that night I moved into the apartment block on Hringbraut where my dope dealer lived with two other guys . . . I started dealing grass, which I told you about before, then I progressed to speed. I dug up hidden packages of the drug and processed it for sale.'

'You told me about the grass, not about the other—'

'I was used to having money, you understand. I was brought up with money . . . When the cops started to tap my phone and follow me around town – which they did within a matter of months – I stopped dealing. For a while

I managed a discotheque on Hafnarstræti, which was a front for laundering money, among other things.'

'What about Egill?'

'He didn't get dragged into any of that. He lived with his parents and was busy going to school, doing his homework. So he couldn't get away on weekdays, but we used to go out at weekends and have a good time . . . After I left home, Egill was my only link to the past, like a connecting thread. I trusted him. Then he began to change, and I had the impression that he saw a difference between us, that he felt *superior*.'

'What gave you that impression?'

'Some of the things he said, the looks he gave me . . . At first I assumed it was the drugs, and I didn't react. Yet I noticed how he always encouraged me to consume more while he held back; he never did anything to prevent me from sabotaging my own life, no matter what I did . . . Not that I wanted any guidance. But to feed off others, to thrive on their misfortune – that's something else . . . I was always more popular, wittier. I made friends easily, and was a quick learner. Egill had never really applied himself to anything, but I already noticed a change in him in our second year, before I dropped out of school. He was different when he came back after the Christmas holidays, as if he had decided that his time had come. It was apparent in everything he did: what he talked about, the way he greeted people in the corridors, the clothes he wore, the books he read by authors with more letters after their names than in them, books on group psychology, management techniques, body language and advertising. He also drank less, went to speed-reading classes, public speaking courses, started talking about "the Chicago School", and attending young conservative meetings at Heimdallur, where he made new friends. After I left, he put himself forward as head of the students' union, and was elected secretary or some bullshit position like that.'

'Isn't it normal to change, especially in junior college? People experiment with different things, try to work out what role they want to play in life . . .'

'Of course. And Egill gave a fine performance – only the script was written by a totally different person, no one *I* recognized. The polite word for it would be ambition; Egill had discovered the social climber in himself, and I found that hard to ignore. The way he saw it, what existed between us wasn't brotherliness, or the desire to help one another, or stand together. No, we were in *competition*, not just with each other and everyone else, but also with ourselves.'

'Did anyone else notice this change?'

Vigdís sounded sceptical, which irritated him.

'Not to the extent I did. I was his only childhood friend, apart from a few mutual acquaintances, none of whom really knew him. I'm not *exaggerating* . . . As you know, I have nothing against being competitive; only I realized how far Egill was prepared to go. Once I lost my temper, I yelled at him, scolded him, told him I missed the old Egill. He responded by sulking for a week – or maybe he was writing new scenes for his character, new postures. Around that time I met the girl I spoke to you about once, the one Egill mentioned during the quarrel.'

'The girl you were in love with?'

Hrafn nodded.

'In my own warped way. I never understood what she saw in me, but I truly wanted to live up to that image. She didn't take drugs, she was different from all the other people around me: kind, light-hearted, gorgeous to look at – all that. I started to use her as a reason to get out of my mess, to become *a better man*. I confided all this to Egill. He said he had never heard me talk that way before, congratulated me, embraced me.

'A month later, the day after the girl told me she wanted to split up – she said she couldn't go out with a drug dealer on principle – I had a call from Egill. He wanted us to meet up. While we were strolling round Tjörnin, the way we did sometimes, Egill told me that he and the girl were in love, that they had spent a lot of time together while I was working, looking after the bar or whatever. They were ashamed, but they hadn't set out to cheat on me – it had happened when they were drinking, and I needed to understand that he wished everything could be different, but unfortunately it wasn't.

'I listened to him telling me how sorry he was, but I didn't believe him – I'm not sure he believed himself. He barely tried to pretend, spoke like someone carrying out a damage-limitation exercise, attempting to save all our faces, or possibly our future relations. He was clearly expecting a knee-jerk response – an emotional outburst, a punch in the face, or worse – but I got the impression it didn't matter to him either way . . . And the thing that really hurt was that Egill showed absolutely no remorse. On the contrary, he seemed to think he had *the right* to take her away from me, because my life was a dirty, ugly mess and I was heading for the abyss, because I didn't know how to appreciate her, and my feelings didn't matter, if indeed I had any feelings. With the girl gone, his worthless friend could go back to taking drugs, and in no time at all he would have forgotten everything.

'That's what he said, or what I heard him say, and in the middle of his speech I walked away. He called after me, but I didn't turn around. I walked out to Vatnsmýri and lay down beside the pond outside the Nordic House. There was a frost, and the grass was white, the stars twinkled in the sky – all terribly dramatic . . . Then I snorted a line and regretted having run away. I went and stood outside Egill's place for an hour, not knowing whether I was spying or planning to do something to him. In the end I went to a party at a friend's house that went on for a month or more, and by the time I sobered up I had forgotten the girl's name.'

They came to the hill that they had walked up the first day in search of a mobile signal, and stopped to drink water. It occurred to Hrafn that the hill was man-made, like the smaller one at its base, and those near the container village, and possibly all the hills around there – born in the earth's entrails from rock that was smashed, ground up and then transported to the surface in trucks. And did that change anything? Wasn't our entire awareness *man-made*?

He took out his bottle and squirted some water into his mouth. The door in the hill was still locked. Smiling at Vigdís, he asked:

'Do you think that's enough?'

'What?'

'Enough of a justification?'

'You needn't justify yourself to me,' replied Vigdís, but he could tell she didn't mean it. 'Were they together for long, Egill and the girl?'

'A couple of months. The time it took me to sink into my personal hell, so to speak . . . With hindsight, I realized I had seen something rotten in him, a coldness, a cruelty that I couldn't understand. But I tried not to dwell on it.'

'When you came to see me at my practice, you told me you had never slept with the girl – is that true?'

He nodded. 'Probably, although I expect we fooled around.'

'Do you think Egill slept with her?'

'Of course. Egill can't be with a woman for more than an hour without at least propositioning her. And if he gets nothing he slinks off, like a dog. They were together until he grew bored of her, after finding out everything he could about me, I imagine.'

'About you?'

'My attempts.'

'How significant is that?'

'I don't know . . . Very.'

'Why has this come up now?'

Hrafn shrugged, squirted some more water into his mouth and tried to recall the events that had led up to the quarrel in the warehouse, but all he could remember were the bones, which he couldn't tell Vigdís about.

'Because there's so much space up here, maybe?' He grinned, then they both laughed and he knew that she had forgiven him. Which was good.

The wind continued to pick up, and not long after they walked away from the hill, the sands seemed to rise as one from the earth. All around them, it grew dark and Hrafn hurriedly wrapped his scarf around his nose and mouth, and saw Vigdís do the same out of the corner of his eye. Instead of blindly following the compass, they decided to head south-west to the ravine and then follow it to the barrage. Vigdís led the way because she was wearing sunglasses and could see better. When they reached the ravine they noticed that the river was much higher than the day before.

They could see better at the edge of the ravine, and the sand didn't sting their eyes as much, because less of it blew out over the water. Hrafn scanned the ground for tracks (he had to amuse himself somehow) and they pressed on, even though he wasn't sure that this was such a good idea. There wasn't much room for error, and one mistake could be fatal – for example, if they assumed that the wind would die down by evening and it didn't, or that it wouldn't change into a northerly one as it got colder, or turn into a downpour or even a sleet storm. They knew nothing.

The ravine curved southwards in a long, sweeping arc. Hrafn took the binoculars, but could see no sign of the barrage. They carried on along the ravine until they stumbled on two rucksacks, next to a path in the rock wall that descended into the water. They opened the rucksacks to make sure they belonged to Egill and Anna. Egill's was crammed with whisky bottles.

Vigdís ripped off her scarf and sunglasses, raised her arms in despair and gabbled something that Hrafn couldn't hear. She was extremely agitated, and he found it painful to watch her. The howling wind made communication difficult. Hrafn pretended not to notice the path into the ravine; he had no inclination to go down there. Vigdís pressed herself against him and shouted:

'. . . down there?'

She screwed up her face, jabbing her finger towards the path. At the bottom was the roaring river. Hrafn took off his rucksack and put it next to the others, walked gingerly towards the path and thought about Egill's bottles, his own inertia, and the invisible glacier which melted, flowing grey and swollen into the world. Finally he indicated that he would go down alone, and ordered her to wait.

'You'll see me!' he shouted, implying that he wouldn't leave her sight, then he set off hurriedly down the path.

It was calm in the ravine although the noise was deafening; the river had risen almost to the edge of the path and was swelling by the minute. Hrafn reached the end of the path, where a huge pipe vanished into the earth. There were two sets of footprints below the pipe, and in the mud inside it. The prints went in but didn't come out again.

26

'ANYONE ELSE?'

Vigdís

She watched Hrafn descend the path. She had been in tighter spots than this, and yet she no longer trusted her responses to anything; if Anna fell, all bloody, from the sky, or emerged giggling from her rucksack, or if Egill appeared trotting across the sands on a goat, she might respond in a myriad different ways to all those things.

Hrafn stood at the bottom of the path with the grey meltwater above his head, or so it appeared, staring at the rock wall. She kept expecting to see Anna or Egill at any moment, but nothing happened; no one stepped out of the rock laughing, or popped their head out of the water and winked. Hrafn turned around and made his way back up the path towards her. She looked at him questioningly, but he shook his head. His face was wet with spray from the river.

He slipped on his rucksack, and they brought their faces close together, noses touching as they struggled to hear one another. Hrafn said he had seen no sign of the others down there, and they agreed that Anna and Egill must have turned around and walked back to the house, either because they had forgotten something, or more likely because Anna had talked some sense into Egill and they had decided they should all travel together. They had left their rucksacks behind because they assumed they would be coming back the same way.

Vigdís moved their rucksacks further away from the edge, in case the wind changed, and she and Hrafn walked back the way they had come, along the ravine.

She had to admit their theory wasn't watertight. For example, Egill would never have veered away from the ravine – his cowardliness made him cautious – and if visibility had worsened, he would have followed the ravine to the bridge, which he knew was only a short walk from the house. Their paths would have crossed.

How well did she really know Egill and Anna? She had been to dinner at their place a few times, had got tipsy one evening and felt Egill's persistent gaze, and Hrafn's silence in the car on the way home.

Her first encounter with Egill, unbeknownst to her, had been through one of his agents, 'someone at the bank', who had once called her father, claiming to be looking after the interests of the bank's 'valued customers'. The agent informed her father that in real terms his non-index-linked account had been losing money over the years, and advised him to make the most out of his capital by purchasing shares in deCODE Genetics. After Vigdís's mother died, her father had received a big lump sum from the insurance company, but apart from buying her a car, Vigdís wasn't aware that he'd spent any of it – he scarcely used up all his wages. Without asking her – or anyone else, apparently, except for the pigs at the bank – her father invested the remainder of the money in the shares, and the day after deCODE Genetics was floated on the stock market, the money disappeared, every last penny. Later, Hrafn had told her how Egill had made his first millions by engineering a marketing campaign to sell shares in Dr Kari Stefánsson's company (which had exceeded all expectations), the consequences of which she worked out for herself. And yet she never said anything, either to Egill or to Hrafn; she was waiting for the right moment, or she was simply unsure what the appropriate response should be.

Didn't one's friends, in some sense, provide an insight into one's own inner life? On at least one occasion she had glimpsed a level of intimacy between Hrafn and Egill that had made her jealous. They had known each other since they were children, and whatever people might say, that created a bond.

They reached the bridge. It was hanging down into the ravine, which meant that Egill must have loosened the ropes the day before. Good, thought Vigdís, there was a *reason* why the bridge was like that. The sand blotted out the village.

From the bridge they headed due north, the wind behind them, but the visibility was worse than the day before, and they could only see a few metres ahead. She timed their walk, and kept checking the compass. If they didn't manage to locate the house within half an hour, they would walk in an ever-decreasing circle, and at the very worst would end up back at the ravine, where they would have to start again. The sand raged all around them, swelling like dark clouds dragged across the Earth's surface from south to north, and who was to say that one winter's day in January the wind wouldn't change, blowing all the grains of sand back where they came from.

'Calm down, calm down,' she murmured inside her hood. She couldn't tell whether the noise from the wind was loud or soft. She thought it must be very loud. Gradually the droning and whistling seemed to be inside her too, in her bones and muscles, in her tiny brain – that smooth grey mass which she was carrying across the sands. For a while, she had the impression that they were walking on a storm-tossed sea; the sands undulated, and she became dizzy from the continuous drone of the wind in her ears. Grit plugged her nose and gathered at the corners of her eyes and mouth.

Vigdís strode ahead, setting the pace, with Hrafn close behind. Soon they made out the shape of the house through the dust. There was no one in the yard and no faces at the window.

'They're not here,' Vigdís murmured to herself. She clasped the handrail to steady herself, before climbing the steps and opening the front door. In the hallway she removed the scarf from around her face, took off her sunglasses and called out to see if anyone was at home. She went upstairs and took a look around. Egill and Anna's room was empty, and there was no sign of them having stopped off on their way somewhere else.

'There's no one here,' she said as she walked into the front room, where Hrafn sat smoking. 'Something must have happened to them. They turned back to fetch us and got lost out on the sands. How could Egill be so stupid?'

'People are always appearing and disappearing up here,' said Hrafn, examining the books on the shelves. 'Like the village and the barrage – first there was nothing, then they appeared, and now there's nothing again.'

'Whatever. We have to wait here,' she said, lighting a cigarette. 'If they don't show up soon, or after the wind dies down, we'll set off on our own.'

Hrafn nodded and flicked through a book he had just plucked from the shelf. He was uncharacteristically silent, and was avoiding her gaze the way he did when he was ashamed about something.

'Otherwise, is everything OK?' she added. 'I trust you, my love . . . You aren't hiding anything from me, are you?'

'Of course not. ' He shook his head. 'I tell you everything I know.'

She looked at the picture on the wall, the one Anna referred to as the picture of the beautiful people. It was hard to believe they had been sitting here only yesterday evening, clinking glasses, speculating about this and that. The things they had been puzzling over last night seemed trivial, as nothing compared to their current situation.

Before she knew it, Vigdís had pointed out the photograph to Hrafn and was explaining to him Anna's theory about the woman in the picture not being Ása, but rather the old man's lover, who was also his sister – or at least, there was good reason to believe that she was, and that they had had a child together, who had been imprisoned in a secret room in the old man's study upstairs and cut out of the photograph.

'There are thousands of books in his study, as well as photos of the old man taken with politicians and other distinguished people. These two aren't farmers; not the old man, at any rate.'

'Are you talking about *incest*?' asked Hrafn. He was sprawled on the sofa, gazing up at the ceiling.

'Yes, or Anna was. I don't know. Why else would they live here? Unless they were running away from something, a scandal . . .'

'And the secret room behind the bookshelves?'

'She saw an old family photo up in the office: the same couple as in this one, only younger. And she found a few clues in a biographical article about the old man. I suppose we could find out for ourselves by looking inside the chamber. She opened it by pulling out a book, as I recall, though she didn't specify which. And I didn't ask . . . She also suggested that the woman in the photo might be buried out there somewhere.'

'I see . . . And what about the child, the spawn of its parents' blasphemous relationship? Where is it now?'

All of a sudden Vigdís had the impression that he was mocking her.

'I think we can safely say the child has grown into an

adult by now. I know it sounds crazy, Hrafn, but don't you *dare* be so dismissive. We haven't exactly come up with any better explanations . . .' She took a deep breath. 'I realize she and I were drinking, but somehow this all seems much more plausible than it did yesterday.'

'So, you think there's someone else here?'

'Did I say that?'

Hrafn didn't reply. He rose from the sofa and walked over to the photograph on the wall.

Had she said that? That someone else, someone they didn't know about, was in here with them?

Hrafn spent a long time contemplating the photograph, then sat down again.

'Where did you say this study was?'

'At the end of the corridor upstairs.'

He stretched out on the sofa and spread a blanket over himself.

'I love you,' he said suddenly, looking straight at her.

She smiled and sat down next to him.

'I love you too . . . What made you say that now?'

'Isn't now as good a time as any?'

He pulled the blanket up under his nose, and closed his eyes. All that was missing was a notepad and pen, and the semblance to the beginning of their relationship would be complete: the doctor and the patient.

Vigdís glanced about the room as she listened to Hrafn's breathing grow deeper. On the shelves beside the sofa were some novels, and an exquisitely bound volume of Jón Árnason's *Folktales*. She reached for the book Hrafn had been reading, or hiding behind – *Tales of Demons and Imps*, a collection of 'new folk tales' that Vigdís had never heard of. A brief foreword, written by someone who dubbed themselves 'Sup Hell', claimed that the stories in the book had been passed down by word of mouth during the twentieth century, and had in common the fact that they were anonymous and 'had actually taken place'.

It wasn't clear if the last comment was intended as a joke. Vigdís flicked through the pages, pausing at one of the tales entitled: 'He has such beautiful clothes'.

The story told of a man who lost his way in a snow blizzard on Hofsjökull Glacier, and became separated from his friends, fellow members of a hiking group from the city. After the weather cleared, the man made his way back down the glacier without any difficulty, for he was well equipped. Soon he came to a deep, green valley on the edge of the glacier, which he couldn't recall hearing of before. The valley was lush and through it ran a river.

The man descended into the valley and followed the river until he came to a farmhouse. He knocked at the door, which was opened by two skinny children who guided him into a room where an even skinnier couple sat alongside a diminutive creature, which was eating its way through a large pile of meat on a plate. The couple welcomed the man and placed a bowl in front of him, into which they ladled a watery soup – the same as the one they and the children were eating, which was very different fare from whatever the creature was having.

The creature was peculiar, both in manner and

appearance. Not much taller than the children, it had a hunched back and a wizened face. Although it never looked up, the creature seemed to see all around, for its eyes were situated unusually high on its forehead. It wore colourful clothes of red, yellow and blue, so bright they dazzled the eye. Upon closer inspection, the creature's skin hung in loose folds, almost as if it had been pulled on in a hurry, and here and there the man glimpsed patches of red, glistening flesh that ripped open and seeped over the creature's skin each time it moved. It exuded a powerful odour, a mixture of excrement and rotten fish, which filled the whole house.

The man drank his soup and tried to work out where he was, but his eyes were hopelessly drawn back to the repulsive creature at the end of the table, as were those of the family, who sat watching it eat as though spellbound. After licking the plate clean, the creature disappeared, and the man asked the couple what it was. 'The little man', as they referred to the creature, had turned up at their house a few weeks before, and they insisted he was a welcome guest whom they wished to do their best to accommodate. The man was horrified; seizing one of the children's arms, which was little more than skin and bone, he demanded to know why they put the creature before themselves when both they and their children were starving. The couple replied as one: *He has such beautiful clothes.*

The next day, around suppertime, the same thing occurred: the creature arrived at the farm, sat down at the table and demanded its dinner, although not a word was spoken. A plate heaped with choice cuts was placed before it, while the others dined on gruel. At this point, the man could hold no longer contain himself; he scolded the creature, which paid him no heed, disappearing after it had licked the plate clean.

The man began to have his suspicions about the situation, and vowed to himself that he wouldn't leave until the family had been freed from their burden. A few days later, it so happened that there was no meat left in the valley, for the creature had eaten it all up. That evening, when (much to the family's dismay) no meat appeared on its plate, the creature started to bellow out loud, rendering those present paralysed. With lightning speed, it grabbed the two children, first the boy and then the girl, and began to gnaw through their bellies, up to their lungs and hearts, smearing their blood on its clothes, which shone brighter than ever before. After it had finished, the creature disappeared through the door.

When the man regained the ability to move, he demanded that the farmer fetch his gun, and that the two of them hunt the creature down. But the farmer and his wife replied in unison *He has such beautiful clothes*, and refused to do anything.

The next evening when the creature returned, it sat down at the table and demanded its dinner. When no meat appeared on its plate, the creature started to bellow, then clambered onto the table and made straight for the farmer's wife, placing its mouth over her eye and sucking until they heard a loud smack as her eyeball popped out of its socket, first one then the other. Next it bared her breasts, gorging on them until there was nothing left, smearing her blood on its clothes until they shone brightly, whereupon it disappeared. When the man leapt to his feet and demanded they find the creature and kill it, the farmer repeated as before: *He has such beautiful clothes.*

The man realized this wouldn't do at all. The next day, before dinner, he poured wax into his ears and let it harden so that the spell wouldn't work on him. As soon as the creature sat down and started to bellow, the man sprang to his feet and set upon it with a knife, only to discover that it had evaporated. Upon closer inspection, he saw that the creature had turned itself into a tiny black fly, which he proceeded to chase round and round first the outside then the inside of the house, until he collapsed, exhausted, on the floor. Hovering above the table where the farmer sat eating his almost transparent broth, the fly alighted on his spoon and disappeared inside his mouth, where it grew back to its normal size. At this point the farmer's head exploded, and the creature re-emerged, straddling his shoulders and smearing itself in his warm blood until its clothes shone so brightly that the man had to avert his eyes.

After that the man went away, for there was no one left alive in the valley. He followed the river until he reached the nearest town, where he told the story of the demon that wore a human skin and draped itself in colours brighter than anything in this world.

27

Vigdís

Vigdís was unaware of how long she sat there. She closed her eyes and was visited by events in the life of the house: its construction out of nearby rocks, the library transported by cart across the sands, a woman combing her dark flowing tresses in front of a mirror, an eye peering through a crack, and a shadow falling onto all fours, scurrying through the darkness. The images arose only to vanish almost in the same instant; she felt she understood everything without being able to describe it in words, just like when she'd dozed off in the abandoned car.

She gave a start as the front door slammed. She heard footsteps, and the old woman trudged across the hallway with a sloshing bucket, before disappearing into the kitchen where she plonked the bucket down.

Rising from the sofa, Vigdís went into the kitchen. She said good morning, feeling that she sounded silly but unable to think of anything else to say.

Ása returned the greeting. She didn't seem surprised to find them there.

'As you can see we're still here,' said Vigdís. 'We were supposed to leave this morning. I think our friend Anna told you our plans yesterday, didn't she?'

'Yes, I remember that well,' said Ása. 'Has something happened?'

'Maybe, maybe not,' said Vigdís, a smile playing on her lips, before instantly fading. 'Our friends seem to have disappeared. My partner and I, Hrafn, the dark-haired one, are looking for them. You haven't seen them, have you?'

Ása shook her head and reached into the cupboard for some coffee.

'You would tell me if you had seen them, wouldn't you? If you knew something we didn't?'

The old woman walked up to Vigdís and stared straight into her eyes.

'All will be well, my dear. Have no fear. Thinking too much can be dangerous.'

She stroked Vigdís's arm, and told her to calm down.

'We're all friends here. Now, I'm going to make you a nice cup of coffee.'

Vigdís longed to ask so many questions, about all the things that were troubling her, but she forced herself to keep quiet. She refused the offer of coffee, went out to the car and took a swig of whisky.

The wind was dropping. While she smoked, she glanced about her, making a mental list of everything they could find up there: stones of varying sizes and types, water, diverse plants, mosses and lichens; a few species of animal, mainly birds and insects. Nothing all that complicated. The only complicated thing here was inside their own heads. Something about this idea awakened her optimism.

On her way back to the house, Vigdís checked her rucksack to make sure the gun was still there. She had decided to take it with her that morning with the sole intention of getting rid of it – digging a hole in the sand where no one would find it. *So why hadn't she?*

When she re-entered the living room, Hrafn had woken up. She lay in his arms and he stroked her hair, and said he felt better than before. He didn't ask about Egill or Anna. Vigdís produced a pack of cards, which she had fetched from the car, and they played Go Fish. They didn't discuss what to do for the best, but Vigdís envisaged staying another night and setting off at dawn.

The old woman locked the front door, even though it was still light, and went back into the kitchen. Vigdís watched her over the top of her cards, and noticed that she kept glancing out of the window.

The wind on the sands had died down completely now, and the sky was filled with low clouds – thick, grey clumps that hung motionless as though waiting for something, merging and separating without ever appearing to move. It was probably getting close to suppertime. The lights from the house could be seen from a long way off across the sands, if anyone needed guiding home.

Hrafn went to the toilet. Vigdís sat listening to the murmur of the radio coming from the kitchen. The old woman had tuned in to the weather forecast, which sounded like meaningless gibberish, a coded message about something entirely different.

Seconds later, the lights in the house went out and the radio fell silent. Ása appeared in the doorway and cleared her throat.

'The electricity,' she said.

'Is there a power cut?' asked Vigdís, as if she had only just noticed.

Hrafn came running down the stairs and Vigdís told him what had happened.

'Unbelievable!'

He raised his hands, as if in anger, and asked where the fuse box was. The old woman led him into the kitchen, where she opened one of the cupboards. Hrafn poked his head inside and tinkered with the fuses for a few minutes.

'Has this happened before?' asked Vigdís.

'Yes,' said Ása.

'Where does your electricity come from – the river?' said Hrafn, closing the cupboard door.

Ása nodded.

'Perhaps the current is too strong with all that meltwater, and it makes the power cut out?'

'Could be . . .' said Ása. 'Sounds about right.'

'Well, I'm glad we cleared that up. Aren't we clever?' said Hrafn sardonically. 'The power cuts out, and it has something to do with the river, *the meltwater in the river*, like I said.'

He bobbed his head up and down very fast, and strode back into the front room, Vigdís following behind. She lit a candle, which the old woman brought for them, and they resumed their card game. Egill and Anna had taken the torch with them, but at least she and Hrafn still had the flares.

They ate sandwiches for supper and Hrafn fetched some tea lights from the jeep, even though the old woman did her best to stop him. Vigdís tried to make it cosy for them in the front room. She drank a beer with their meal, which didn't seem to bother Hrafn.

Later, as the light faded, a noise reached them from across the sands, like the roar of an engine or a low growl. Hrafn suggested it might be a power saw, coming from the village on the far side of the ravine.

They asked the old woman, who was sitting in the kitchen knitting, and she said she thought it was the roar of meltwater in the ravine.

'In that case, why didn't we hear it before?' asked Hrafn. 'The noise only started when it got dark.'

'There are certain things we only notice in the dark, my dear,' said the old woman, smiling at him tenderly.

They returned to the living room, where Vigdís proposed that the water level had risen so high in the ravine as to become audible.

'Or after the wind died down.'

At that instant the noise stopped. They sat on the sofa, discussed going to bed, but neither of them made the first move. Hrafn said he needed a piss and disappeared upstairs, not for the first time, although Vigdís wasn't aware that he had drunk enough liquid to warrant all those trips to the bathroom. She wanted to relax, to stop watching him, and yet she couldn't. Her perceptions were tense, on high alert. The beautiful people gazed down at her reproachfully, but also expectantly – like the clouds.

Ten minutes later, Hrafn came back downstairs, and she refrained from asking him why he had taken so long. He stood next to the window for a moment before beckoning her over.

Fires were burning out in the darkness.

'The village,' said Hrafn, and fetched the binoculars, pointing them into the blackness before handing them to Vigdís. The fires were near the bridge. If more fires were burning in the village they were obscured by the hill next to the ravine.

She gave back the binoculars.

'Do you think it's them?' she asked, her pulse quickening.

'Anna and Egill?'

'Yes.'

'I don't know.'

'If they were stuck on the other side of the ravine,' said Vigdís, 'wouldn't they send us a signal to come and pull up the bridge? So that they could come back across?'

'They couldn't have crossed the ravine in the first place without pulling up the bridge. In which case they'd be able to get back, wouldn't they?'

'It might have collapsed after them . . . Every moment counts, if that's them.'

He shook his head but said nothing.

'What are you thinking, Hrafn? Say something, you're so silent—'

'I'm not silent, stop *obsessing* about me!' he shouted.

She snatched up one of the candles and went out into the hallway, only remembering what she was going to do when she got there: check to see if the front door was locked.

She was beginning to understand something that she couldn't put into words: why the house was locked at night; why the bridge hung from a cable; why a wire fence spanned the barrage, cutting it off.

She went into the kitchen, let the tap run in the sink and contemplated the old woman: the eczema on her face, the incessant jerking of her shoulders as she knitted. It occurred to her (based on Anna's theory) that Ása might be a later child of the same parents, the sister of the one that had been locked away. And she featured in none of the photographs because she'd been conceived after her parents moved to the countryside.

'What's going on out there?' Vigdís asked the old woman. 'Have you seen the fires?'

'The fires?'

Ása went on knitting. On the table in front of her a candle was burning.

'On the other side of the ravine.'

Hrafn entered the kitchen.

'Someone's out there,' he said, looking at the old woman.

No one spoke, until Ása opened her mouth:

'Your friends?' she whispered.

Hrafn burst out laughing.

'There's something very wrong going on here . . . What the hell are you doing in this place? This is no farm – where are the animals? Do you keep invisible cows and invisible sheep!'

'Calm down, Hrafn,' said Vigdís.

Hrafn ignored her. He leaned across the table to where the old woman was sitting and rapped the wood with his knuckles, as if for effect.

'The phone is broken, the jeep is broken, the electricity cuts out. When did the phone stop working? There are no telegraph poles around here, which means the wires must be underground. Who cut them? Underground wires don't cut themselves. There's someone out there, isn't there? Someone else, as my girlfriend put it.'

The old woman remained motionless.

'You aren't a lucky man,' she said, staring straight at him.

'I don't believe in luck, old woman,' he said. 'I believe in myself, and I demand to know why we can't get *away* . . .'

He went on rapping on the table until Vigdís could bear it no longer, and seized his hand, much the same way Hrafn had grabbed the old man after he overturned the table. Hrafn shrugged her off, and Vigdís begged him to come away, to go upstairs to bed.

'You make things so difficult!' she cried, louder than she had intended. 'Get dead drunk if you want, but stop hiding it! I don't give a damn what you do, it doesn't matter any more!'

Hrafn stood in the kitchen doorway, his eyes glazed and shiny.

'Do you think I've started again?'

'Of course you've started again. I don't think, I know. I know you—'

He turned on his heel, and she heard him go upstairs.

Vigdís slumped onto a chair by the table, facing the old woman.

'Be careful, my dear,' the old woman said after a brief silence.

'Careful . . . Why? Careful about what in particular?'

'He's branded.'

'What are you talking about?'

'You know, my dear. Anyone with eyes can see.'

'What the hell do you mean by "*branded*"? You mean the nick in his right earlobe? That's a hole from a pierced earring he wore when he was fourteen. And the pullover he's wearing is a Lacoste his mother gave him . . .'

She fell silent, and clasped her head in both hands, doing her best to control herself. She was good at controlling herself. Then she thought she heard the engine noise start up again out in the darkness, and she put her hands over her ears. The old woman sat down beside her and caressed her back.

'We have to get away from here,' said Vigdís, and she sat up straight. 'But I'm not really sure about anything any more . . .'

She realized that the tap was still running. What she had thought was the engine noise was the burble of water.

She rose and walked into the living room to fetch a cigarette, saw the photograph of the beautiful people, swung at it with her hand and watched it drop to the floor. The glass smashed, and when Vigdís bent to pick up the photograph she saw that it was torn across the middle and stuck together with tape on the back.

'Why has this picture been torn in half?' she screamed, finally losing control, letting the tears flow as she leaned against the wall, screaming once more before slumping to the floor, indifferent to whether she cut herself on the broken glass. She heard the old woman approach from the kitchen, and she thought about the desert, the child, the house that was locked, defended like a castle, about the fence across the barrage, and the hanging bridge – for something out in the darkness wanted to come in, from the far side over to this side.

28
DEVELOPMENTS

Hrafn

Hrafn stood motionless in the gloom upstairs, debating whether to go down and fetch a candle, but he decided that would be stupid after the quarrel.

He heard something break downstairs, doubtless Vigdís's famous composure, followed by a scream. She could come to him if she was scared; she owed him an apology after what she had said.

At the far end of the corridor he saw a faint sliver of light seeping under a door. He tiptoed towards the door and pressed his ear to it, but heard nothing, then he pushed the handle gently and the door opened. Tiptoeing across the floor, he saw immediately that this was the study Vigdís had told him about. In the dim light, he could make out thousands of leather-bound books lining the walls. Over by the window, on the far side of a large desk, the old man sat in an armchair, an open book in his lap, reading by candlelight. Hrafn didn't announce himself at first, but instead watched the old man pick up a pair of scissors from the windowsill and trim the candle wick as it began to sputter, before he resumed reading.

Hrafn cleared his throat. The old man looked up, and his face broke into a smile, his eyes twinkling as though he was seeing an old friend. Hrafn felt an echo of contentment.

'Hello,' he said, 'forgive the intrusion. Am I interrupting you?'

The old man shook his head.

'I was on my way to bed when I saw a light under the door. A fine study you have. And so many books – it must have been quite a job, ferrying them all up here.'

The old man's face twisted into a grimace as he tried to speak, a frozen smile on his lips.

Smiley face, Hrafn thought, laughing to himself. That was a good name for him: *Smiley face*.

Hrafn fell silent and glanced about. No harm in taking a looking around, he thought, since he was there. A red-brick fireplace stood between two bookcases, and in front of it an empty bucket and a poker. On the wall above the old man hung the photographs the girls believed proved their bizarre incest theory.

'Well, well, old man,' said Hrafn, sensing the devil in him rear up on its hind legs. The old man gazed at him, smiling, and Hrafn perched on the edge of the desk, opposite the wall with the photographs.

'I see you have quite a few photographs. Your family, I presume?'

Without saying anything, the old man rose slowly to his feet, took down a framed diploma and handed it to Hrafn.

'Princeton, no less. Excellent. Bravo,' said Hrafn, stifling a giggle. 'Doctor of Physiology, it says here. That must have been a difficult subject. I always wanted to study, but my father didn't believe in it. He said it would take too long. There was no real tradition of education in my family. We were *entrepreneurs*, you see.'

The old man nodded, assuming an air of seriousness for the first time since they had met, which Hrafn almost found even funnier. Then he walked over to a shelf stacked with ring binders, took one out and placed it on the desk.

'The family album?' asked Hrafn, putting down the diploma, which he wished he could steal, take with him back to town, hang on his study wall and laugh at. He was struck by how rudely he'd spoken to the old man, making no concession to his infirmity.

'I'm sorry about what happened between us the other night—' he began, then broke off, deciding he couldn't be bothered. He had nothing to be ashamed of; he was no intruder in that house, he was there out of unfortunate necessity. He clenched his jaw and fists, angry at the thought that Vigdís didn't trust him and his good intentions. She obviously couldn't cope with the strain, as demonstrated by all that nonsense about incest. It was typical of her to fly into a rage like that – not because of their actual situation, but because someone else had lost their temper. Now she was taking a holier-than-thou attitude, making him the culprit, rather than facing up to the problem.

The old man retired to the window, while Hrafn browsed through the album. Clearly he had been successful in his day, a respected citizen, but what did any of that matter in the grand scheme of things?

He was overlooking something in that room.

Hrafn closed the album, took one of the lighted candles and moved along the shelves, contemplating the books. Most pertained to science, but there were also tomes on philosophy, anthropology, psychology and history, as well as a few volumes about magic. He remembered about the secret room, and from time to time crooked his finger over the top of a book, half-tilting it towards him, then grew bored and resolved to forget about incest, scandals and secret rooms, which in any case were no more than subconscious metaphors for Anna's cunt, small and shrivelled like a frightened piglet after Egill hadn't penetrated it for months.

At that precise moment, he knew what was bothering him about the room. Not the musty smell, which pervaded everything, but rather the odour of soot, or *burnt hair*, which reminded him of when he was younger and used to set fire to the rubbish or singe his own body hair.

The smell was coming from the fireplace.

Hrafn crouched in front of the hearth and ran his finger across the floor. The brickwork scarcely bore any traces of soot, nor was there any sign of coal or logs, or of anything having been burned recently. He leaned forward and poked his head up the chimney. The smell grew stronger. If the damper was open he should be able to see the night sky, a pale square amid the darkness, or even feel a draught.

He found the lever that operated the damper, changed

its position and looked up the chimney again, but nothing had changed.

'There's something in there,' he murmured to himself. Reaching for the poker, he thrust it up into the darkness, encountered an obstacle, and felt the bulk of something above his head that might topple onto him at any moment. A sprinkling of soot fell on his face and a few long black hairs floated down from the darkness. He grew impatient and began to thrust the poker up the chimney as hard as he could, until he heard a noise like a balloon bursting. Something heavy dropped into the grate, and a cloud of soot rose into the air. Hrafn turned away, spluttering. A foul odour of burnt, decomposed flesh wafted from the fireplace, and he pulled his shirt up over his nose and mouth.

Once the soot had settled, he reached for the candle and peered into the fireplace. In the grate lay the bloated carcass of an animal, gas oozing from a slit between its grotesquely splayed hind legs. On its head were two small, curved horns, its eyes were charred black holes, and it legs tapered into cloven hooves.

Hrafn gazed at the carcass for a while, wiped the soot off his face then spat copiously to rid himself of the stench, marvelling at the strength needed to push an animal all the way up a chimney, the heft of the man, the length of his arms . . .

Still sitting with his book by the window, the old man seemed oblivious. Hrafn walked over and sat down in the chair opposite him.

'There was something blocking your chimney.' He gestured towards the fireplace and lit a cigarette. 'How do you get a sheep up a chimney?' he added, and laughed. It sounded like the beginning of a joke, the punchline of which he had forgotten. 'I'm sure you and the old woman have a perfect explanation. Santa Claus comes down the chimney. Sheep are roasted. Ergo: Santa Claus is a sheep. Is that the way things work around here?'

Far away across the sands, he saw the blaze from the fires. That wasn't Egill out there – he was too gutless to put on such a show. Besides, he wouldn't know how to light a fire like that. No, everything pointed to this being *someone else*. But that was problematic, utterly incomprehensible, and yet not. Hrafn was amazed at his ability to see two points of view simultaneously, and it wasn't the first time he had noticed this – part of it he had known for a long time without knowing it. For example, something had happened when he was young, and yet it hadn't.

'*Something else*,' he murmured, rising from the chair and fumbling in his pocket for the photograph of Vigdís, the one from the pyramid of bones in the village. The image was less grainy, less shadowy, as if it were still developing. Vigdís's hands lay by her sides and one side of her face was bathed in the kind of soft light that might seep through a crack in the door. Someone on their way to an adjacent room might have noticed the door open, or opened it themselves, by accident or on purpose, seen her lying there, pulled the sleeping bag down to reveal her breasts and taken the photograph. Her breasts looked like eyeless heads, dead suns floating in space.

Unless it had been taken earlier, a week or even a month ago? Who was to say that this was her sleeping bag and not her duvet back in town, or that Egill had found the photo in the village rather than it falling out of his shirt pocket when he crouched over the bones. Were her hands by her sides, or between her legs, rubbing herself for the man who was watching, the man who took the photograph when her lips parted and her face relaxed as she came?

Hrafn switched his gaze from the photograph to the old man. The candle next to him had started to sputter, and yet he didn't move, merely sat with the book open on his lap. Hrafn finally understood what he was doing. He wasn't reading – he hadn't so much as turned a page in all that time. He was listening.

'Are you waiting for someone out there?' asked Hrafn. The old man looked at him, his smile fading as he bobbed his head.

'Don't open,' he said, reaching out his hand and placing it on Hrafn's knee, leaning towards him, a look of intensity in his eyes that hadn't been there before.

'Don't open the door.'

29

WHAT APPEARS

Vigdís

Vigdís peered inside their bedroom and saw instantly that it was empty. She held the candle out towards the corners, just to make sure, then looked along the corridor, but saw no glimmer of light. Doubtless Hrafn was sitting somewhere sulking, avoiding her; at any rate he hadn't come back downstairs.

She closed the door and slumped onto the bed, took another swig from the flask and hoped she would fall asleep. She and Hrafn seldom quarrelled. And yet, she felt calmer; the buzz in her head from the whisky served to dampen her unease.

She turned over onto her stomach and rubbed her face. When she'd last looked out of the window, the fires were no longer blazing. She had decided that all change was bad; from now on, she would lead an even quieter, more conventional life than before they came up to the highlands.

She heard a knock coming from somewhere in the house. Vigdís lay motionless, listening, as she felt her skin go cold, contracting over her body. She stood up, walked to the window and peered out. It was too dark for her to see if anyone was standing outside the door.

She hurried into the corridor, where she immediately saw Hrafn. Judging from his expression he had heard the sound too, for he was standing motionless, candle in hand, gazing down the stairwell.

'*Psst*.' She caught his attention and beckoned him over with a wave of her hand. 'Do you think it could be Anna or Egill?' she whispered.

'They wouldn't just knock,' he whispered back, 'they'd call out to us.'

His face looked strangely black, as though covered in soot, and it merged with the shadows. She refrained from asking him what had happened, and went back into the bedroom where the two of them peered out of the window together. A dim light spilling from the kitchen should have allowed them to make out a person on the steps, but there was nothing. Further along, at the end of the porch, Hrafn said he saw something that looked like a stick.

'*A stick*?' said Vigdís, glancing sideways at the gun beneath the bed. She wasn't sure Hrafn would know how to use it, and she herself had never fired a gun. They listened again, but heard nothing, then left the room and went downstairs to the hallway, where they found the old woman. She was holding a candlestick, her staring eyes shining.

'Why don't they knock again?' asked Vigdís.

'Don't open it,' the old woman said, fixing her gaze on the door.

'Why knock only *once*? It's dark outside – people don't just knock once and then stand there in silence . . .' Vigdís went on, but the old lady shushed her, and implored them to go back upstairs.

Hrafn made a move towards the door, but Ása grabbed him by the shoulders and begged him to stop. As he wriggled free, the old woman's candlestick dropped to the floor and the flame went out.

'Should we be doing this?' said Vigdís feebly, aware that she couldn't dissuade him. The old woman turned on her heels and vanished upstairs. Hrafn slid back the bolts and opened the door a crack. He peered out then flung the door wide open and stepped onto the porch, glancing left and right, while Vigdís followed close behind. The wind had dropped and the darkness encircling the house was deep and impenetrable. No moon or stars shone in the sky.

At one end of the porch, a long, thin stick rose straight up in the air. Dangling from the tip was a fine cord, like a beam of light or a spider's thread that vanished into the darkness.

'A fishing rod?' said Hrafn, and Vigdís saw the reel at its base, the wire threading through the eyes up to the tip. While she was looking at it, the tip of the fishing rod jerked suddenly. She clasped hold of Hrafn to steady herself, and tried to say something but her mouth wouldn't open. Hrafn crouched down beside the rod, yanked it out of the hole it had been forced into and turned the reel. Vigdís's eyes moved between the rod and the darkness beyond the house.

The rod gave another jerk, and arched forward before straightening up again.

Aware of something hot on the back of her hand, Vigdís looked down and saw that her hand was trembling so much that wax from the candle she was holding was spilling onto it.

'Something's moving,' said Hrafn, as they glimpsed a dim shadow amid the darkness, which slowly began to resemble a human. It was moving towards the light coming from the kitchen, and Vigdís knew that it was her even though everything about her was different. Her body was startlingly white against the darkness, her eyes like two black circles, her face almost unrecognizable. Her chin, neck and breasts were covered in a brownish muck or half-congealed blood that had oozed down her naked body. Her hands were wrapped in white rags, and she walked with her arms stretched out in front of her, as if she were blind. The fishing wire disappeared into her mouth, and each time the reel turned, she gave a low, painful, hollow moan that seemed to come from deep inside her belly. Her once-fair hair was now white. And yet there was no doubting who it was: Anna.

30

'IS MY FACE GRUBBY?'

Vigdís

Between them, they guided her into the house. She resisted when they touched her, but hadn't the strength to push them away. She lost consciousness at the top of the steps, and as they carried her the rest of the way to the front room she made no sound.

They laid her out on the carpet, where she came round. Vigdís resolved that from now on *action* was the way forward, and she strode into the hallway to fetch the first-aid kit from Hrafn's rucksack, slamming the door and sliding the bolts across before returning to the front room. Hrafn was crouched beside Anna, holding her down. A coil of fishing wire still dangled from her mouth, and Hrafn bent over and bit through it with his teeth. Vigdís became mesmerized by the remaining stub, the beam of light, until Hrafn cried out to her. She took some codeine tablets out of the packet, ground them up and fed them to Anna, after which Hrafn held her mouth closed, forcing her to swallow. The tip of Anna's tongue appeared to have been cut off, which would explain her bloodied neck and breasts.

She continued to whimper feebly, and then started having convulsions, her limbs flailing so that they had to pin her down to prevent her from hurting herself.

When she grew calm, Vigdís held the candle up to her face, peered inside her half-open mouth and saw the hook glinting inside her throat.

'Best to leave it there,' she murmured.

Anna's eyes were open, but had been poked with something, because blood had run into the whites and congealed, and her ears were plugged with brownish blobs. She didn't respond when Vigdís shouted in her ear, nor when she waved her hand in front of Anna's eyes and asked her to blink if she could hear her. Her breasts, belly and genitals were covered in tiny cuts and bruises that resembled bite marks.

Vigdís turned away and retched. When she looked back, Hrafn had unravelled the rags on Anna's hands to reveal darkened stumps: her fingers had been snipped off above the knuckle, and her wrists tied with plastic cord to staunch the bleeding.

They cleaned her wounds with iodine, bandaged the stumps with gauze, then lifted Anna onto the sofa and spread a blanket over her. Vigdís retched a few more times, but forced herself to keep going. She took a swig of whisky, rummaged for the scissors in the first-aid box and used them to cut the stub of fishing wire poking out of Anna's mouth, as close to her lips as possible. Around her neck, she noticed a small tube or lozenge, fastened with a piece of fishing wire and caked in blood. She snipped the wire, and wiped away the blood to reveal a smooth white bone.

'*A bone*,' she said, fingering it.

Hrafn took the bone from her and examined it. It was hollow, and at one end he glimpsed a bit of paper. He fetched a knife from the kitchen, and they managed to snag the paper, easing out a tight scroll the size of a cigarette. As they unfurled it on the floor they discovered a drawing in red ink: rectangles ranged around a square, itself made up of four rectangles, and an 'X' in the centre traced in blood. Scrawled at the bottom of the map, also in blood, was the word: H E L P.

As she took another swig of whisky, Vigdís had the impression that she was impervious to getting drunk. Her thoughts condensed like whale backs rising from beneath a dark, shimmering surface.

'It's a map of the village,' said Hrafn, leaning over the scroll. 'The huts in two semicircles round the main building, which is made up of four huts around the "X".'

'What does the "X" stand for?'

'Egill, or . . . I've no idea. But, given the state Anna is in, it seems unlikely that he's OK. He's either asking for help, or someone has made him ask for help.'

'What if he did this?' She lowered her voice, glancing sideways at Anna on the sofa. 'And he wants us think it was someone else?'

'Why ask for help, then?'

'To make us go to the village.'

Vigdís thought about the fires, the engine noise they had heard that evening, and she found it increasingly painful to look at Anna – her truncated fingers, her white, witchlike hair. *Her toes are intact*, she reflected, trying to be positive. Anna's toes poked out from beneath the blanket. Toes were good; if there was anything encouraging in this world, it had to be toes.

Hrafn sat on the floor and leaned back against the wall. Vigdís sat beside him. Every now and then, she took a swig from the bottle, and almost passed it to Hrafn but didn't, playing along with his game.

'What happened to your face?' she asked.

'What do you mean?'

'It's grubby.'

He wiped his chin and examined the soot on his fingers.

'I don't know . . . Sand?'

'Is my face grubby?'

He inspected her face and shook his head.

'In that case it can't be sand.'

A thud came from the floor above. Vigdís gazed up at the ceiling and then at Hrafn. They sat motionless, listening out for further noises, but heard none. The thud had come from the far end of the house, above the kitchen.

'The old people,' said Vigdís.

She had forgotten all about Ása, and felt a flash of anger, her fists clenching as she remembered the old woman running upstairs. Ása knew something they didn't, and had done right from the start; she knew precisely what was going on and yet she said nothing.

They left Anna asleep in the front room and went upstairs, each carrying a candle.

'Let's talk to them,' said Vigdís, heading straight for the

door at the end of the passageway where the noise had come from. Hrafn tried to protest, she didn't know why, as she opened the door on to a gloomy, dank room full of books.

'Do you think they're hiding?' she whispered, aware of Hrafn entering behind her as she raised her candle and stepped gingerly into the room. She paced the length of the bookshelves, glancing about, up at the ceiling and into the corners of the room, but saw no one. Examining the photographs on the walls and the desk, she soon found the black-and-white family portrait Anna had mentioned: two grown-ups and two children sitting in front of them. One of the children resembled the old man, and the other was a young girl, but the image was faded and she had difficulty making out her face.

'*Of course*,' Vigdís hissed, realizing in a flash where they were hiding: in the secret room Anna had told her about.

'I give up!' she shouted, and moved into the middle of the floor, adding that she knew about the room, and that they were hiding.

'We aren't angry with you, we're scared! We simply want you to tell us what's going on!'

She went on to assure them that the coast was clear and the door downstairs was bolted, adding that they would be grateful for some help with their friend, who was injured.

A window on one of the walls reflected two minuscule candle flames, and behind them the dark outlines of her and Hrafn. They stood motionless, and Vigdís listened out for any sound the old people might make but heard nothing. She wondered about the significance of their going into hiding. As far as she could tell, only two or possibly three of the walls could conceal a secret room. She told Hrafn her plan, walked over to the nearest bookcase and started to pull out the books. A moment later Hrafn did the same. They made their way along the shelves, sweeping their entire contents onto the floor, and attempting without success to dislodge the bookcases, which were securely bolted to the wall. Then they tried to smash or kick them down, and Vigdís overturned the freestanding ones at the centre of the room, before falling breathless to her knees. She had a sudden impression of being completely drunk, which soon passed.

Action, she thought, gasping for breath. All the shelves were empty, and there was no sign of a secret room.

'That's enough,' she said, thinking she heard Anna downstairs then realizing she must be mistaken. For Anna was like nature itself: blind, deaf and dumb.

They left the room, closed the door behind them, and wedged a candlestick above the handle so that they would hear if the door was opened from the inside. Before going downstairs they checked the bathroom and bedrooms but saw nothing there either.

Anna remained prone on the sofa. Vigdís felt her pulse and considered doing something to her before they left (anything was better than to live like that), but she hadn't enough cruelty in her. Or kindness.

She sipped from the bottle, and a warm sensation spread

over her chest and down her arms – even the tip of her nose felt good. She sat down on the floor next to Hrafn.

'Egill is still alive,' he said, contemplating the map they had found inside the bone.

'It's a trap,' said Vigdís. 'We were meant to find this map.'

'I don't care . . . If Egill is responsible for this,' he gestured with his head towards Anna, 'all the more reason to find him. I'll go on my own, if you like.'

She pressed up against him, and had the impression that he was so afraid he was barely able to speak.

'We'll go together,' she said, sensing that Hrafn was right; all they could do was to find Egill, save him, or cut off his fingers and stick needles in his eyes. Or shoot him.

She stood up to fetch the gun.

31

BEAUTY

Vigdís

By the time it grew light in the living room Vigdís still hadn't fallen asleep, despite all the alcohol she had drunk. And yet she was calmer than might be expected. Hrafn dozed off for half an hour without realizing it. They'd heard no sound from the old people.

The sky was cloudless and there was no wind, for the time being at least. The sands lay motionless and black as far as the eye could see. Anna murmured, and had another seizure, and Vigdís administered more codeine. They left written instructions for the old woman about dosages and how to care for Anna while they were gone, adding that they would hold her responsible if anything went wrong.

'They had better crawl out of their hiding place once we've gone,' said Vigdís, leaving the note standing in the kitchen.

Hrafn slid the bolts back and opened the front door. They put on their rucksacks and descended the steps together, closing but not locking the door behind them, in case they needed to turn back for something.

The sun was rising fast in the sky and seemed to bear down on them while at the same time appearing very far away.

Hrafn had tucked the gun into the waistband of his trousers, underneath his shirt. He told her that when he was twenty, living in voluntary exile in Suðurnes, he'd spent his days working for his father's company, practising at a shooting range outside Grindavík and taking potshots at seagulls on the beach.

They fell silent and Vigdís tried to clear her head, not in order to analyse their situation, or to plan. She had done too much of that in her life. She should have left more things to chance. What was she afraid of? In death everything happened automatically, like when as a child she somersaulted over the handlebars of her bike, rising slowly up into the air, and gazing down at the blue sky, marvelling at the calm; or rolling over in a car when she was a teenager, seeing the sky spin in slow motion outside the window, and then finding herself on all fours at the side of the road.

Pain came later. But in death there was no later, no pain, and no choice; the body went numb, squeezing out the mind, or the soul, or whatever it was, and in the rear-view mirror, our life (all our different bodily needs and desires) became like a hitchhiker you sped past in the rain, who aroused in you a sense of shame, pity, remorse even, only to be forgotten.

She heard the river up ahead, and they arrived at the bridge, which no longer hung into the ravine but was stretched across it, fastened to the posts on either side. She asked Hrafn whether he had been over it the day before, and he said he hadn't.

They crossed one at a time, Hrafn first. When he had reached the other side Vigdís set off; she felt the bridge give beneath her feet, and took care not to look down into the roaring water, which had risen even higher, and at that moment she knew the answer to the question she had tried asking herself a moment ago: *No*, she didn't wish to die, there were too many things she hadn't done. She wanted a child, for example; her eyes grew moist at the thought.

She stepped off the bridge. Either side of it stood a pair of charred iron drums, in which, judging from the smell, oil had been burning during the night. They walked up the hill by the ravine, which overlooked the village, and took turns with the binoculars. Vigdís pointed them at the huts, and at the building in the centre of the village marked with an 'X' on the map, but saw nothing suspicious. Hrafn took out the gun, and ran his fingers over it with the expression of someone conjuring a genie from a magic lamp. The barrel was long and smooth. He flipped the safety catch and spun the cylinder a few times, pulled the hammer back then released it again.

At the foot of the hill was the door Vigdís had found while Hrafn and Egill were in the village, only this time it was open. A broad, paved path sloped into the earth. Vigdís called down the passageway, then turned on her heel and followed Hrafn into the village. They agreed not to lose sight of each other.

As they passed one of the huts, Hrafn came to a halt, raising his hand to signal her to stop.

'What?' whispered Vigdís, but he gave no reply and kept staring at the hut. The paintwork on the outside was flaking. The silence was so intense, the air so bright and pristine, that for a moment Vigdís had the impression the whole world was transparent.

'What?' she repeated. 'Did you hear something?'

Hrafn remained motionless for a while, eyes fixed on the hut, then he lowered his hand with an exaggerated gesture that made her think for a moment that he was play-acting.

'In the hut,' he whispered. 'A thud, like something hitting a wall.'

'Are you sure?'

'The door's open . . . It was shut the last time I was here.'

She glanced at the hut, and was about to protest – convinced that the door was shut, but to her surprise she saw that he was right, it was wide open. For some reason she remembered the little potting shed in her mother's garden.

They edged towards the door. Hrafn clasped the butt of the gun, hugging the wall, before peering inside. Vigdís followed him silently into the hut. They found themselves in a central corridor with eight or nine rooms opening off it. The one closest to them looked like a kitchen, with a sink, cupboards and a dining table.

Hrafn entered the kitchen, holding the gun as if he was going to shoot off his penis. Vigdís stifled a giggle, clasping her hand over her mouth, and backed out into the corridor.

There were more rooms than she'd expected. Moving one foot in front of the other, she inched her way along the corridor, even though she knew this was foolish.

To the very end.

All the windows had the curtains drawn across, but enough light filtered through them for her to make out the furniture: a single bed, bedside table and wardrobe.

Before she reached them, she could see that the doors to the end two rooms were closed, and she knew instantly that they weren't alone in there. She glanced over her shoulder, along the corridor, but couldn't see Hrafn. Pausing in front of one of the doors, she grasped the handle and opened it. The curtains were drawn and the room was empty.

Then she swung round, walked over to the other door and opened it onto a white room, ablaze with sunlight. In the centre of it a reindeer stood gazing at her with meek, round eyes. On its crown were two red circles where its antlers had been ripped out; blood was spurting swiftly and rhythmically out of its head and trickling down the walls, and yet the animal didn't move. Its fur was golden in the sunlight, and the beauty in the room was so poignant and cruel that Vigdís felt something give way inside her, she couldn't bear it any longer. She watched the animal slowly turn pale, merging with the brightness, before sinking to its knees and finally lying down on its side on the floor.

32

SACCADES

Hrafn

On the table in the kitchen was a camping stove with a grimy pot on top of it. Hrafn picked up the pot and saw that it had score marks around the rim, and the bottom was gouged out.

Soon afterwards, he heard a screech coming from deeper inside the hut. He poked his head out of the kitchen and saw Vigdís standing at the far end of the corridor, hands by her sides, gazing into one of the rooms.

'Vigdís . . . ?' he said, moving towards her.

Her expression was oddly vacant, and she didn't look at him as she continued staring into the room. The screech seemed to come from between her clenched teeth.

Hrafn heard a rustle behind him, like feet running across the sands, and he saw something shoot past the door of the hut. He raised the gun, and ran outside in time to see it disappear round the corner. He shouted out what was intended to be both an order to stop and a warning to Vigdís to be careful. Flipping the safety off, he sprinted round the corner. He gave chase between the other huts in the direction of the ravine, and occasionally caught sight of what he was following: a small person with short legs, and arms that dangled grotesquely from its shoulders. Although it appeared to be running fast, this could easily have been an illusion caused by the strange jerking and lurching movements, which also made it difficult for Hrafn to be sure which direction it was going in, or what shape it was. His eyes moved ceaselessly as he tried to pinpoint the creature (he quickly decided it probably wasn't human), and yet when he looked straight at it, he had the disconcerting impression that he was seeing it out of the corner of his eye. The only thing he was somehow sure of was that it had thick white tresses that fell like a mane down its back, and its body was covered in fine red hairs.

The creature disappeared behind the large warehouse close to the ravine. Hrafn ran round the corner and found himself looking at the bridge, where he saw it scramble up one of the posts and unfasten the rope. Hrafn gave a roar, levelled the gun and fired. The blast was so loud that it deafened him. He ran in silence towards the bridge and saw the creature bolt across it. Two of the ropes were loose. As he fastened them, he saw that the creature had almost reached the far side, where it would have nowhere to hide. It looked different somehow, as if it had shrunk. He tucked the pistol into his waistband, clutched the guide ropes with both hands and ran across the bridge. The creature paused, then moved off again the moment Hrafn drew near.

After a brief pursuit across the sands, the creature stopped, turned around, and sat down on its haunches.

Hrafn also came to a halt, caught his breath, and saw what it was he had been chasing. A fox, one of the two that had made their home at the farm.

He raised the gun once more, aiming it straight at the tiny, rust-coloured head. Nudging the safety off, he caressed the trigger with his forefinger, and in his mind's eye saw the creature's brains spatter across the sand, congealing in the heat, gluing together a few grains of sand that would otherwise have remained separated for eternity, its death a meaningless addition to Europe's biggest wilderness.

The fox stared at him blankly, ears pricked above its black eyes, and as he lowered the gun Hrafn let out a long, resounding laugh that he himself couldn't hear. When he looked up again the creature had vanished.

He turned around and saw Vigdís on the far side of the ravine. She was standing in front of the wooden posts, and everything was different. The bridge no longer spanned the ravine, but plunged vertically into it on his side. Vigdís shouted and waved to him, and Hrafn waved back. His hearing had returned.

The bridge was still attached to the posts on his side, but had clearly been unfastened on the other side. It occurred to him simultaneously that he could jump into the river and try to swim across, throw the gun to Vigdís, or press it to his forehead and pull the trigger. He shouted back to her, but the roar drowned out his voice, and so he waved his arms exaggeratedly upstream before setting off along the edge of the ravine. Vigdís waved her hand once briefly above her head, as if to say she had understood, and set off herself along the other side. Hrafn wanted to run, but held back; if he got too tired he wouldn't be able to aim the gun straight. Occasionally he looked ahead, but most of the time he kept his eyes fixed on the far bank, in case Vigdís got into difficulties.

The sun continued to rise in the sky and soon it was so bright he could scarcely see across the ravine, and the sweat made his eyes sting. He had once read in *Living Science* that even when the eye is apparently still, it moves three times per second in order to pinpoint objects more accurately, the way someone in a dark corridor might wave a torch around in order to see better. These movements were called *saccades*, and in the moment they occurred everything 'went dark' for between twenty and two hundred milliseconds while the brain tried to 'gloss over' this gap in perception, interweaving casual bits of information into that spool of images we perceive as reality. But it didn't always work, and occasionally time seemed to 'freeze', as if life slowed for a moment, or even stood still:

When the person known as X takes his or her eye off the page and looks at the clock, he or she has the impression that the second hand pauses for a while before moving again. The reason for this is 'saccades'. In order to compensate for the temporary blindness caused by these saccades, the brain 'guesses' at what it sees, based on what it has already seen: the eye stops seeing for approximately one tenth of a second while the saccades take place, during which time the brain produces an image of what was there before.

If the saccades occurred when the second hand was

moving, one second would last approximately 10 per cent longer – or so it would seem – and consequently about a third of everything we saw with our eyes was guesswork, sometimes real and sometimes not.

But, now that he thought about it, the most important thing in Hrafn's view wasn't the apparently inherent imprecision in the workings of the brain, but rather the fact that people should be able to notice a detail so trivial as a second being a few milliseconds longer or shorter than it should be. What was this higher power of perception, seemingly so intrinsic to the brain's functioning and yet outside it? The brain received information from our senses, but wasn't 'taken in', knowing instantly when something was amiss, when the result contradicted our past repeated experiences stored up over time: for example thirty-five years' experience of how long a second lasted.

What did this mean? That in some ways the brain was able to perceive itself, and so, besides sight, hearing, taste, smell and touch, we had a sixth sense? But what might that be? Well, what else but *intuition*, wordless and unsubstantiated, but which nevertheless scrupulously encompassed our entire experience, the past workings of our brain, and compared them to the present ones? What other tricks might our intuition play on us? Did it have any limits? If so, what were they? And what about the past? Could it know anything about *the past*?

He laughed and quickened his pace. They came to the bend in the ravine, where Hrafn saw that the river had risen above the drainage tunnel, as if it had never existed.

The ground started to slope up towards the barrage. He lost sight of Vigdís for a few seconds as he climbed, but then she reappeared and waved. A crack ran down the middle of the barrage, like a drawing of a lightning bolt; the wall itself was coated in sand, and beneath it Hrafn glimpsed a large area where the outer layer had broken away. On the far side of the ravine a winding track led up to the barrage, doubtless the same one they had seen from the village.

The closer they got to the barrage, the further they were from each other, until finally Hrafn reached the top, where he lost sight of Vigdís again. He ran the last stretch towards the road that crossed the barrage. Above it, instead of a reservoir, there was a vast labyrinth of dried clay and mud, stretching as far as the eye could see. The clay reached halfway up the wall, and was riven with fissures, faults and crevasses, the biggest of which lay towards the centre where the river ran along the bottom. The edge of the crevasse was lined with huge blocks of clay, towering edifices, some of which jutted out over the river and looked as if they might collapse at any moment.

Hrafn half-ran half-walked along the top of the barrage until he reached the wire fence shutting it off in the middle, which he had put out of his mind. He hurled himself against the fence, and shook it, but it wouldn't budge. The mesh was tightly woven and extended out on metal pipes either side of the barrage. A roll of barbed wire ran along the top of the fence, and the bottom was bolted to the floor.

Vigdís appeared at the other end of the path and

approached the fence. Hrafn seized the gun and aimed it at the wire mesh; with any luck he might be able to shoot a hole in it – big enough for their heads to pass through, but that would be too small. He could take his shoes off and scale it, but the roll of barbed wire was too thick and high for him to heave himself over. He tugged harder on the fence, rocking back and forth until Vigdís reached him. They clasped fingers.

'We're together, my love. We'll find a way out of this,' he said, and they kissed through the fence. She tried to speak but couldn't, and wept as she pressed herself up against the wire. He had never seen her cry like that before. He said something reassuring and she nodded.

'I'm coming over to you,' he said, pulling away. 'Wait there . . . I'll be back. Don't move, my love.'

He made his way back across the barrage, but turned round instantly, held up the gun and told Vigdís she should keep it for her protection. He tried to slip it under the wire, but only the muzzle would go through. Then he took off his pullover, wrapped it round the gun and threw it over the fence, explaining how to flip the safety off and that she should clasp the butt with both hands to take aim.

'I love you,' she said, and her face started to droop, her mouth contorting, until he could no longer bear to look at her. He ran towards the house at the far end of the barrage, where he hoped he might find a tool, an iron bar perhaps, with which to tear through the fence. A stone path led up to the house, which was box-shaped, grey and windowless. Around it lay slabs of stone. The door was locked.

On the reservoir side, built into the barrage itself, Hrafn noticed another door with a sign saying *Staff Only.* He walked over, grasped the handle and opened the door. He was met by a wave of heat and a metallic odour, like engine oil or paraffin. In the light seeping through the doorway he made out a long passageway, painted white, which disappeared into the darkness.

He slipped off his rucksack, took out the emergency flares and read the instructions, then edged forward until he could no longer see in front of him. He reckoned each flare should last a few minutes, and with any luck the passageway would lead straight through the barrage to an identical grey door on the far side. He loosened the wire on one of the flares, pulled the cord and held it away from his face. The passageway was illuminated by a bright red flame and sparks, which stung the back of his hand. As he hurried along the passageway Hrafn saw mice skitter across the floor – tiny, squeaking field mice that disappeared into the walls, even though he could see no holes. Soon he came to a sharp bend, and a steep staircase leading deeper into the barrage. He clasped the rail on the wall with his free hand, raising the flare with the other as he ran down the steps. The passage opened out into a large room where he dimly made out water tanks and thick pipes running down the walls. Hrafn managed to get his bearings, and followed the right-hand wall as far as the corner, then the next wall leading to a door into another large room.

Once inside, he noticed a third door facing in the right direction, and which might lead to another staircase like the ones he had just descended. He walked diagonally across the floor, stopping halfway between two waist-high tanks. A deep silence reigned inside the room. He looked up, but couldn't see the ceiling. The water in the tanks was still and dark, and it occurred to him that they reached all the way down into the barrage, possibly as far as the tunnel where the river flowed under the bridge.

The light from the flare began to dim, but to Hrafn it seemed more like the darkness was closing in around him rather than the flame burning out. The walls had vanished, and he could scarcely see the outlines of the tanks closest to him. He pulled another flare out of his waistband, glancing at the door leading to the staircase and to Vigdís. He thought he heard the sound of footsteps and a door slamming somewhere above. Then came a shout, or perhaps it was more like a *scream*. Hrafn suddenly felt himself go cold, and almost immediately he heard another scream, louder than the first, followed by a short, sharp explosion as from a gun. After that, everything went quiet.

33

Hrafn

The flame had gone out and Hrafn was no longer holding anything. His arms hung by his sides, his heart was pounding, and red and white spots swam before his eyes. He felt as if he couldn't get his breath properly, and he screwed up his eyes, even though he could see nothing in the darkness.

He crouched, inhaling great gulps of air as he fumbled around on the ground, crying out softly as he grasped the burnt-out flare, which was still hot. He flung it away from him.

Someone entered the room. Hrafn clasped his hand firmly over his mouth in order not to give himself away, and stared motionless into the darkness in the direction of the door. He heard a faint rustle, like bare feet dragging slowly across the floor. Then it stopped.

No sound came from the darkness, but Hrafn knew that he wasn't alone; close to him someone was standing, motionless, listening like him. He cautiously felt the floor with his free hand, closed his eyes and heard a splash from one of the tanks, as if the water had been disturbed. He no longer knew which direction he was facing, and was becoming confused about what was up and what was down, when he felt something touch his palm.

He leapt to his feet, held the flare away from his face and pulled the cord. A red light filled the room. The walls and ceiling blazed, the pipes slithered down the walls, and the water in the tanks shimmered like a sunset. Shielding his eyes from the flare, Hrafn glanced around the room but saw no one. On the floor in front of him was a pool of water, and the surface of one of the tanks rippled slightly, as if something had dived into or crawled out of it.

Wet tracks led from the pool to one of the doors. He followed them, as though in a trance, and came to yet another large room, similar to the first two, which meant that either there were three rooms, or he was heading back the way he had come. The tracks crossed the floor diagonally, and Hrafn followed them, calling out Vigdís's name. Tiny red eyes glinted in the darkness. Mice. He reached the door, behind which was a flight of steps, leading down, not up. He hurriedly descended them, thought he heard Vigdís sobbing ahead of him, and quickened his pace until he came to a long passageway with pipes snaking along the walls. As he ran, he saw them zooming past out of the corner of his eye, rising and falling, separating and merging again.

The passageway ended in a room, smaller than the ones higher up in the barrage, and the heat inside it was stifling. In the centre of the room was a tank, and over by one wall, rising through the ceiling, a contraption resembling a church organ hummed. In front of it were three cone-shaped mounds level with his chest. They were made out of bones and hollow at the front, like the pyramid in the village where he and Egill found the photograph of Vigdís. Scattered on the floor were more bones, dry and brittle, which crumbled beneath his feet.

Once again the light from the flare started to dim. Hrafn walked over to one of the mounds and saw that the bones were glued together with some sort of liquid or slime. In the first mound was a tool that looked like a pair of wire-cutters, and some of Anna's jewellery and clothes, which were in tatters. A bloody trail emerged from the second mound, as if something had slid, or been dragged, across the floor. In the third a figure sat cross-legged with its back to him, but the bones obscured its head.

'Vigdís,' he whispered, kneeling beside the mound. 'Is that you?'

Darkness descended as the flare went out. He waited for an answer, reached out and felt his hand plunge into water, almost as if he were being dragged. The water was acrid and thick like saliva. He sank slowly deeper until the slime covered his face and he started to fight back, digging his heels into the ground, and flailing about. Then he heard a crack from one of the mounds as the bones toppled onto the floor, and whatever had been inside it shot past him.

He grabbed the last flare, and pulled the cord just in time to see something disappear into the tank in the centre of the room. He ran over to the tank. Bloody fingers and teeth lay strewn around it on the floor. The inside of the tank was empty except for a ladder. Hrafn put the flare in his mouth, holding it between his teeth as he climbed down the ladder into a narrow pipe. The walls were made of iron and there was just enough room for him to walk upright. In one direction the pipe climbed steeply towards the barrage, in the other it sloped gently downwards, and from there he could hear the thud of footsteps running away. Hrafn gave chase, sprinting down the pipe until he reached a place where several pipes converged into one and the floor became level, meaning that the hills were now behind him. The iron pipe disappeared, giving way to black, glistening rock. Hrafn lost his footing on the slippery surface, and it dawned on him that whatever he was chasing had no light to guide it between those walls.

The tunnel split in two. The one on the right sloped downwards and was filled with water. He couldn't see what colour the water was, but assumed it came from the river, and that this was the tunnel into which Egill and Anna had disappeared. Around the opening was a thick steel frame, and he glimpsed a hatch, probably for regulating the flow of water from the reservoir.

He didn't feel afraid. In less than a minute the flare would be extinguished, and then he would see nothing, although he would doubtless get used to it – like one long, dark *saccade*! He hurried along the tunnel, and soon he sensed a movement close to him; something pressed itself against the wall before disappearing into it. Hrafn lifted the flare and saw another side tunnel, also with a steel frame and a hatch, which at that very moment was closing over the hole. He tried to seize the hatch, but it was too late, the tunnel closed, and soon afterwards the flare went out.

He stared ahead into the darkness, but all he could see was Vigdís's pale, expressionless face as she vanished into the tunnel. No paw over her mouth, no gun to her head. Just her. *Alone.*

34

WHO STUFFED A SHEEP UP THE CHIMNEY?

Hrafn

He sensed the weight of the rocks around him, the deep silence that wasn't calm but hissed in his head. Suddenly, he realized that they had never finished the game they started in the car, just before the accident: I spy with my little eye. No one ever knew what Anna had spied. In any case, according to the rules, Skimmi Stokkur, the little man who lived in the rocks near the student residence, didn't count because he was invisible. And neither did they! They no longer counted in the material world; they were stuck in a kind of limbo between life and death, unable to find their way in either direction.

Hrafn forced himself to keep going, feeling the ground with his feet, arms outstretched to avoid bumping into the wall. And he came to an abrupt halt, stepping resolutely into the centre of the tunnel where the darkness was thickest, determined to walk upright, back straight, instead of groping his way forward like an insect. This was what had always set him apart from others. He never let his surroundings get the better of him; he had a strong sense of who he was, of self-respect: *self-control*.

Presently, he had the impression that the darkness either side of him was becoming more impenetrable; the tunnel opened out, branching into other tunnels that plunged into the earth or up to the surface, shrank to nothing or opened out into vaulted domes. He couldn't care less where he ended up: back at the barrage, popping out of the old man's nose, or a toilet in Egilsstaðir. Hrafn thought about the Minotaur, and about the drill that had bored these tunnels, the diamond tips turning in one direction on the end of a steel probe that turned in the other, spinning in frantic circles like a wounded animal, burrowing through the rock. He imagined himself calmly operating the machinery from a tiny cockpit, pushing buttons, pulling levers, watching on a screen as the rock face crumbled relentlessly beneath the glowing diamonds, driving through the earth, creating a void where people could lose themselves, round and round, until it imploded in the middle.

After walking for a long time in the dark, Hrafn felt the air stir; a fresh breeze was wafting towards him from one of the side tunnels, and the floor become smooth then started to slope upwards.

He made his way to the surface and gradually it grew light. When his eyes had become accustomed to the glare, he stepped out onto the sand at the foot of the hills from which they had first spotted the barrage. In the distance, he could see the cowshed and the barn, and beyond them the house.

As he made his way towards the house, he was no longer sure about anything that had happened: he imagined Vigdís still waiting for him by the fence on the barrage, or even better: letting herself be lured inside, struggling as a hairy paw covered her face, forcing her into submission. Who?

Who put the photograph in the mound, stuffed a sheep up the chimney, cut their own fingers off in the barrage, drove a car into a house?

He started to run slowly, and the closer he got the more he felt as if something were pulling him along, that he could run as fast and as far as he wished. He leapt into the air wielding an invisible axe, buried it in someone's temple, stepping sideways to muddle his tracks, leapt brandishing the axe so it came down on his enemy's head, cleaving it asunder; then all at once he paused, watching the axe slice through the head and body before plunging into the ground, where he left it.

The old couple were standing in front of the barn, as if they had been expecting him. The man was grinning like a halfwit, but the old woman's face was expressionless. Hrafn walked up to her, shaking his finger in her face, and told her he would hold them responsible for anything that might happen to Vigdís, whom he referred to as 'my wife'.

He laughed as he turned to the old man:

'As for you, smiley face, where's your wife?' he demanded, remembering Anna and Vigdís's theory about incest. 'Who was in the secret room in the study? Where is the child?'

They didn't reply. Hrafn told them he knew how to

make them talk. He strode over to the silver-grey barrel containing the moonshine and tipped it over. The spigot snapped off, and the clear liquid flowed out of the barn door where the old woman was standing. The old man had disappeared.

'No more smiley face!' said Hrafn, and saw the old woman cast a sidelong glance towards the cowshed.

'Has he gone to hide in the stalls with the invisible cows?'

The old woman remained silent, and Hrafn seized her by the shoulder, dragged her over to the pool of liquid and stood her in the middle of it. Then he took out his lighter and lit a cigarette.

'What have you done?' whispered the old woman, who didn't seem afraid of him. 'Where are your friends?'

'I'm the one asking the questions,' he told her, and she shook her head. *'Don't shake your head at me!'* he yelled, waving his cigarette at her. He demanded to know about the barrage, the village, Vigdís and Egill, and what had befallen Anna, heard himself ask all those questions, and felt as if he was getting closer to the heart of the matter, although he wasn't sure how. 'We're not alone up here, are we? Who else is out there?'

'There's nothing out there,' said the old woman, and carried on shaking her head. 'It's here.'

She reached out her hand, placing her palm against Hrafn's chest and patting it gently. Hrafn seized her wrist, twisting her to the ground.

'Look at the photograph,' she said, without moving from the pool.

The liquid had stopped flowing out of the barrel and yet the pool was getting bigger.

'What photograph?'

'The one in your pocket. Of your wife.'

Hrafn reached into his back pocket and pulled out the photograph of Vigdís. Rising from her head were two faint lines that seemed to grow thicker and whiter by the minute and resembled animal horns. Her face had changed too; her eyes were open, but only the whites were showing, and her mouth gaped as she tore bright red strips of skin from her breasts.

'What is this?' he asked, tearing his eyes from the photograph. 'What are you doing to her?'

'We've done nothing,' said the woman, and her smile broadened as if she could sense his uncertainty.

He crouched over her, took a drag on his cigarette and blew the smoke in her face.

'I'm going to set fire to you. What do you say to that, you old witch? Then I'll set fire to your old man, the hay and the house. There'll be nothing left, no sign of anyone having been here.'

Hrafn looked up and saw the old man emerge from the cowshed. He was clutching a long, sharp scythe. His smile had disappeared, and the rash on his face formed a triangle from the bridge of his nose to the corners of his mouth, the flesh beneath glistening pink as if the skin had started to peel away.

'And what have we here?' said Hrafn, standing up

straight. 'You found your scythe and you're off to reap? Where's your field?'

The old man swung the scythe with short, sharp movements. He took a step closer, and swung it again, releasing his grip from the middle of the pole and holding the end of it so that the scythe almost touched the back of Hrafn's head, grazing his neck as it swung the other way.

Hrafn flicked the ash from his cigarette and tossed it into the pool where the old woman was sitting. He wheeled round, heard an explosion like a sheet flapping in the wind, and ran away from the barn, feeling the heat on his back, as the old woman started wailing.

'Are you angry about something, old man?' he shouted over his shoulder, laughing at the old man, who was tottering after him, rather slowly, still wielding the scythe.

When Hrafn was halfway to the house he paused, hearing the crackle of burning timber from the barn as the flames licked through the doors. Close by he saw the streetlamp and beneath it three holes in the sand, long and deep as graves.

The old woman's cries fell silent, and were succeeded by the high-pitched yelp of foxes flowing out of the barn, no longer just two, but a whole horde, hundreds or thousands of the creatures. They spread across the sand like a dark-red flame, past the old man, and round the corner of the house just as Hrafn ran into the yard. They nipped at his ankles, leapt yelping on to his back, digging in their claws, crawled up onto his shoulders, and sank their sharp little teeth deep into his flesh. He fell to his knees, and crawled on all fours up the steps to the house. Blood spurted from his neck and face, and trickled down the steps. He dragged himself the rest of the way, opened the front door a crack, and forced himself through before closing it behind him.

35
DIMENSIONS IN THIS WORLD

Hrafn

He leaned his back against the door, catching his breath, fumbled in his pockets for a cigarette, and lit one.

'Anna,' he cried. 'I'm home!'

He raised his arm and slid one of the bolts across.

There was a thud on the door as the scythe pierced the wood, narrowly missing his head. Hrafn rolled away from the door, stood up and discovered that not only was the floor covered in blood, but it was also dripping from the ceiling and streaming down the walls. The scythe appeared like a long, sharp beak, in and out, in and out, and sporadic yelps came from behind the door.

He penetrated deeper into the house and saw Anna sprawled on the floor in the kitchen. She seemed to sense his movement when he stepped into the room, and she curled up in a ball.

He slumped onto a chair and sighed, rubbing his face with his hands to try to rid himself of the exhaustion overwhelming him.

'I'm going to give you some tablets, Anna dear. To stop

the pain,' he said, no longer recognizing his own voice. 'Then I'm going to fetch some wire cutters for the fence. Vigdís is at the barrage. I'm afraid it's too late, I don't believe this any more . . . It's all gone, dear Anna. Yet there never was anything, and now it's gone . . . Nothing's gone.'

He dropped his cigarette on the floor and crushed it underfoot.

There are dimensions in this world that we cannot see.

He stamped his foot on the floor a few times, causing Anna to curl up even tighter.

'I don't know, Anna . . . Have you heard the story about Jonas Whalesnatch? One day, some men were walking along the shore in the Westfjords when they came across an enormous beached whale. They all clambered on top of the animal, when a man called Jonas suddenly disappeared inside it until only his head and shoulders were sticking out. He had stepped straight into the whale's snatch, and it was all the others could do to pull him out again. From that day on, he was known to everyone as Jonas Whalesnatch.'

Hrafn stood up, closed the kitchen door, walked over to the window and looked out at the shining white landscape. He had never had any real knowledge of himself, only that he was alone. They all were. They saw themselves in everything, and yet found themselves in nothing.

The photograph Vigdís had knocked off the wall lay on the windowsill, together with a few shards of glass and a broken picture frame. The woman in the photograph was beautiful, but her eyes were dull. She feared the man next to her, but compensated for it with shopping trips to New York and London, babysitters, friends and an occasional love affair; too fragile to care for anyone but herself, she was still a teenager, her face a mask that concealed nothing. And the old man was a crazed rat who dragged around his pus-filled scrotum, and required nothing from society save a bullet in the head.

His parents.

They were to blame, for all of it. Others were to blame.

He stooped over Anna, lifted her writhing to her feet and laid her on the kitchen table. She lashed out with her stumps, and the gauze on her hands started to come undone. He fetched the tablets, ground some into a powder and told her to stop struggling, although he doubted she could hear anything. He tied her hands behind her back with some strips of her T-shirt, forcing her jaw closed until she had swallowed the powder, and afterwards her mouth opened so wide he could see into her throat. After she had calmed down and her muscles relaxed, he examined her bloody stumps: her fingers had been cut off with clean, precise incisions. He stroked her warm, moist belly, running his fingers gently over her wounds, which were more swollen and bruised than before, and sensed how she at once welcomed and recoiled from his touch. Her body was moist and open, every last pore gaping like a tiny mouth, her breath came in short gasps, and she gave off a thick, warm odour, of mud and blood. He stroked her breasts, gazing down at her crotch and the mound of downy blonde hair, and felt her respond to his caresses as she came out in goosebumps, lifting slightly off the table then arching her back abruptly, as though convulsing.

Outside the house, the yelping had become a deafening babble. The kitchen walls were turning red, as blood started to stream down them, oozing out of the pot on the stove. Casting about for a better place to hide, Hrafn saw a door in the wall that he hadn't noticed before. He opened it, and found himself confronted by a narrow staircase leading to the cellar. The stairs were steep, with lots of shallow steps – either that or the staircase was longer than it appeared. He lit a candle stub he found in the kitchen and made his way gingerly down the staircase.

At the bottom was a corridor running the length of the house. On either side were rooms, and at the far end a door, exactly the same as on the top floor. The first room was filled with crumbling cardboard boxes that spilled their contents onto the floor: photographs of carcasses strewn across the sand, a two-headed calf, a tethered sheep eating its own entrails, a fox with a shaved torso and a bird strapped to its head. In the next room, bright red and green plants gave off a sickly smell like rotting fruit, and perched on their fronds were birds with huge beaks and tiny slits for eyes. The room reverberated with a sound like people cheering at a match or rain pounding on a rooftop.

Hrafn was no longer sure where he was. A few planks of wood, mouldering in the dank cellar, were nailed clumsily across the door at the far end of the corridor. A rhythmical drone reached him from within. Stretching out his hand, he began to tear away the planks, felt them crumble between his fingers, and opened the door. The draught that blew back into the room snuffed out his candle and the droning stopped.

He peered into the dark interior, where someone lay on a bed. The curtains were drawn across the windows, and through them he glimpsed the courtyard at Hraunbær where he could hear the creak of the swing. Daylight tried to penetrate the room but couldn't, because it was too far away. A thick, acrid smell pervaded the room, and in the gloom a red ember glowed, as from a cigarette. Someone murmured something, and then the door closed behind him. Next to the wall, a lamp went on, revealing the figure of a man who sat up in bed, and started to speak in strange, hushed tones. His eyes were two slits in an oversized head swivelling on his shoulders, his curly black hair rose like smoke into the air, his body was withered and his skin sagged so that the flesh beneath showed.

Hrafn turned towards the door and pulled the handle, but the door was locked from the outside. His body was starting to feel numb and heavy, and something inside him snapped; he felt the tears streaming down his cheeks and heard himself call out for help, for his mother, saying he wanted to go home, but he couldn't move, and felt the void inside him grow bigger until it swallowed everything. He was floating in the air, looking down on the shadow moving over him, as though looking down on a tiny house from a rain cloud; he could hear the rain beating on the roof and saw it sparkle as it fell through the darkness. After that there was nothing to say – or at least he didn't know how to say it.

Later he was at home in Selás. He lay in bed gazing out of the window at a tree he had never noticed before. The branches were black and shiny.

His dad walked through the door; he was angry and started to scold him. They went into the bathroom, where his dad washed off the blood running down his legs. Afterwards they talked about what had happened, his dad dressed him in his pyjamas and he got back into bed. The light made the room blindingly white. His dad sat on the floor at the edge of his bed and wept. Hrafn looked away from him at the tree outside the window. Its branches swayed back and forth in the wind, faster and faster until everything went dark and was obliterated.

NATURE

36

Vigdís

First there was darkness, and then a line appeared separating the sky from the earth, a dark grey band that slowly pulled apart. The wind dropped, the grains of sand settled close to one another, and for a while the earth seemed to take on a darker hue. At the same time, a deep silence descended over the world, not of tense expectation, but more like what lingers after a door has been slammed so hard the room shakes. Listening closely, one could hear a murmur or drone amid the silence, something so insistent and heavy with despair that matter seemed unable to contain it, and the senses furled out towards the edges, where it flowed like a raging river over the rock of the world.

Her face was the first thing to emerge, shiny and dirty, as if she were peering through a hole in the darkness. The rest of her body followed, moving jerkily across the sand, as though it were a question of chance whether her feet went in the same direction. She didn't look down, but instead stared straight ahead to where the outline of the glacier touched the sky. The summit glowed, although the earth below remained in darkness, and she reached out her hand as though wanting to caress it.

There was a flapping sound in the air, and a pair of swans flew overhead, craning their necks and beating their wings before disappearing into the glacier. The world was flat and smooth, swamp-like, but still she went on walking. She couldn't remember when she had got undressed. A pair of white antlers sprouted from her head, branching gracefully, meekly, into the air, looking as if they'd been polished. She couldn't remember when she had got undressed.

The sun floated across the sky and Vigdís followed. When she stepped on the ground a fine, shimmering dust swirled up into the air, trailed in the wake of a car that had come to a halt near to her. She was surrounded by people, and a voice on a radio was calling for help, she could smell petrol, and felt something pressing down on her head as if she were wearing a bulky helmet. She was lifted up, a mask placed over her face, and she soared high above a white immensity, which was the glacier or what had once been her life.

Looking back, she was astonished at how hard she had struggled in life, how seriously she had taken all her suffering and joys. Why? She was haunted by images of the past that had caused her so much pain, but she took them less personally now and no longer allowed them to weigh her down. Above her all was still. Her breathing was slow and deep. Everything that had once been her was fading, and the notion of *individuals* seemed increasingly absurd. Where did this endless defensiveness against the world come from?

She saw cities, houses, all those boxes lining the streets, which people spent their lives filling with joy, regret, sorrow, objects, everything but themselves; because there was no other way. The way lay outwards and from there inwards, and that was why matter existed: to cut oneself loose, go to extremes, shake off one's self, with everything that was in bottles and tins, on screens and wheels; things that glittered and moved, other people's bodies, music, ideas, words – imaginary closed pockets forming a seamless whole.

'*Nature*,' she said as she glanced about her, sitting in a white bed while someone shone a pen in her eyes. Her chest was bandaged in gauze up to her neck. Once more she swooped down over the glacier and saw a man with a gleaming white crown; he reached out to catch hold of her but she evaded him, flowing away like a stream. Something inside her had changed, become simpler.

She woke up in bed with a start, breathing rapidly, and saw that her wrists were fastened to the sides of the bed. All night she had been adrift on the sands. '*Where are your friends?*' asked a man in a suit, who was sitting beside her, and he showed her pictures of a jeep that had been driven into a rock, of police tape surrounding the rock, of a man on all fours shovelling sand into his mouth.

Before wandering alone on the sands, she had been in the village, the one she hadn't dared enter before. She couldn't remember why she dared now – she had been fleeing someone. She was naked, and in place of her breasts were two red circles the size of an outstretched palm, glistening like strawberries, her ribcage showing beneath. In the centre of the village was a sort of park, with fires burning along its walls, and the night was dark red, lighting up and dimming by turns. Everything was in constant motion, nothing was still; she was part of that motion and didn't try to resist. Sitting across from one another at a table, Hrafn and Egill were passing something between them. The lower part of Egill's face was missing, his jaw an open wound as if a wild animal had attacked him and devoured half his face. She ran her hands over her chest, shook her antlers, hips swaying as she sashayed around the table. There was a heavy thud as Hrafn's head disappeared, and he slumped forward. A moment later, Egill's head was enveloped in a pink mist. She touched her face and discovered that she was bathed in sweat.

She was being spoon-fed, and she recognized the warm, sweet aroma of the food before it was brought into her room. Her friend sat weeping by the bed, someone shouted and her hands fell free from the sides of the bed. Her mother came to see her, floated above her bed with a yellow plastic shopping bag in each hand, and during the daytime she sat beside the window gazing out. A gentle smile played on her lips, and her face was serene. She gazed out at the garden, watching as the sun rose in the sky and the shadows crept slowly across the lawn before disappearing into the wall. In the corner of the garden stood a little shed with a red, corrugated-iron roof and rectangular windows. High up above the shed, a tree that was coming into leaf spread its boughs, and the newly sprouted leaves fluttered sweetly in the breeze, all in their right place.

TRANSLATOR'S ACKNOWLEDGEMENT

I would like to thank Ösp Viggósdóttir for her invaluable collaboration.